"Two hund

Jocelyn hea
bid then doub   veral
steps towards   ne full
complement of   was staring at her.
The bid kept goi

As the applause continued, she did a slow, seductive turn. The cheers rose to a deafening pitch.

"Eight hundred!" someone shouted.

"Two thousand dollars!"

Jocelyn froze, and the entire audience fell silent. The auctioneer cleared his throat. "Would the bidder identify himself, please."

Everyone turned as a man in a three-piece suit rose. "Rob Donnelly," he said.

Across the sea of faces, Jocelyn met his eyes filled with lust—and definite purpose.

Sitting high above, on a cloud of billowy softness, Cupid smiled . . . and patted himself on his back.

Dear Reader:

It's Valentine's Day. . . and to celebrate this we are offering you a Sensation which includes an earthly visit from Cupid himself!

Experience all the passion and excitement of falling in love as you follow the story of Jocelyn Foley and Rob Donnelly—who don't believe in romance. They both present a challenge—one that Cupid is going to meet!

Happy Valentine's Day.

Jane Nicholls
Silhouette Books
PO Box 236
Thornton Road
Croydon
Surrey
CR9 3RU

MURIEL JENSEN

Valentine Hearts and Flowers

Silhouette Sensation

First published in Great Britain in 1993 by Silhouette Books, Eton House, 18-24 Paradise Road, Richmond, Surrey TW9 1SR

© Muriel Jensen 1992

Silhouette, Silhouette Sensation and Colophon are Trade Marks of Harlequin Enterprises B.V.

ISBN 0 373 58744 9

18-9302

Made and printed in Great Britain

Prologue

"Got mine. Have you made a choice?" Perched on the marquee of the Liberty Theater, Percival ran a hand lovingly over his bow and tested the tension of his string. He heard a satisfying, flat-noted *ping*.

"Yes," Rupert replied, withdrawing an arrow from his quiver. "Her."

"Where?"

"The redhead."

Percival peered down. Twenty feet below them, on the corner of Water and Twelfth streets, a young woman in a long, loose trench coat waited for the traffic light to change.

He frowned. "A little...serious for our purposes, don't you think?"

Rupert examined the point of his arrow. "Our job is to help those who need it, isn't it? People who can find love on their own don't require our services."

"Rupe, think a minute," Percival cautioned. "I mean, you've already lost your stripes for that attitude."

Rupert shook his head, unconcerned. "So I hit a slump. I'm coming back. I know I am."

Percival reached back for an arrow. "Slump? Charles and Di, Madonna and Sean, Liz and the last four of her seven husbands? Those were all yours."

Rupert nodded regretfully and nocked his arrow. "Who can stay in love when your every move is front-page news? And anyway, the success of this depends on the man you've chosen for my redhead."

Percival spotted the tall, young man who'd been his choice the moment he'd laid eyes on him. He had all the requisite qualifications, *and* he looked lonely. Percival had had a sexy, willowy blonde in mind for this subject, but maybe that would be doing him a disservice. The man walked with square-shouldered confidence. Maybe he needed more of a challenge.

Percival glanced at the redhead just as an older woman stopped beside her, also waiting for the light to change. She greeted the woman with a hug and a smile. A warm woman deserved a strong, capable man—even if she looked a little serious for romance.

"I'm trusting you on this, Rupe," Percival said to his companion, taking aim. He hadn't wanted to be paired with Rupert. The cupid business could be iffy, and Rupe had called a few bad ones. Still, there was an advantage to having someone else to blame.

"You won't be sorry," Rupert promised, smiling as he drew back on his bowstring. "This pair's going to make us legends."

Chapter One

"It's really very simple." Nathan Foley smiled at his granddaughter across the desk that separated her from the Senior Center Committee. Then he cleared his throat, scratched his temple and sat up a little straighter—warning her that it probably wasn't simple at all. "All you have to do is come up with a fund-raiser that'll make twenty thousand dollars."

Jocelyn Foley almost choked on her coffee. Twenty thousand dollars! In Salty Harbor, Oregon, population 4,004, in the dead of a rainy January, raising that much money would require a bank and a sawed-off shotgun.

She tried to think. In the summer, Salty Harbor filled with tourists anxious to see its turn-of-the-century architecture, and the city's beautiful situation at the mouth of the Columbia River filled with commercial fishing craft and sailboats.

In December, shoppers came from Portland and from the cities across the river to shop in the harbor's unique boutiques and to take in its sumptuous Victorian lights and decorations.

Drawing crowds to Salty Harbor in January and February, however, was another matter. It was that time of the year when rain fell constantly and everyone settled happily in front of their fireplaces or wood stoves to enjoy the post-holiday calm.

But as community-development director, Jocelyn enjoyed no such luxury. It was her job to conceive a money-raising project that would finance a new furnace and a new roof for an old storefront bequeathed two years ago to the senior citizens of Salty Harbor by a long-time Harborian. Age and a pre-Christmas snow had finally decimated the heating system and the ancient shingles.

"Let's have a bake sale!" Frederika Lund suggested in a high, bright voice. At eighty-one, she was the oldest member of the committee.

"Freddie, that's stupid!" an irascible male voice replied. "That wouldn't even pay for a bucket to put under the smallest drip." John Whittaker, newly retired and the youngest of the group, was not known for his amiability.

"It's not stupid." Mary Maloney, champion of everything and everyone, put an arm protectively around Freddie's shoulders. "It simply doesn't go far enough. We have to think bigger."

Freddie raised an arthritic index finger. "We could sell Mary's chocolate truffles for a dollar apiece and—"

John turned on her, but before he could speak, Nathan said reasonably, "Freddie, we'd have to sell five truffles to every man, woman and child in town."

"And they cost fifty cents apiece to make," Mary said. "We need a *big* fund-raiser. But what?"

"Let the girl think." Nathan, chairman of the committee, crossed his long, lean legs and folded his arms, staring at Jocelyn as though his faith in her would help somehow. "The city council and the merchant's association hired her because she's an idea woman. It'll come. Give her time."

Four pairs of eyes stared at Jocelyn as she sat in the old green Naugahyde chair she'd resurrected from the city hall basement when she'd taken the job. She felt a strong sense of responsibility toward them.

Senior citizens were a growing percentage of the population everywhere, but here, where people stayed for generations or went away and almost invariably came back, they were all relatives, friends, neighbors. It was impossible to look at them as statistics.

Freddie had been Jocelyn's second grade teacher, John Whittaker had owned the drugstore where her family had traded for as long as she could remember, and Mary had bought every raffle ticket, every chocolate bar, every magazine subscription Jocelyn had ever peddled in the name of Salty Harbor Grade and High schools.

Nathan was more dear to her than she could ever explain to anyone. With her sisters married and her parents retired to San Diego, he was her anchor to family. He loved her, encouraged her, frustrated and infuriated her. And he was always there when she needed him.

Jocelyn doodled on the yellow pad in front of her, trying desperately to force a flow of ideas. The sharp tip of her number two pencil made a smiley face. *We need something to shake the doldrums out of the middle of winter,* she thought.

She drew long, flowing lines like whiskers on the face and added triangular ears. *Something to touch people—to make them come out and spend a little money, even though they're right between Christmas and tax time.*

She put a bow under the face. *Something semiformal? A dance with a band?* Frustratedly, she scribbled through the face. That was an idea she could never support wholeheartedly. She'd hated dances since the Valentine Ball she'd resolutely attended alone in her senior year. She was sure no wallflower had ever been so conspicuous or so lonely.

As though her brain held on to the idea though she'd thought she'd dismissed it, her pencil drew a slightly lopsided heart in the middle of the page. She looked at it, surprised to see it there. She poised her hand over it to cross it out, but couldn't put pencil to paper. Who could scratch through a heart, the eternal symbol of love and charity and all that is generous about us?

Charity. Generosity. The idea slapped her in the face then rolled over her like a wave.

"That's it!" She looked up from the page and smiled at Nathan. "An all-community Valentine's Day project!"

"Sugar-cookie hearts!" Freddie said.

With a small groan, Nathan put a hand over his eyes. John said something that made Mary elbow him.

"Cookies would be wonderful," Jocelyn said, hastily making notes. "We'll have a bake sale or a craft show or a whole bazaar, if we can put it together. But the bigger money will come from charming the city's service groups into earmarking a portion of their funds to restore the center, or into holding their own event with the proceeds going toward making the Senior Center habitable."

The four committee members straightened in their chairs. "How do we approach the groups?" Mary asked.

Jocelyn looked up from her notes. "I'm always in touch with the various groups. I'll explain what you're up against with that building and what you need. And a bazaar does get a lot of people out—we shouldn't discount that. Maybe that could be the seniors' project."

"I'll talk to the city about using the armory," John volunteered.

Mary frowned. "That's such a big, cold place. I wish there was somewhere else we could hold it." She sighed wistfully. "Wouldn't it be nice in some smaller, cozier place where we could hang lacy hearts and flowers and not have them lost under a thirty-foot ceiling?"

"Good idea." Jocelyn doodled lace around the heart and looked up at the committee with a broad grin. "We'll make everything really schmaltzy and old-fashioned, just like you guys.''

Three pairs of eyes looked back at her in consternation. Only Freddie hadn't taken offense.

''You know what I mean,'' Jocelyn hastened to explain. ''Not *old* old, but seasoned, vintage, classic.''

''You might better serve our cause,'' Nathan said quietly, ''by telling these people you hope to influence how much is accomplished at the center, rather than making it sound as though we sit around like antiques. We write letters to Veterans' Hospitals, Mary teaches a ceramics class to the retarded, John keeps up the library's clippings file....''

Mary frowned at him. ''Don't be so sensitive. She didn't mean we were antiques, she just meant an old-fashioned theme would coordinate with the fact that the beneficiaries of this fund-raiser are old-timers. We can't deny that, no matter how young we feel.'' She nodded to Jocelyn. ''I agree. It's an excellent idea. Your grandfather doth protest too much.''

''I—'' Nathan began heatedly.

''What about having the bake sale in the center court at the Old Cannery Mall?'' Freddie suggested cheerfully, cutting into the little fracas. ''My daughter works in the restaurant there, and it's such a pretty place. And it already looks old-fashioned with all the wooden beams and the plank floor.''

Everyone turned to Freddie in surprise—even the combatants. She did have a one-track mind, but she'd made an excellent suggestion. The center court would be ideal.

''It's only been open two months,'' John pointed out. ''Do you think they'd want to be bothered by something like this so soon?''

Nathan frowned. ''The man who built the mall and opened the restaurant comes from Los Angeles. He might not want any part of our quaint small-town festivities.''

A valid point. But Jocelyn was beginning to see the potential in the project. "He might," she said hopefully. "He may come from L.A., but he lives in Salty Harbor now. Just choose someone from your group to go and talk to him. I'll bet he'd be happy to help."

Freddie, John and Mary turned to Nathan. Nathan turned to Jocelyn. "We choose you," he said with a smile.

Jocelyn laughed and shook her head. "Gramps, it should be someone from your committee...."

"You know all about us," Nathan insisted. "You volunteer at the center. You've seen all the problems firsthand, and you know what'll appeal to him. We'll do whatever else you want, but we'd better leave the big-city dude to you. Don't you know him already, anyway? You always call on the new businesses to welcome them to Salty Harbor."

Since Jocelyn's work often depended strongly on the generous support of the local merchants, her job also involved acting as a sort of advocate for their causes and a one-woman welcoming committee.

Jocelyn shook her head. "When I called on them, I spoke to Griffin Donnelly. He's the chef and a partner in the restaurant and mall, but he said his cousin makes all the business decisions."

Nathan shrugged. "Then talk to his cousin. You can do it, Jossie. I know you can." He stood and tucked his clipboard under his arm. "Well, that's a relief. I knew you'd come up with something. We'll meet again after you talk to the service groups and the man who owns the restaurant and plan our strategy. Why don't you..." Nathan lowered his voice as John helped Freddie to the door. He cleared his throat. "Why don't you borrow something from Charlie to wear for your meeting with this man?"

Jocelyn pretended she wasn't offended. She was used to the wincing glances of women, the dismissing looks of men and the pressure from her family to reconsider her style of dress. That didn't mean it didn't hurt.

"Gramps, this is me." She spread wide the long, heavy denim skirt and tugged on the hem of the natural wool fisherman's sweater that reached almost to her knees. It also bunched the shirt bulbously around her hips, but she didn't care. "I dress for comfort and warmth."

He shook his head at her. "You dress like a bag lady."

"Perhaps," Mary, who'd overheard Nathan's comment, suggested gently, "a little curl in your hair."

Jocelyn put a hand to her bright red hair. It skimmed her eyebrows and was blunt cut to the length of her chin. "The man isn't going to care what I look like," she said patiently. "I'm seeing him on business."

"Every man," Nathan said, putting an arm around Jocelyn's shoulders as he walked to the door, "notices what a woman looks like. And, deep down, it affects how he reacts."

"That may have been true in your day, Gramps," she replied, stepping aside to let Mary and Nathan pass into the hall. "Today, men are less sexual in their thinking."

Nathan raised an eyebrow. "Who told you that?"

"It's fact."

"It's hooey."

Jocelyn ignored that and gave her grandfather a hug and the group an all-encompassing wave. "I'll be in touch when I have news."

She closed her door and leaned against it with a groan. She was setting herself a difficult task. She would do her best, but stirring interest, much less enthusiasm, at this time of year would require a miracle, and it would take considerable enthusiasm to raise the kind of money the seniors needed.

While a schmaltzy Valentine theme was the perfect note for the project, it was not a comfortable platform for a woman who didn't believe in romance. She believed in love: familial love, the love of friends and the charitable love that made people care about and help strangers—the kind of love upon which this project depended.

But the love of man for woman was a simple urge that filled a need. Men wanted a pretty, cuddly being to warm their dens, and most women wanted a strong, sexy man who would let them get close and feel needed. She didn't see why hearts and flowers should be attached to it. Besides that, for those who didn't fit the pattern, it was a heartless system.

Jocelyn wandered to the window and looked down on the river visible from her second-floor office. A lone sea gull rode a piece of flotsam downriver. He was hunkered down against the wind and rain, looking resolved to his solitary plight. Jocelyn felt a strong sense of kinship with him.

"ISN'T THAT A LOT OF oregano?" Rob Donnelly looked over his cousin's shoulder into the fragrant pot of soup simmering on the burner. He reached for a spoon and dipped it into the mixture.

"Hey." Griffin Donnelly balanced his spoon on the rim of the pot and pushed the chef's hat back on his head. "You've got the charm and the business brains. The kitchen is my turf. Beat it."

The minestrone was robust and delicious. Rob gave Griff a wry grin. "It's perfect. My humble apologies."

Griff put a scrupulously clean hand to Rob's white shirt-front and pushed him backward so that he could reach a large stainless bowl filled with a creamy green mixture. The aroma of crème de menthe rose from the bowl.

"You're going to have to start tripling this recipe," Rob said, pushing a lineup of chocolate-cookie crusts Griff's way. "Your grasshopper pie is a hit."

With a spatula, Griff transferred the pale green cream to the pie pans with a careless precision that filled each one perfectly and left a decorative swirl in the center.

"Booze and sugar," Griff said without looking up from his work. "What more could anyone ask of a recipe? Don't forget, that woman's coming to see you."

"Right." Rob glanced at his watch, then took the gray, pin-striped jacket that matched his vest and slacks from the back of Griff's stool and slipped it on. "Run it all by me again."

Griff shaved chocolate curls onto the tops of the pies. "Some community thing for old folks. She wants to use the center court of the mall for a bazaar."

Rob considered that as he adjusted his tie, "You foresee any problems with that?"

"Not as long as you keep the old ladies out of my kitchen."

Rob laughed, downed the last mouthful of a cup of coffee that had grown cold and headed for the double doors that separated the kitchen from the hostess's station. "What's she look like?"

Griff looked at him over the refrigerator door. "Prince Valiant," he replied.

Frowning, Rob took a step back into the kitchen. "She carries a sword?"

Griff grinned. "They share the same hairdresser."

"Ah." Rob walked out into the restaurant, his eyes going over the tables set for dinner, the globed candles reflected back in the wall of glass that looked out on the river, the few early diners talking quietly against the cloudy dusk and the flashing lights of the channel markers.

The Old Cannery Restaurant's atmosphere of comfortable elegance was subtle but pervasive, and the food was outstanding. After a short two months in business they enjoyed the patronage of regulars, they were booking large banquets, and several service clubs had moved their monthly luncheons to the Old Cannery. So far, so good.

Rob tried not to think about how important the success of this venture was to him. Two restaurants had been taken out from under him in his lifetime, and he wasn't going to lose this one. Not to mention the fact that he'd talked Griff into joining him in the venture and had moved him a thousand miles up the West Coast from a land of sunshine into one that in winter looked like an artist's rendering of the edge of doom.

"Mr. Donnelly?"

The hostess, a little blonde dressed in a dark wool suit stepped out from behind the cash register and handed him a business card. "She says she has an appointment to talk to you about some Senior Center project?"

Rob glanced down at the card. "Jocelyn Foley," it read. "Community Development Director. Stoveman Building, 12th and Water Streets." Prince Valiant had arrived.

He pocketed the card. "Thank you, Abby. Where is she?"

"I put her on number 10. Shall I bring some coffee, or will you need a waitress?"

Rob glanced to the far corner of the restaurant where the features on the woman in question were indistinguishable, except for her hair. Even from that distance, it was clear that it was very red.

"Coffee, please." He smiled a thank-you at the hostess and started across the green-and-beige-carpeted floor, down the few steps, to the tables near the window.

JOCELYN WATCHED THE MAN come toward her with long-legged grace. Before he'd come halfway, her seldom-used but always reliable man sensors flashed on. *No,* she thought. *Oh, no. don't let it be* him.

She liked men, she really did—at least, as far as business was concerned. As a rule, they were straightforward, logical and pleasantly succinct. But *handsome* men were another matter.

They made her nervous. Every time a handsome man crossed her path, she felt as though a sign appeared on her forehead in four-inch-high neon that read Dumped In Favor Of Her Beautiful Sister. It was stupid, she knew, but she was powerless to do anything about it.

No she told herself resolutely as the man's long stride ate up the distance between them. *One is never powerless.*

Her resolution wavered as he approached and she got a clear view of rich, dark hair, thickly lashed brown eyes, well-defined eyebrows that slashed dramatically across a broad forehead, a strong nose with just a suggestion of the Roman hook and a smile and a demeanor that could only be described as sexy.

The years rolled back and she was thirteen again, taller and larger than all the other girls in her class, her bright hair the object of ridicule.

Forcefully, she took herself in hand. She was a competent woman in a position of responsibility, entrusted with a mission that was important and worthy.

She stood and offered her hand across the table. "I appreciate your time, Mr. Donnelly. I'm Jocelyn Foley."

Rob smiled and shook her hand. Griff's assessment of her coiffure was very much on target, he decided, the cut every bit as angular as it appeared on the character in the Sunday comics. But there the resemblance ended. Had Prince Valiant ever found it necessary to mount his horse or leap into combat in the clothes this woman was wearing, Queen Aleta would have become a widow years ago.

Coming from Los Angeles, he'd thought he'd seen everything in the way of clothing as a form of expression. But he'd never seen a message delivered so clearly. "Don't look at me," it screamed at him, from the baggy sweater over the plaid shirt to the long denim skirt that hung formlessly almost to her ankles. When she'd stood to greet him, he'd caught a glimpse of brown Birkenstock sandals over socks. The woman-loving male in him recoiled.

Then he looked into her dark blue eyes and was disarmed. She was nervous, uncertain, even a little frightened.

For a moment that unnerved him. He didn't usually have that effect on people. As a man, he'd grown used to seeing approval and interest in a woman's eyes. As a restaurateur, he'd built his reputation on his ability to put people at ease.

He reached around her to hold the back of her chair. "It's my pleasure, Ms. Foley. Please, sit down."

Abby appeared with a carafe of coffee, poured, then left the black-and-stainless-steel jug in the middle of the table.

"I understand you have a project underway," Rob said, hoping to ease the way for the woman opposite him, "that would involve the use of the Old Cannery's center court."

"Yes." Wide blue eyes touched his face, darted away, then looked back at him again with an expression of determination. He smiled encouragingly, and she began to explain.

"Two years ago, a storefront was donated to our senior citizens as a place where they can get together, play cards, do crafts, watch television, whatever they like. For some of them, it's the only social contact they have." She lifted a shoulder in a gesture that seemed to ask, *Isn't that sad?* Rob's attention focused on it. It was the first move she'd made that said "woman."

"Unfortunately," she went on, "the roof leaks badly and the furnace died just before Christmas, making it uninhabitable. And the cost of repairs is going to require a major fund-raising effort. I'm trying to coordinate a community-wide program of events, and a bazaar is always a pretty sure thing. It's also something the seniors can get involved in. We were wondering if you'd let us hold it in the mall's center court."

He sipped his coffee, seeing the relief in her eyes that she'd finally gotten that much out. "I'm not objecting," he said, "but aren't these things usually held in church basements or school auditoriums?"

She nodded, reaching to the small, rectangular bowl that held a tight squeeze of artificial sweetener packets. "In our case, the armory, but it's so dark and cavernous. Since we're going with a schmaltzy Valentine theme—" She yanked on the pink packet and it exploded from the bowl, raining other packets all over the end of the table.

Rob ignored the little mess, concentrating on her explanation.

"We . . . we thought it would be more in keeping with our theme." She talked on hesitantly as she stuffed packets back into the bowl. "The mall is so rustic and cozy and would be perfect for our purposes."

"What would you want to do?" he asked.

"Set up about a dozen tables," she replied, looking into his face despite a blush that betrayed her embarrassment. "If you'd let us string some streamers and hang some hearts and flowers, that'd be wonderful, but we could manage without that. Your mall traffic would help us, and I think our strong community support would help you."

Rob nodded. "I think we can work something out. The idea sounds fine to me, but I'd like to check it out with the shops renting space in the mall."

"That's wonderful." Jocelyn relaxed just a little. This wasn't quite as painful as she'd imagined. Though she'd seen Robert Donnelly give her the dismissive once-over she'd grown used to, he seemed genuinely willing to be helpful.

"We carry insurance for such projects," Jocelyn went on, holding one corner of her sweetener packet and flapping it back and forth to force the contents into the other end before she tore it open. "You won't have to worry about—" She stopped in horror as the packet flew out of her hand and landed with a plop in her host's cup of coffee.

"Oh, God," she groaned. "I'm sorry!" Instinctively, she reached across with her spoon to fish the packet out. She dropped the soggy mess onto his saucer.

He raised quiet brown eyes from his cup to her face, one eyebrow slightly elevated as though he couldn't quite believe what he'd just seen. *I've blown it,* she thought. *It's the armory or the basement of the Foursquare Church. We'll raise eleven dollars. I'll be fired and forced to move in with Gramps.*

"Miss Foley," Rob said, pushing his cup aside as he leaned toward her. "Why are you afraid of me?"

Jocelyn usually appreciated directness, but not in this case.

"I'm not afraid," she replied, "I'm—I'm just nervous."

"Why?"

Because I know I'm lacking something all men look for in a woman. Because I know I dress funny, and despite all our contemporary claims that we look beyond appearance to the person within, men still appreciate perky bosoms and tight bottoms and I have neither.

"You're from Los Angeles," she said, grasping at an excuse he might believe.

Both eyebrows went up. "Does that make me the Night Stalker or something?"

She shook her head, realizing the absurdity of the excuse. But it was all she had. She refused to tell him the truth. "I expected you to be very big-city and condescending," she said with an apologetic shrug. "And this project is important to a lot of very special people who are counting on me to put it together. I guess I just arrived prepared to be sneered at."

His eyes were so dark. At the moment, they were looking into hers as though he wasn't sure whether or not to believe her. Then he smiled and leaned back in his chair. "If the other shops in the mall have no problem with it, the court is yours. Now, aren't you ashamed for having misjudged me?"

Close call. She nodded contritely. "Very."

"Do you have a date?" he asked.

A date? Her heart lurched and color flooded into her cheeks. Her eyes widened and she asked in a small voice, "A date?"

"For the bazaar," he clarified. "Have you set a date?" It took him a moment to understand what was going on in her eyes. A little explosion of excitement seemed to collapse on itself and he realized that she'd misinterpreted his question. Despite his innocence in the matter, he felt responsible. What had happened to this woman? he wondered.

She lowered her lashes for an instant, then looked at him with a cool smile that was suddenly all controlled professionalism. "Valentine's Day. February 14." She stood and offered her hand again. "Thank you so much, Mr. Donnelly. I apologize for the sweetener in your coffee and for misjudging you because you're from Los Angeles. Salty Harbor is happy to have you here, and we appreciate your community spirit."

Rob stood and took her hand. It felt small and very cold. "We're happy to help, Ms. Foley. I'll call you as soon as I've polled my tenants. I'll see you out."

Gently but firmly, Jocelyn drew her hand back, the stiff smile still in place. "I've taken a lot of your time already. I'll see myself out, thank you. I'll wait to hear from you. Good night."

Rob watched her leave, the heavy, shapeless clothes hitching and buckling around her as she hurried from the restaurant. He paused at the kitchen door for one last look as she disappeared into the mall.

Griff appeared on the other side of the batwing doors, following Rob's gaze. "What're you looking at?" he asked.

"Princess Valiant," Rob replied absently.

Griff frowned at him. "Not your type."

Rob ignored a lingering curiosity and pushed his way into the kitchen. For a man whose taste ran to leggy brunettes, he had to concur.

Chapter Two

"Have you talked to Charlie in the past few days? I called her yesterday to—"

"Vrrooom! Vrroooooom!" A four-year-old girl on roller skates, black braids flying out behind her, sailed past the kitchen table on her way to the back door.

Jocelyn's older sister, Phyllis, stopped in midsentence to catch the child by both arms and stop her. "Lindsay Marie, this is the last time I'm going to tell you to take off the skates or go outside onto the patio. One more time and you go straight to bed."

Lindsay, doll-faced and devious, turned from her mother to her aunt with a bright smile. "I'll go live with Aunt Jossie."

"Good. I'll help you pack."

Jocelyn, sharing a slice of bundt cake with seven-month-old Robin, put a crumb-sized piece to the baby's mouth. It was drawn in and gummed. "Sorry, Linds," she said. "I live in a second-floor apartment. You wouldn't be able to skate indoors there, either."

Phyllis, three inches taller than Jocelyn and Nordic-goddess beautiful, though three years older, looked imploringly at her sister. "Now, don't be hasty. If you'll take her, I'd be willing to buy you a big condo."

"Really?"

"Mommy!" Lindsay climbed into Phyllis's lap and took her face in both hands. "You don't want me to leave you. You're teasing Aunt Jossie."

"Think so?"

"Yes. I know you love me."

I know you love me. Lindsay, speaking the words in her high, baby voice but underscoring them with her father's gray-green eyes, knocked Jocelyn out of time and place. She was no longer at her sister's kitchen table. It was six years ago, midnight, and she was in the front seat of Jeffrey's car, parked on a bluff overlooking the bay. They'd met at Clark Community College where she was taking business classes and he taught English.

Jocelyn remembered vividly her surprise and alarm when his quiet speech had begun with, "There's just no easy way to do this, so I'll just say it."

"I know you love me," he'd gone on, his sensitive, bespectacled face reflecting the reluctance to which he'd already confessed. "Or, you think you do." He had looked her bravely in the eye. "But, I think . . . I'm falling in love with Phyl."

Phyllis, an assistant buyer at Salty Harbor Fashions and spare-time costumer for the college's theater group to which Jeffrey belonged, had mentioned working with him on a production, but nothing more.

"Don't be angry with her," he'd said quickly. "I haven't even told her how I feel." He'd put his arm around Jocelyn and drawn her close. "I love you like a buddy, Joss, but what I feel for her is already robbing my appetite and my sleep and generally making me crazy. I think this is it."

Whenever Jocelyn felt inadequate or thought poorly of herself, she remembered that moment and felt somewhat vindicated. That she had finally hugged him back and wished him well had been a tribute to her affection for him and the love and devotion she felt for her older sister.

She'd been deeply, wholeheartedly in love with Jeff. He had everything she'd wanted in a man—kindness, wit, intelligence. He was tall and shy and a little awkward, but she wasn't deluded by looks and charm the way her friends were. She wanted a practical, dependable man.

The pain had taken time to heal and been greatly aggravated when Jocelyn served as Phyllis's smiling maid of honor.

When her mother had learned the news, she'd taken Jocelyn to an elegant restaurant in Cannon Beach. She'd patted her hand across the table and said, "I'm so proud of you. Not many women can take that kind of..." she had groped for the right word, and Jocelyn had waited patiently, stoically. "Disappointment" was the word she'd finally settled on. Jocelyn had thought it inadequate, but less hurtful than the other words that came to mind. "...And continue to be a loving sister and a good friend. That's what's so special about you, Jossie. Phyl has the glamour, Charlie has the beauty, but you've got the heart. And the brains! Your father and I are so proud of you."

Because I have heart, Jocelyn had thought. *And brains.* What was a brainy woman without looks? A spinster. A woman a man would compare to another woman and find inadequate.

"...Little devil manipulates every situation to her benefit," Phyllis was saying as the slam of the kitchen door brought Jocelyn out of her thoughts. "Just like her father. More tea?"

Jocelyn focused on her sister and saw her expression change from one of teasing pride to uncertainty.

"You okay?" Phyllis asked.

A cross word had never been spoken between them over Jeffrey, but Jocelyn knew Phyllis remained sensitive to her feelings to this day—despite her every effort to pretend that her feelings for Jeff had been nothing more than friendship and that she was delighted with their relationship. Sometimes, in the privacy of her room in the middle of the night, she could admit to herself that that little edge gave her a small feeling of power over Phyllis, who'd been born first, who was taller, prettier and more accomplished.

"Of course, I am," she said, frowning. "Why wouldn't I be?"

Phyllis poured more tea into her cup from a fat, brown pot. "I don't know. I had the feeling I'd lost you there for a minute. Here. Give me Robin. She'll be happy in the playpen for a little while."

Jocelyn waited while Phyllis put the baby in the cube of nylon mesh near the table. "You started to say something about Charlie," she said as Phyllis sat down again.

"Right." Phyllis leaned toward Jocelyn and lowered her voice conspiratorially, as though they had an audience. "I think something's wrong," she said.

"What?" Jocelyn demanded, straightening in her chair.

Phyllis shook her head. "She didn't say, and I didn't ask."

Jocelyn rolled her eyes. "Great way to find things out. You think something's wrong with the pregnancy?"

"No. She looked a little pale and tired, but you know Charlie. That platinum hair and porcelain skin make her look like she's about to shatter."

Jocelyn's sisters shared their mother's blond elegance. Jocelyn favored her redheaded, portly father.

Phyllis went on. "She just seemed sort of... I don't know... removed, I guess. Like she wasn't quite with me. We'd met to look at baby furniture, and she couldn't have been less enthused. Remember when we went shopping for *my* furniture?"

Jocelyn had to laugh. "You'd have tried the crib if I hadn't threatened to leave you there and let you walk home. And after you charged two thousand dollars..."

"All right!" Phyllis waved her sister into silence with a feigned frown. "It was a rhetorical question." She grew serious again. "The point is, she should be aglow with excitement now. Her first baby is due in less than a month. But her mind is on something else. That isn't normal."

Jocelyn didn't want to consider the other most obvious reason for her younger sister's distress, but Phyllis was less reticent. "I wonder if she and Chris are having problems," she said with a thoughtful frown. "He's a darling, but that fun-loving, devil-may-care outlook can wear on you."

"He's been with Gibson and Dunn Accounting for over a year now." Jocelyn sipped her tea. "He's outgrowing that. He adores Charlie. He wouldn't do anything deliberately to hurt her."

"Not deliberately, no." Phyllis nibbled on a piece of cake. "But you know how men are."

Jocelyn didn't—at least, not in any detail. She'd pretty much given up on them after Jeff.

"Well, I shouldn't worry," Phyllis went on. "She'll call you eventually and tell you. Then you can relieve my mind."

Jocelyn detected the smallest trace of resentment in Phyllis's voice. She'd always thought it an interesting fact that her beautiful, charming sister confided in the ugly duckling.

"She's always admired you," Jocelyn said tactfully. "She doesn't want to admit to you that she has any problems. You make life look so effortless. It's easier to tell me. I screw up all the time, and I don't have your looks. I don't threaten her."

"You have looks," Phyllis said. Then with sisterly candor she added, "You just don't have any style."

Jocelyn replied with sweet sarcasm. "Thank you, Phyl."

Phyllis shrugged off any feeling of guilt. "If you'd been born without fashion sense, I'd have never said that.

This—'' she gestured toward Jocelyn's rolled neck sweater under oversize coveralls, apparently unable to find a word to describe them ''—is a choice you've made. I feel a responsibility to be brutal.''

''I've always dressed to please myself!''

''No, you used to. And your tastes always were a little bizarre, but now you dress not to please yourself but to *dis*please other people, and that's cause for criticism.''

''Now, look—'' Jocelyn pushed her cup away and prepared to stand, but Phyllis caught her hand.

''Stay right where you are, Jossie,'' she said with a grin, ''or I will send Lindsay home with you. Have you heard from Mom and Dad? What's new on Coronado Island?''

That was Phyllis, Jocelyn thought as she forced herself to relax and report on the latest phone call from their parents. It occurred to Jocelyn with a sense of gentle malice that Jeff deserved her sister.

ROB, DRESSED IN OLD JEANS and a new down vest, pried up the rotten board with a crowbar, wrestling a sturdy, seventy-year-old nail for possession of it. The nail gave with a suddenness that dropped him on his backside.

Griff squatted on his knees beside his cousin, a tulip glass of Zinfandel in one hand, a new slotted board in the other. He toasted him. ''That's how I like to see you—flat on your butt.''

Rob swung himself onto his knees again and snatched the board from him. ''Stick around,'' he said, positioning it in the long, rectangular hole on the front porch. ''That happens to me regularly.''

Beyond the overhanging eaves, rain fell in a torrent down a grassy slope into a quiet little bay. Griff looked from it to Rob in quiet contemplation.

''Sandy was selfish and stupid,'' he said. ''And you're well rid of her.''

Rob hammered in the nail. "Well, selfish, anyway. You can't call living on Maui in a mansion with a retired movie producer stupid." He reached for another nail. "But I was talking about the restaurant I lost in the settlement."

Griff straightened to his feet and tossed the rotten board onto the pile of discarded wood in a corner of the porch. "Your bad luck to get a divorced female judge to hear your case. Anyway, the Cannery's doing better than we had any right to hope for. Lighten up."

Rob pried the lid off a can of sealer. "People who lighten up don't get anywhere."

"Where is it precisely you want to get?"

"I want to get to a place where your investment and mine are secure," he said, stirring the oily mixture with a stick. "Then I can lighten up."

Griff leaned a hip on the porch railing and watched as Rob painted on the clear liquid. "Nothing's ever secure. If you wait for that perfect point in time to start enjoying yourself, you never will."

"I enjoy working." Rob glanced up at him midstroke. "I thought the man who can spend five days perfecting a moussaka did, too."

"You know I do," Griff said, leaning back against a pillar and planting the flat of his foot on the railing. He took another sip of wine. "But I need a woman."

Punching down the lid on the can, Rob gave him another grin.

"You know what I mean," Griff said with mild impatience. "I need . . . an important woman."

Rob sprang to his feet and handed Griff the can, suggesting, "Margaret Thatcher's out of a job."

"A woman," Griff clarified with a glare as he followed Rob into the small cottage's kitchen, "who would be important to me."

"So find one," Rob said. He dropped his tools into a box in the service porch off the kitchen, and took the can of sealer from Griff and placed it beside the toolbox. He led the way back into the kitchen.

It was a large, multipurpose room that included a plaid sofa set before a picture window with a view of the bay. "The situation's perfect for you. You do the cooking, I do the worrying. When you're off, you're free to scour Salty Harbor for the mother of your children."

Griff sank onto the sofa and crossed his feet, clad in British Knights, on the Sunday paper on the coffee table. "I want my children to have cousins."

"That's impossible." Rob topped off Griff's wineglass and poured one for himself. "You're an only child."

Griff leaned his head back and closed his eyes. "Like you don't know what I'm talking about."

"My kids would be second cousins to your kids," Rob said, sinking down into the opposite corner of the sofa. "Or once removed or something. I never understood how that works."

"You don't understand a lot of things." Griff's voice grew grim and heavy. "What would we have done without each other when we were kids? Hell, what would we have done in the last couple of years?"

Rob squared one leg on the other and made himself think about that. He could handle business with calm and logic, but his personal life had always been another matter. Mostly, he supposed, because it made him angry and everyone else involved in it was gone, so all consideration of it was not only aggravating, but futile.

He and Griff had grown up in the back of The Brahmin, a restaurant their fathers had built together in Boston. Griff's mother had died young, and Rob's mother, warm and hardworking, had mothered Griff as her own between long shifts in the kitchen. Then Rob's father, tired of the long hours and small returns, had left. Rob had been four-teen.

"If it hadn't been for you," Griff said quietly, "I'd have probably died in a gang fight after my father died, or be doing ten to twenty in Attica. And you have the scars to prove it."

"I knew how you felt. My father hadn't died, but he might as well have. He left that large a vacancy in my life."

"You ever going to get over that?" Griff asked mildly, sitting up and putting his wineglass on the table. "You're so determined not to be like your father that you're..." Griff paused, apparently to rethink what he'd been about to say. His grimness suddenly turned to teasing censure. "You're no damn fun anymore."

"Sure, I am," Rob laughed lightly, more than willing to put away thoughts of the father he'd never seen again. "Laurel Parker thinks I'm a stud."

Griff barked a laugh. "You've got the worst taste in women. All she has on her mind are the clothes in her shop and sex."

"I thought you wanted me to lighten up."

"All things in moderation, my son. She's only throwing herself at you so you'll lower her rent." Griff got to his feet and zipped up his leather jacket. He looked at Rob a moment as he, too, stood, then asked carefully, "You two been...?"

Rob didn't need the word. He raised an eyebrow, surprised by the question. "Why?"

Griff turned to the door. "Just curious."

Rob leaned against the doorway as Griff stepped out onto the porch. "Watch the wet board," he cautioned. Then he asked pointedly, "Curious or jealous?"

Griff's gasp of indignation told him instantly. Well, that was interesting.

"No, we aren't," Rob replied. "You know what working until 2:00 a.m. does to a man's social life."

"She called yesterday, incidentally. Something about a problem with the heat in her shop."

"I'll check it out tomorrow."

Griff stopped on the third stair down and turned to smile, ignoring the rain beating down on him. "You need somebody like Princess Valiant. She's as serious about business as you are."

Rob laughed. "You know me. I need a lady who wants romance but not love. She may be very nice, but she does not look like a romantic."

Griff shrugged a shoulder. "Hard to tell what's under all that. A little like you. Under that suave exterior is a guy who'd take on three lunatics with knives and chains to save his kid cousin. She could be hiding things, too." He waved. "See you tonight."

Rob went back into the cottage, thinking that could very well be true. A '57 Buick could be hidden under those clothes.

"IT'S THE THERMOSTAT." Laurel braced her palms on the glass counter that separated her from Rob. Eyelashes thick with mascara dropped once, then rose slowly as chocolate brown eyes smiled into his. Her torso in a black mohair sweater leaned toward him, her long, glossy, black hair falling over one shoulder.

Rob turned away and through racks of colorful clothes to the back wall near the dressing room. The dial had been set to seventy degrees—precisely what the thermometer read.

He turned to frown at Laurel and found her right behind him. "Looks fine to me. It's comfortable in here."

Perfectly outlined red lips parted in deliberate invitation as she ran her index finger under the lapel of his jacket. "Not that thermostat, silly," she said huskily. "Mine."

He caught her hand and lowered it gently. "Turn it down, Laurel. It's eleven o'clock in the morning."

Laurel pouted prettily. "Control's broken."

He grinned. "Shall I get a glass of ice water?"

Laurel dropped the pose and gave him a genuine sulk. "What time of the day is a woman supposed to approach you? When I tried to pick you up at 2:00 a.m. after work, you said you were beat. When I tried to have a late lunch with you before your shift, you said your mind was on business. Are you ever . . . accessible?"

Rob folded his arms to force a distance between them. "Sorry. No. But Carstairs—" with an inclination of his head, he indicated the jeweler's across the mall "—has made it more than clear he's interested. And he has diamonds."

"I'm not after diamonds," she said softly, blocking his path as he tried to move past her. "I'm after a man."

Rob took her firmly by the forearms and pushed her backward between the racks. "Then you'll have to find another one."

She leaned against his grip until her mouth was a mere inch from his chin. "But I like them tall and gorgeous and forceful."

The loud clearing of a throat caused Rob to drop his hands and turn guiltily. Princess Valiant stood in the doorway, her red helmet of hair gleaming like a setting sun, her body maligned this morning by a long, purple skirt, a shapeless, pink jacket over a lavender shirt, the collar turned up. The obviously curious but slightly disappointed look in her eyes distracted him from her clothes.

"Now that's an interesting look, Jossie." Laurel's eyes went over her in pity. There was as much genuine dismay as sarcasm in her voice. "Annie Hall was put to rest a decade ago. And the Haight-Ashbury look went long before that."

Rob saw the hurt register in Jocelyn's eyes, followed immediately by a pitying look of her own. "Hello, Laurel. I'm sorry to interrupt…" Jocelyn's gaze turned back to Rob. "I came to leave you some things, and Griffin asked me to tell you you have a phone call. He's alone in the kitchen." She looked from one to the other with an air of innocent mischief. "Shall I tell him to take a message?"

"Yes," Laurel replied.

Rob caught Jocelyn's arm as she turned away. "No," he said. "I'm coming."

"Well, here. I was just going to leave—" She tried to force a manila envelope on him, but he pushed it back at her.

He smiled over his shoulder at Laurel. "Coffee this afternoon?"

Her eyes brightened perceptibly. "What time?"

"Three. In the kitchen."

Rob walked out into the mall, still holding Jocelyn's arm.

"Mr. Donnelly, I have to go back to work," Jocelyn said, resisting as she tried again to make him take the envelope. "This includes a map of Salty Harbor, a brochure of places of interest, a few coupons for—"

He pushed it back at her. "Certainly you have time for coffee. Don't you want to know how my poll of the other shops went for your bazaar?"

"Well, yes…."

"Then come on."

While Rob spoke on the phone with a supplier who was apparently having difficulty with an order of place mats, Griff put a dessert plate holding one tiny strawberry chiffon tart under Jocelyn's nose. "Try this," he directed, pulling her toward a stool. "Tell me what you think, but be kind."

Jocelyn hiked up onto the stool and took a bite. It was sweet and succulently fresh and made her wish she could have another. "It's wonderful," she said emphatically.

"Good." He took the plate from her and handed her another that contained a small wedge of something velvety dark. "Chocolate Mousse Grand Marnier."

Jocelyn rolled a bite on her tongue and closed her eyes in ecstasy before swallowing "Exquisite," she said. "I don't suppose you ever burn anything. Or make a mistake with the ingredients."

Griff smiled and handed her a glass of champagne. "No," he said airily. "I'm a gifted genius with food."

"Then shouldn't you be in Paris?"

He shook his head. "Rob and I came here via Boston and Los Angeles. We're ready for small-town life and genuine people."

Jocelyn wondered why that was. "Our good fortune," she said. "But certainly, real people are found in the big city, too."

Griff nodded. "They're just harder to keep there." He handed her a cookie wrapped in a napkin. "Parisian tea cakes to serve with ice cream. What do you think?"

Rob came to stand beside Jocelyn's stool, a hand braced on the counter behind her. "I begged you for one of those," he said to Griff, "and you told me they were still too hot."

"Oh, don't whine," Griff said, handing him one. "They've cooled."

Jocelyn tasted sweet cream, butter and almond. In the center was a chunk of chocolate. "Your customers won't want to go home," she predicted. "And you'll probably get several marriage proposals."

"I am available," Griff said, smiling as he pulled off his apron. "Pass the word among your friends. Be back in ten minutes, Rob. Jackie's in the back if you get an order."

The moment Griff left the room, the comfortable ambiance evaporated. Jocelyn was acutely aware of Rob's arm behind her and his shoulder just inches from her face. She leapt off the stool and snatched her purse from the counter.

The empty plate near it fell to the floor and broke in three large pieces.

"Oh, no," she groaned, and reached down to pick them up.

Rob caught her arm and pulled her up. "You'll cut yourself. I'll take care of it."

When she tried to insist, he tightened his grip. "Relax," he chided quietly. "I thought we'd established that I want to help you."

This behavior was bad—even for her. She smiled and tried to look in control. "Yes, of course." She splayed a hand on the envelope on the counter. "These things should help you get acquainted with Salty Harbor. I've included a map because some of the roads on the hill are pretty impossible, but the view of the harbor from up there is breathtaking."

Jocelyn swallowed. Rob's undivided attention was making her heart beat too fast. "And we're steeped in history. Did you know that Lewis and Clark camped right across the harbor?" she chatted on. "I know you probably haven't much time between the restaurant and Laurel, but there's so much to . . ."

The moment the words were out of her mouth, she knew they were inappropriate. When she was nervous, she reacted like a disc jockey with dead air to fill.

"I'm sorry," she said quickly. "I meant . . ."

Rob was smiling despite himself. This was, indeed, the most unusual woman he'd ever met. "I know what you meant," he said. "I gather you know Laurel."

"We went to school together." Jocelyn tried to reply without inflection, without betraying how she felt about Laurel.

He folded his arms and leaned a hip on the stool she'd just vacated. The action eliminated the disparity in their heights and Jocelyn found herself looking into deep dark eyes. For an instant, she lost awareness of her surroundings. She saw strength, humor, sadness and lazy sex appeal.

"Then you know that her...enthusiasm," he said, bringing Jocelyn back to the conversation, "often outdistances the reason for it."

Rob looked into a small, pink-cheeked face with rounded contours and not the least suggestion of cheekbones. A pretty pink mouth smiled shyly, and blue eyes focused on him with an absorption that unsettled him just a little. He took a moment to wonder why he'd bothered to explain about Laurel.

He stood, suddenly, curiously needing the advantage of his height and the edge of discomfort he knew he could inspire. He saw it fill her eyes immediately.

"You have the center court for February 14," he said, "for as long as you need it."

Jocelyn put her hands in the pockets of the strange jacket and became all business. "We were hoping to run the bazaar from ten until four, but we'd probably need an hour before and after to set up and take down."

"You've got it."

"About the streamers and the decorations..."

"No problem."

"We'll have baked goods. Some of our committee are concerned you might consider that competition for the restaurant."

He grinned. "Not unless you prepared chateaubriand or Chocolate Mousse Grand Marnier."

She laughed. "More like brownies and snickerdoodles."

"You're welcome to bring your committee by to look things over if you like." He put a hand on her shoulder and walked her through the kitchen and out into the mall. "We can help with banquet tables if you need them, and I'll show you where the outlets are."

"Thank you." At the double doors that lead out onto the pier, Jocelyn smiled and offered her hand. "We appreciate your help, Mr. Donnelly. I hope the bazaar will do a little for your restaurant, as well."

He shook her hand. It was soft and strong and felt good in his. "Rob," he corrected.

"Jocelyn," she said. "Or Joss. If I can do anything for you in my capacity as community development director, please call me."

The question formed in his mind and he couldn't stop it from reaching his lips. "Only if I need you in that capacity?"

She opened her mouth, then closed it, obviously surprised. He smiled, more intrigued than amused. What was he doing?

She cleared her throat. "I'm . . . I'm as busy are you are, Mr. . .Rob."

Rob pushed the door open for her. Cold air rushed into the mall. "No male counterpart of Laurel in your life?" he asked.

The wind ruffled the angular cut of her hair, and he caught a glimpse of how it could have looked with a little effort.

The ingenuous nervousness he so enjoyed changed suddenly to a jaded fatalism that both startled and upset him. "Be serious, Mr. Donnelly," she said quietly, and turned away.

Rob stepped outside and caught her arm as she started for her car. The January chill seeped through his suit coat and shirt.

She turned on him angrily, cheeks as aflame as her hair. "Will you stop doing that?" she demanded, yanking her arm away.

For a moment, they stared at each other, each surprised by her small show of temper. Then she sighed and put a hand to her forehead. He smiled. "So there is a woman in there," he said gently.

She looked up at him, still annoyed, a hand on her hip. "Well, what do you think? That every female on the planet looks like Laurel? Some of us weren't blessed with such obvious femininity. Look—"

He opened his mouth to reply, but she stopped him with an outstretched hand. "This conversation is out of place."

"Why?"

"Because I came here on business."

"You came here to bring me an envelope of things that would acquaint me with Salty Harbor. That sounds like a friendly gesture to me."

"It's my job to be friendly."

Rob shifted his weight. The weather and the woman were chilling him to the bone, but it went against the grain to relinquish anything without a fight. "We are now outside of my place of business. I terminate the professional call. I'm now getting personal. Will you come back tonight and have dinner with me?"

She pulled her jacket around her. "No," she said, simply but firmly.

"Why not?" he persisted.

She sighed as though he were dense. "You're having coffee at three with Laurel. No woman, even a plain one, wants to be part of a menu, Rob. Goodbye. I'll be in touch."

That was stupid, he told himself as he stood in the middle of the pier and watched her drive away. He'd forgotten about the coffee date with Laurel. Jocelyn would never believe he'd intended to find a last-minute emergency that would leave the field clear for Griff to spend the time with Laurel.

What did he need with a hung-up little redhead who might weigh three hundred pounds for all he knew? It was anybody's guess what was under those clothes.

Not that he was a man whose sole concern was physical. He wanted more. He just didn't want it forever.

He remembered Jocelyn standing there in her bright-and-awkward pink-and-purple outfit, holding him coldly at a distance, her eyes wide and hurt. He definitely didn't need that. He pulled the door open and felt the warmth from inside rush out to lure him in.

Chapter Three

"I—I wanted us to s-start thinking about... about buying a house." Charlene gulped and wept and stammered as she poured her heart out on her sister's sofa. "But he says we don't have the money!"

Jocelyn, an arm around Charlene, patted her shoulder. "Well, Charlie, you're always telling me how tight things are," she pointed out gently. "I know how much you want a house, but maybe he's right."

"All I want to do is think about one!" Charlie said tearfully, her porcelain complexion puffed and blotchy from an hour of crying. She waved a much-abused tissue in the air. "Is that so much to ask? Just to *think* about it?"

"Honey, what I wish you'd think about is the baby," Jocelyn said, reaching to the coffee table for Charlene's discarded teacup and putting it in her hand. "If you deliver early on my sofa, I'll never forgive you. Now, drink this and try to calm down."

"Chris wouldn't care," Charlene said, staring into the half-empty cup. "His mind is on something else." She dropped her head onto Jocelyn's shoulder as she dissolved into deeper sobs. "Or some*one*."

As Charlene wept, Jocelyn held her close and tried to offer comfort.

She'd always loved and admired her younger sister, but under the affection was a jealousy, however benign, that simply wouldn't go away, no matter how logically she reasoned with herself.

It wasn't Charlie's fault she'd been born ethereally blonde, slender and petite, with an air about her that made everyone rush to help her, whether she needed it or not.

It was no one's fault that Jocelyn had been preceded by gorgeous Phyllis, who'd guilelessly stolen the only man she'd ever seriously cared about.

Jocelyn didn't doubt her womanliness. She knew she was strong, capable, caring. She was simply lacking whatever made men feel protective and romantic. She drew them, all right, but as friends and allies, not as lovers.

She accepted that fact with the practical common sense with which she did everything.

Charlene looked up at her and sniffed pitifully. "Maybe he doesn't love me anymore because I've gotten fat and ugly."

"You're not fat and ugly. You're pregnant," Jocelyn said reasonably, giving her sister her full attention. "And instead of crying and worrying, you should just ask him straight out what the problem is."

"I tried that," Charlene said. "He says I'm imagining things." Her chin began to quiver dangerously again. "Isn't denial of a problem the first sign of a deteriorating marriage?"

"No. It could just be a sign that there is no problem and your raging hormones are reading more into this than is really there."

"Then why does he work late three nights a week?"

"Maybe to make more money so that you *can* start thinking about a house."

"Then where is it going? It's not in the budget, and wouldn't he tell me about it if he knew that was what I wanted?"

Jocelyn poured Charlie a fresh cup of tea and handed her a new tissue. "I want you to stop this and ask him all the questions you're asking me. If he insists nothing's wrong, ask him about the late nights and where the money's going. Then you should know if you really have a problem or not."

"What if I do?"

Jocelyn didn't have to think about it. "Phyl and I will kill him. Drink your tea."

JOCELYN GLANCED AT HER watch and rang her grandfather's doorbell again. She checked on him every day at lunchtime, sometimes with a phone call, sometimes with a visit. Today, she'd wanted to deliver the news in person that the Service Clubs Cooperative had agreed to stage all events for the Senior Center, and that Robert Donnelly had approved the use of the mall's center court for the bazaar.

The front door was suddenly yanked open and Jocelyn was pulled inside. "Hurry up," Nathan Foley said, waving her to follow. "I've got three Russkie subs in my sights. I don't want to lose them."

"Gramps..." Jocelyn tried to call him back as he hobbled arthritically across the living room to the small room off the kitchen where he slept and kept his computer. Since her grandmother's death three years earlier, her grandfather had chosen not to use the upstairs bedroom they'd shared.

"Hurry!" he said over his shoulder.

Reluctantly, Jocelyn followed. She had no idea how his *The Hunt for Red October* computer game worked, but she could be left cooling her heels for half an hour while her grandfather destroyed the Russian submariner force. Apparently, the game would continue when a player left it unattended, and treacherously lead him to defeat at the hands of the enemy or by collision with an iceberg.

"Got 'em in my sights," Nathan cackled gleefully as he worked the keyboard. "Just be a minute."

Ten minutes later, he slapped the tabletop, shouted victoriously and turned to her with a wide smile. "I rule the North Atlantic. What can I do for you?"

Jocelyn, sitting in an ancient overstuffed chair in the corner perusing a *Playboy* magazine, looked up from the centerfold.

"Gramps, I'm going to have to call the ambulance for you one day. How does your pacemaker deal with this?"

He rolled forward in his desk chair, snatched the magazine from her and tossed it aside. "I had a booster put on it. What do you want?"

Jocelyn leaned forward with a smile. "To tell you that the Senior Center project is underway. All the service groups are going to donate to the cause, and the Old Cannery Mall gave us the center court for Valentine's Day. So get Freddie busy with her cookies."

"You're a genius," he said, reaching out of his chair to hug her. "I knew you could do it."

"You want to call the committee and see when we can get together again to look the place over and decide what we'll need?"

"Sure. When are you free?"

Jocelyn stood. "Just call me, and I'll make time. You have something for dinner tonight?"

"John's picking me up and we're going to McDonald's."

"You need groceries?"

"Jossie, stop fussing."

"You know," she said cautiously, "if you'd let me have a key, you wouldn't have to interrupt your game when I come to visit. I could just let myself in. Or you should replace this ancient lock with a more modern dead bolt. No one has a door that has to be locked from both sides anymore.''

Nathan got to his feet, his expression both scolding and knowing. "If it was good enough for the guy who built it a hundred years ago, it's good enough for me. And if you could get in, you'd start doing my laundry when I wasn't here, checking my pantry, leaving casseroles and taking over my checkbook. I'd lose control of my life. No, thank you.''

Jocelyn sighed. They'd had this argument so many times. "Gramps, I don't want to take over your life. I just want to make it more comfortable.''

"It's my life," he said gently but firmly, offering her a hand up. "And I'm comfortable with it the way it is. When I go into a coma, you can make yourself a key." He kissed her cheek and pulled her toward the door. He opened it for her and frowned down at her. "Is that what you wore when you called on Mr. Donnelly?''

Jocelyn looked down at her clothes.

"Mr. Donnelly," she said calmly, "had nothing to say about how I was dressed." He'd wanted to, she knew, but he hadn't. "I told you the nineties man takes a woman at brain value.''

John nodded sadly. "Lucky for us. I'll call the committee this afternoon and be in touch with you tomorrow.''

Jocelyn drove away in her vintage Volkswagen Beetle, unsettled by the memory of Rob Donnelly asking her to dinner. Heading home to a lonely meal, she wondered why she'd turned him down.

JOCELYN HEARD THE RING OF her telephone and growled in frustration. She stood halfway up a rickety ladder in her bedroom closet, a large box of seasonal decorations in her hands.

She balanced the box on the top of the ladder, then dove across her bed and yanked the phone off the side table.

"Hello," she said, the sound taking on a little lilt as the mattress bounced under her.

"Joss?"

She recognized the voice instantly as belonging to the last person she'd have expected to call her on a Friday night.

"Yes, Laurel," she replied. She braced herself. All her dealings with Laurel since the fourth grade had had a negative outcome for her.

"I took your request to direct the proceeds of our fundraiser toward the Senior Center to the River Belles," Laurel said. The Belles were a group of professional women whose support could be important.

"I appreciate that, Laurel," Jocelyn said politely. "Thank you."

"The reaction was mixed. Part of the group would like the money to go to putting wrought-iron benches downtown."

Jocelyn made herself count to ten. Laurel was baiting her. She had something up her sleeve. "It is the River Belles' money, after all," she said amiably. "And your talent-and-services auction would make enough money to line both sides of Water Street with benches—if you think that's important."

"Benches would have our name on it."

"So would the bronze plaque in the Senior Center."

Laurel's husky laugh made Jocelyn stiffen. "I think I can sway the vote to your side, but you'll have to help me out."

Jocelyn hated to ask. "How?"

"By offering your services at the auction."

She finally understood. Laurel knew she'd declined the invitation to participate for the past four years. It was a trick to embarrass her. Though the auction was set up as a donation of professional services for charity and community betterment, the young men and women who volunteered were teased mercilessly from the audience. Jocelyn got a mental image of herself standing there in her bibbed overalls while total silence came from beyond the lights.

"Every business in town is entitled to my services through their Community Association dues." She tried to sound unruffled. "Why would anyone want to pay for them?"

"You forget that your former employer, Janice Reston, is one of our members and she's dying to get you back. She promised to bid big if you'll sign on."

Jocelyn closed her eyes and grimaced. She'd loved her work as office manager for Reston Decorators, but she'd wanted to do something with her life that would make a difference, however small. Then the job of development director had come up two years ago, and she'd applied to the city council.

"Last year, we netted eight thousand dollars," Laurel said, prodding. "The take'll be bigger this year."

Almost half what the seniors needed! Jocelyn put a fingertip to the growing ache between her eyes. "The auction's in February?" she asked.

"Saturday night, February first," Laurel replied.

Jocelyn caught the smug note in Laurel's voice. She was caught. She couldn't turn down the invitation and risk losing such a large contribution. "Sure," she said brightly. "Thanks for the opportunity."

There was an instant's silence on the other end of the line, followed by the husky laugh. "I knew you'd want to help. I'll tell Janice. Have a nice weekend, Joss." There was a small, malicious pause. "Doing anything special?"

"Alec Baldwin's limo is picking me up in ten minutes," Jocelyn said. "Gotta run."

She dropped the receiver gently, then pounded her fists into the mattress. "Damn!" she shouted.

The telephone rang again and she snatched it up. "The limo's here!" she growled. "I don't have time—"

"Limo?"

Jocelyn closed her eyes and pressed hard on the aching spot between her brows. "Hi, Gramps. Alec Baldwin's limo."

"Jossie, are you tippling?"

Jocelyn smiled. Any other man her grandfather's age might have been expected to ask, "Alec who?" But Nathan Foley had seen *The Hunt for Red October* four times.

"No, it was a joke," she exclaimed with a sigh. "I thought you were someone else. What is it?"

"I talked to the committee and we all agreed Wednesday would be a good day for us to look over the Old Cannery's court." He still sounded worried. "Would that work for you?"

"That'll be fine. Want me to pick you up?"

"No, I'll pick up the committee and meet you there. Mary has her grandchildren until three-thirty. Is four o'clock too late?"

"It's fine."

"Get some rest, Jossie," Nathan advised in concern. "And don't wait for the limo. Isn't Baldwin seeing Batman's girlfriend?"

"Good night, Gramps."

ROB CAUGHT SIGHT OF Jocelyn and the Senior Center Committee wandering across the center court when he arrived for work. Everyone was talking at once while Jocelyn patiently took notes and parried questions.

"We'll need a minimum of twelve tables. The Scandinavian Brotherhood has already reserved space, and the Fishermen's Wives want a table with an outlet to keep their chowder hot.''

"We don't want to blow any fuses."

"Jossie, can we have plug-ins?"

She was wearing black tights today, Rob noticed, following the line of her leg up with interest, only to stop with disappointment at midcalf when he encountered a brightly striped sweater that didn't stop till it reached her chin in a turtleneck and made her shoulders look like Refrigerator Johnson's.

He looked at her earnest expression as she replied to one of the women's questions, and found himself smiling. He couldn't help himself. Princess Valiant fascinated him.

He approached the group. "Hello, Jocelyn," he said, then nodded at the ladies and offered his hand to the men. "Good afternoon. I'm Rob Donnelly. Are there any questions I can answer?"

"Hi." Jocelyn's eyes registered surprise followed by an instant of pleasure, then clouded almost immediately with the shy nervousness he always seemed to inspire in her. "Several dozen," she replied. "Let me introduce you."

She went around the small group, finally pulling forward a tall, lean man wearing a baseball cap with the insignia of the USS *Lexington*. "This is my grandfather and chairman of the committee, Nathan Foley."

Rob pointed to Nathan's hat. "You serve on the *Lexington?*"

Nathan squared his shoulders. "World War II."

"I was on her in '77 and '78."

"What rating?"

"Quartermaster."

"I was assistant air officer."

"Please don't get him started," Mary said, interrupting gently. "At least, not until we've finished what we've come to do. He could go on until breakfast."

Nathan didn't take offense. "No fun having war stories if you can't tell 'em."

Rob smiled. "We'll have to compare notes on the *Lexington* another time. Did I overhear a question about outlets?"

Jocelyn tagged along behind the group, taking notes as Rob pointed out the outlets, showed them where the banquet tables were stored, offered the use of white table covers and a seldom-used second refrigerator in the back of the kitchen.

Jocelyn admired and resented his kindness and easy warmth. In a gray suit over a white shirt with a subtly elegant tie, his tall body moved with easy grace, insidiously distracting her from her task. Her eyes, lowered to her notes, glanced up at every opportunity to admire long legs, broad shoulders and a smile that could upset her equilibrium.

When the tour had been completed and all questions answered, Rob asked Jocelyn, "Can you stay for dinner?"

She stared, first pleased, then disappointed. How dare he do that to her a second time—and in front of her friends. The foursome waited interestedly for her reply.

"Thank you," she said, "but I have to take these people—"

"I'm taking them home," Nathan interrupted.

Thwarted, Jocelyn glanced at her watch, looking for another excuse. "I have to call—"

"It's after five-thirty," Mary put in. "Everything's closed."

Rob put a hand on Jocelyn's shoulder and drew her toward the restaurant. "Pleasure meeting all of you," he said to the group. "Mr. Foley, we'll have to get together and talk about the *Lexington.*"

"You're on!" Nathan, looking pleased, began to shepherd the committee toward the door. "Bye, Jossie."

The moment they were out the door, Jocelyn turned to Rob, the line of her lips firm. "I am not staying for dinner."

He put a hand to her chin and ran a thumb lightly over her mouth, completely unsettling her. The sternness she'd hoped to convey turned to open-mouthed surprise. Her lips tingled and she had to resist the need to rub them.

"That's better," he said, lowering his hand. "Why do you do that?"

"What?" she asked. Her voice was a croak.

"Stiffen up around me like a spinster with a traveling salesman. What do you think I'm going to do to you, particularly in the middle of a restaurant?"

Jocelyn had no idea how to answer that. Everything that came to mind had possibilities she'd almost like to consider if she weren't sure she was just providing him some spur-of-the-moment amusement.

"Why me?" she asked. "Is Laurel busy?"

Temper flared in his eyes. He looked over her head at the late shoppers wandering through the mall and replied quietly, "Laurel's in the doorway of her shop, staring at us right now. If you'd like her to see you run off like a scared rabbit, that's fine with me. But I invited you to dinner because I'm new here and so far, every meal I've had has been snatched standing at the counter in the kitchen or alone in front of my television at home. I thought company across a table would be nice, but perhaps I was mistaken."

Jocelyn caught the sleeve of his jacket as he tried to turn away from her. She felt small and shrewish. "I'm sorry," she said quietly. "I thought you were...teasing."

He frowned in confusion. "Teasing?"

She shook her head. "Never mind. May I reconsider?"

His expression softened and he offered his arm. "Yes, you may."

Jocelyn, her hand on the soft wool of his sleeve, caught a quick glimpse of a pouting Laurel ducking behind a rack of jackets. Jocelyn had never been in a position to best her nemesis before, and she told herself it was petty and unworthy to enjoy it. She had to tell herself twice.

Chapter Four

"Griff sautés the oysters in butter and garlic," Rob explained as a waitress placed oval platters before them. "Then he sprinkles them with Parmesan and broils them for a few seconds. Tell me you've ever tasted anything better."

Jocelyn took a bite, closed her eyes to savor the delicate flavor, then made a soft sound of approval. "They're wonderful. How can you eat what he prepares day after day and remain..." She hesitated. She was willing to unbend because he'd made her feel so guilty for rebuffing his invitation. But she wasn't willing to admit she thought him gorgeous. "And remain in shape?"

"Why, thank you, Jocelyn," he said with a teasing grin. He seemed to know what she thought despite her careful choice of words. "Efficient metabolism, I guess. I spend twelve hours on my feet here, then go home to a wreck of a cottage overlooking the bay. My little fixer-upper is as time-consuming as my work."

"Don't you get tired of being here?" she asked.

He pushed a small bowl of sauce her way. "Try that," he said. "It's spicy but wonderful. No, Griff and I grew up in the back of a restaurant our fathers owned. I don't think either of us could function without the aroma of a roux simmering or the sound of water sloshing in a dishwasher."

Jocelyn smiled at him, almost surprised to learn he had that kind of a past. He always looked as though he'd sprung fully formed from Nordstrom's window. "No kidding? Brothers and sisters?"

"No. Just me."

"Griffin?"

"No. Just him."

Jocelyn dipped an oyster into the sauce and found it more than spicy. It was hot. Tears sprang to her eyes, and she reached quickly for her water.

Rob stopped her, pushing her coffee toward her instead. "It's better to drink something hot."

Once the fire abated, she realized the flavor was delicious. She tried it again, dipping more cautiously this time.

"Do your father and your uncle still have the restaurant?"

"No. Our family's gone now. Griff's mother died when he was seven. My father got tired of the struggle and left when I was fourteen. My mother worked nonstop until my uncle passed away two years later and we had to sell the restaurant."

Despite the carefully casual way in which that small speech had been delivered, Jocelyn heard the bitterness. "I'm sorry," she said softly.

He dismissed the past with a shrug and offered her a basket of rolls, folding back a hunter green napkin. "It was a long time ago."

She selected a fat butter-flake roll. "In Los Angeles? Griff said you came here via Boston and L.A."

"Boston." He passed her the iced rack of butter curls. "I went to Boston College, then did a couple of years in the navy while Griff went to the CIA."

Both eyebrows disappeared into her bangs. "The Central Intelligence Agency?"

He laughed. "No. The Culinary Institute of America. That's Griff's favorite joke."

She make a face at him and went back to her meal. "Then what?"

"Then he was sous-chef at a trendy place in Hollywood, and I opened a restaurant on La Cienega Boulevard."

She frowned. "And you left that to come here?"

"After a messy divorce." He looked grim for a moment, then asked with a smile, "Aren't you pleased?"

She dropped her fork, took a sip of wine. So, he'd been married. "Salty Harbor is delighted to have you," she said noncommittally.

He laughed softly. "But you aren't?"

She had to get tough now, she thought. He was going too far, but she knew how to deal with that. "You're flirting, Rob," she said candidly.

He nodded equably. "Yes."

That surprised her. Most men retreated when their tactics were brought out into the open. "Flirting is out of favor," she said, concentrating on a forkful of rice.

"With whom?"

"Everyone. People don't play games anymore."

He frowned. "Flirting's not a game. It's a method of approach."

"It's artificial."

He folded his arms on the table and leaned toward her. "And what did the direct approach get me with you? A rejection followed by the suggestion that I'd invited you to dinner to tease you."

She put her roll aside and fiddled with her fork. "I apologized for that."

He said gravely, "And I've forgiven you. So, if we've ruled out honesty and flirtation, what approach do you prefer?"

She made herself smile politely while looking him firmly in the eye. "I don't have time to *be* approached. I'm very busy."

He returned her look steadily, and she had the uncomfortable feeling he wasn't impressed with her declaration.

He leaned back in his chair and picked up his wineglass. "With what?" he asked politely.

"Work," she replied, dabbing at her lips with her napkin and replacing it carefully in her lap. "Family. The usual stuff."

"That's it?" His question expressed disbelief that those could be enough.

She was becoming defensive. "My work is satisfying, and my family is dependable. What else is there?"

He related completely to the satisfaction of work one enjoyed, but only partially to a family that was dependable. But he couldn't understand a life without romance.

"Man and woman," he said quietly, putting his glass on the table and leaning toward her. "Magic. Romance."

She rolled her eyes. "That's nonsense."

He widened his. "Ms. Foley, you blaspheme." He looked at her closely and reconsidered. "Or you've been stung."

Stung. She repeated the word to herself. An insipid word for the way she'd felt at the time.

"He married my sister," she explained briefly.

"Ah." Rob nodded sympathetically. "There are other men in the world."

"But they all want the same thing—beauty, glamour, a sort of—" She waggled her hand as she searched for the right word. She finally said quickly, "I don't know. Sex appeal, I guess, and I'm just not like that."

"*Every* man?" he questioned with an innocent stare. "Have you really polled all of them?"

She gave him an exasperated smile. "No, but I've observed many."

"I don't recall your getting around to me."

"No, but you weren't here."

"Then here's your chance to prove or disprove your theory." He poured more wine into her glass. "I volunteer to be the subject of your thesis, your experiment."

"You mean I may observe you?"

"Observation does not constitute an in-depth study. You'll have to spend time with me."

She put a hand over her heart. "Too selfless of you, Rob, but I'm not after a Masters in Men, or a Nobel in Nineties Relationships. I told you, I'm a nonbeliever."

"Because of faulty data." He pushed her wineglass toward her. "You might be interested to know that a woman's physical attributes are not a priority for me."

She sipped her wine. "I'm not rich, either," she said, "or well connected."

He ignored her mild sarcasm. "I like sensitivity, humor, a cheerful attitude."

Jocelyn put her napkin on the table and tried to look fierce. "Will you please stop? You can not convince me for one moment that you have any romantic inclinations toward me. This is only our third meeting, and we're too opposite to—"

"Jocelyn," he interrupted calmly, "If you understood romance, you'd know it can strike on the *first* meeting, and that being 'different' is what the game is all about. I told you. You're working from a faulty study. And how do you know we're too different? Do you know me?"

She leaned toward him, her expression smug. "How can you claim attraction for me when *you* don't know *me?*"

He grinned. "Attraction doesn't require knowledge, just hormones. We both have them, Joss."

Alarmed and completely out of her element, Jocelyn picked up her purse and stood. "Well, I'm taking mine home. Thank you for a lovely dinner."

Rob reached across the table, caught her hand and pushed her back down in her chair. "Can't leave now. Here comes Griff with dessert."

The sound of oohs and ahs made her turn her head. Griff was coming toward them, something flaming on a cart. Jocelyn perched on the edge of her chair, trapped.

Griff served Cherries Jubilee, poured coffee, looked approvingly from one to the other, then retreated.

Rob added cream to his coffee. "What are your plans for the weekend?"

Jocelyn took a bite of the exquisite dessert and cast him an impatient glance.

"What?" he demanded with a light laugh. "I didn't ask to be included in them, did I? I was just making conversation."

She sighed and reached for her coffee cup. "Friday night, I'm baby-sitting my older sister's girls. Saturday, I had hoped to attend the high school production of *Steel Magnolias,* but I've a lot of planning to do for the fund-raiser. I'll save that for next weekend. Sunday, I'll go to church, have brunch with my grandfather and spend the afternoon finishing an afghan I'm making for my younger sister's baby. Anything else you want to know?"

"Which sister took your boyfriend?" he asked gently.

"Phyllis, the older one." She sipped coffee and sat back in her chair. "And she didn't take him. He fell for her like an anvil off a roof."

"So you don't blame her?"

"Of course not." She looked at him levelly, then succumbed to a weak smile. "At least, not when I'm being rational."

Jocelyn pushed away her half-eaten dessert and stood. "I really have to go. Please thank Griff—"

Rob got to his feet. "I'll walk you to your car."

"You needn't bother. You're supposed to be working, and I'm per—" She stopped because he wasn't listening. They were already at the door to the mall. Rob signaled the hostess that he'd be right back.

He rested an arm on Jocelyn's shoulders and led her slowly across the polished planks. On either side of the mall was a long stretch of dark shop windows, closed for the night. Many of them were decorated with hearts and cupids for Valentine's Day.

"Are we going to be colleagues in the name of science?" he asked.

Jocelyn had to concentrate to breathe. The comfortable burden of his arm and the closeness of his body were robbing her of air. *Attraction doesn't require knowledge,* he'd said. *Just hormones.* Hers were definitely acting up.

She pretended interest in a stationery-store window to break the contact. He simply came up behind her and looked over her shoulder. Were she to move her face an inch, their lips would have touched.

She moved nervously to the next window. It belonged to Carstairs Jewelry. All the precious baubles had been removed for the night and she found her face reflected back against the white silk drapery on which a collection of garnets rested during the day.

Rob's head was reflected above hers.

"I consider that a very pretty face," he said.

She looked at Rob's reflection, his chin even with the top of her head, and saw that his eyes were focused on her face. The seriousness she saw there startled her. He thought she was pretty.

She lowered her eyes to herself, trying to force them not simply to look, but to *see.*

Red hair, bright and glossy, but cut like a helmet. She looked into her eyes and flinched, the movement forcing her back against Rob's chest. It was hard and warm, a barrier against escape. With a sigh of reluctance, she looked again.

The competent director of community development she usually saw in the ornate mirror over her dresser at home appeared to have been replaced by a woman with wide, slightly sad, enormously vulnerable blue eyes—dark blue, like that brief period between dusk and darkness.

Her nose was ordinary, her complexion clear and free of freckles—a rare victory for a redhead. At the moment, there was hectic color in her cheeks. Her lips, without makeup, seemed to have gained color from her blush. Unfortunately, they'd lost their usual no-nonsense line and were now parted in confusion and distress.

"Well?" Rob asked.

Her eyes strayed down to the turtleneck of the baggy, brightly striped sweater, and she saw her own eyebrows ripple in dismay.

"Don't look at the clothes." Rob placed both arms across her, covering what was visible of her sweater. "Just look at the face."

For an instant, Jocelyn couldn't make her brain or her eyes work.

Her senses were filled with awareness of his touch. She felt muscle and energy in his arms. The hands closed around her shoulders were warm through her sweater, and gentle, despite their strength. His spicy scent wafted around her, and she felt his breath against her temple as he dipped his head to ask, "What do you see?"

"Just . . . me," she replied in a small voice.

She felt a rush of air in her lungs when he dropped his arms from around her, then lost it in a tiny gasp when he combed both hands through her hair, teasing it out of its stiffness. Gooseflesh rose on her scalp. He reached around her to ruffle her bangs, then rested both hands lightly on her arms.

"Now what?"

She struggled to regain presence of mind. The disarray was a little flattering. The hair stirred away from her face brought out its shape, and her eyes seemed more prominent.

"A cross between Red Skelton," she said, "and Phyllis Diller."

Rob dropped his forehead against the back of her head with a thunk.

"If how I look isn't important to me," she said, "why should it be important to you? I'm not looking for... for... romance."

Rob put his arm around her again and pulled her toward the double doors. "Because I think your appearance *is* important to you. For some reason I can't imagine, you use it as a way of keeping people—or, rather, men—at a distance. And because it isn't going to work with me."

Jocelyn stopped to look up at him as they reached the doors. "Then what are *you* hiding, Robert Donnelly, that you insist on cultivating the feelings of a woman who's told you several times that she isn't interested in you?"

He nodded and replied with hesitation. "Fair question. I married a flawlessly beautiful woman. She fell all over me with dramatic declarations of love and devotion and left me after fourteen months for a little bald guy with a bankroll."

Jocelyn felt sadness for him and a return of indignation for herself. "So now you're opting for a plain Jane who won't give you the time of day?"

He closed his eyes a moment, as though summoning patience, then pinched her chin between his thumb and forefinger and leaned toward her until their faces were only inches apart.

"You're not plain. You're camouflaged," he said. "And you're as interested in me as I am in you. And you're looking for romance just like everyone else on the planet."

Jocelyn felt a hot blush rise from her turtleneck. He was right. And he knew she knew it.

"Fifty percent of marriages end in divorce," she said. "That's an appalling statistic."

"You're right," he conceded with an inclination of his head. "But that's love. I'm talking about romance."

"Doesn't one stem from the other?"

"The semantics are tricky," he said, "but I think romance is an emotional attraction, an exploration of the soft side of what we are. It doesn't make the same demands as love. It's caring and kindness and excitement and sweetness—a sort of adventure into putting all those things together and enjoying them."

Jocelyn raised an eyebrow. "That is love, Rob."

He shook his head. "Love is for the purpose of permanence and an acknowledged disappointment to half the people who try it. Romance is for as long as it lasts."

That statement jangled discordantly in Jocelyn's ears, but before she could refute it, Rob said, "Joss, you're planning a Valentine bazaar. You've got to believe in romance a little or you'll never pull it off."

She finally felt on familiar ground. Work. She understood her work. "I'll pull it off because I believe in the people who'll benefit from it. I don't have to swallow any hearts-and-flowers claptrap."

She was about to push the doors open when the sound of Griff's voice filtered clearly down the hall that led to the restaurant's kitchen.

"I'm afraid he's still busy," Jocelyn heard Griff say. "But I'll tell him you came by on your nightly hunt."

There was an indistinguishable reply in a feminine voice.

"Well, you are after prey, aren't you, Laurel?" Griff asked.

Laurel's reply was defensive. "I was after a dinner companion."

There was the sound of something being dragged. "Put your pretty backside on the stool," Griff said, "and we'll share a plate of oysters."

"When hell freezes over, cookie," Laurel replied.

They heard the smile in Griff's voice. "If anyone can make that happen, sweets, you can."

High heels clicked angrily away, then Griff wandered into the corridor and out into the quiet mall, a mug of coffee in his hands, a preoccupied frown on his face.

"You weren't very nice to her," Jocelyn scolded gently, casting Rob an accusatory look, as though he, too, had been somehow responsible for what they'd overheard.

Griff laughed grimly. "She doesn't need nice," he said. "She needs a couple of days with a man with a short temper and a broad spatula. You left half your dessert."

"I was stuffed. Everything was wonderful." She put an arm around him and kissed his cheek. "Thank you. Good night."

Rob tried to follow her into the parking lot, but she stopped him with a hand to his chest.

"Good night," she said firmly.

He watched through the glass doors until she was safely in her car and on her way. Then he turned to Griff with a frown.

"I get a lot of sass," he said. "And you get a kiss."

Griff shook his head. "God created women to protect men from excessive self-confidence."

"I AM HAPPY!" Jocelyn wiped the steamy mirror in her tiny bathroom and found her towel-clad reflection. "Happy!"

she continued aggressively. "And no smooth-talking hunk is going to mess that up."

After fifteen minutes under the shower's hot spray, she'd lost that sense of disorientation with which she'd arrived home from her dinner with Rob. She didn't know what he was up to, but she wasn't falling for it.

Recovering from rejection was too difficult and took too long. After Jeffrey, she'd isolated herself in her comfortable protective armor, and she wasn't shedding it for anyone.

Toweling off, Jocelyn pulled on a lavender velour robe that had been a gift from Phyllis and dried her hair. She swept the blow dryer quickly back and forth, combing her fingers through the wet, redwood-colored strings of hair.

As it began to dry, lightening in color and gaining curl and volume, she stopped, staring. There she was. The woman reflected in Carstairs's window—the one with the wide eyes and the ingenue-siren face.

Who was that? And what was she doing in Jocelyn's body? Not only could she see her, she could feel her invading the armor plate of her protective cocoon. "Let me in," she said. Then, clearly, gently, "Let him in."

Jocelyn yanked the blow dryer's cord out of the socket, wrapped it around the appliance with a firmness that would have strangled anything living and dropped the instrument into the belly basket near the sink.

She crawled into the twin bed that had been hers since childhood and pulled the blankets up to her eyes. "No one is getting in," she said aloud to the darkness. "No one."

IN A KHAKI-COLORED trench coat, the collar pulled up against the wind and rain, Rob walked to the restaurant. It would have made more sense to drive, but it was only half a mile from his cottage and he'd never smelled air like this in

Boston or Los Angeles. Besides, he needed the exercise. Princess Valiant was getting to him.

Jocelyn had been on his mind since they'd had dinner together a week ago. He was usually good with women. He prided himself on knowing how to treat them. He could make them feel special because he truly believed they were. He could encourage them with subtlety or extravagance, whichever they preferred, or he could let them down easily or play out a dramatic scene according to the woman's taste. But he didn't understand being unable to make contact at all.

Several times over dinner that night, he'd thought he'd caught Jocelyn's interest, only to have her scurry away from him before he could arrange to see her again. The image of the woman had been on his mind ever since. Something had permeated his consciousness and refused to let him go— something in the wariness in her eyes, in the softly parted lips he'd seen reflected in the jewelry-store window.

This hilly, isolated little town at the mouth of the Columbia River was the kind of landscape where a man needed a woman. It was moody and elemental—the protective, forested hills at one's back; the river spread out for transportation, sustenance or simple drama. The atmosphere could make a man feel alone and lost. A woman in his arms could make him feel comforted, supported and somewhat important. He missed being important to someone.

"Donnelly!"

As Rob stepped onto the pier where Griff's car was already parked, he looked up at the sound of his name. A tall man in a blue nylon jacket and a brimmed cotton rain hat waved at him from the railing. It took Rob a moment to recognize Jocelyn's grandfather.

He joined the man, who was now leaning over the railing, looking down into the water flowing away from the restaurant toward the mouth of the river and the open ocean. It was spiked with broken pilings from a cannery that had burned in a long-ago fire.

"Hello, Nathan," Rob said. "Forgot your pole."

Nathan pointed to a sea lion weaving its way among the pilings. It's slick, rich brown back curled in a reptilian hump as he dived and disappeared. "I never get tired of watching them," he said, then pointed to the distance where the sea lion, finally free of the pilings, broke the water with a loud snuffle, his bristly whiskers visible from where the two men stood.

From its perch on a bobbing green channel marker in the middle of the river, another sea lion barked loudly.

"I can hear them from my cottage at night," Rob said, leaning his elbows on the railing. "I've come to listen for them and wonder what they're talking about."

Nathan laughed. "Oh, probably the kids and the bills and the infrequency of sex, just like the rest of us."

Rob laughed. "You think wildlife is as mundane as everyday life?"

Nathan pointed to the sea lion swimming toward the channel marker. "Must be. She rang the dinner bell and he's running home. Speaking of dinner . . ." Nathan continued to stare at the water, but his tone changed subtly. "How was your evening with my granddaughter?"

Rob thought a moment. "She's . . . an interesting young lady."

"Interesting to you?"

Rob didn't have to think about that. He didn't understand it, but he didn't have to think about it. "Yes," he replied. "I'm not sure the interest is reciprocal, though."

Nathan nodded without surprise. "Prickly girl. Her mother is beautiful. Her older and younger sisters are pretty."

"She's not unattractive," Rob said.

John turned to look at him, a smile of approval coming slowly. "She never much cared how she looked. Young men, unfortunately—or maybe all of us—pay more attention to a pretty face than we should." Nathan straightened away from the railing and dug both hands into his jacket pockets. "Jossie's feelings run deep, but she doesn't share them easily."

A gust of wind blew across the pier and Rob hunched deeper into his coat. "Yes," he said. "I'm aware of that."

"So—" Nathan grinned conspiratorially "—maybe if you really are interested, you won't let yourself be too easily discouraged. Jossie can be a cussed young woman, but she can be a sweetheart, too. She tells me men these days are more interested in a woman's brain than her body. That true?"

Rob laughed. "I don't think we've come quite that far. Let's say, equally interested."

Nathan nodded, as though what he'd suspected had been finally confirmed. "She needs a man who'll show her how much woman she is. Can you do that?"

"I like to think I can do anything I put my mind to."

"Without hurting her?"

"Trust me."

Nathan put out his hand. "I think I do."

Rob shook it. "Do you have time for a cup of coffee?"

Nathan walked with him toward the double doors. "Thanks, but I'm supposed to meet Mary here to take measurements for streamers." He gave Rob a wry smile. "To think an independent, hard-living ex-marine mill-worker would come to this—helping with cupids and buying crepe paper."

Rob pulled the door open and gestured the older man through. "What we do for the ladies."

Nathan waved as he caught sight of Mary, waiting for him across the court. He turned to shake hands with Rob. "Rain check on the coffee?"

"You bet. If you don't see me in the restaurant, ask the hostess to check the kitchen and my office."

"Thank you. I will."

Rob walked into the restaurant to find everyone eating a late lunch. The hostess sketched him a wave before seating a party of eight, waitresses rushed between kitchen and tables, and the cash register rang melodically. It was music to his ears.

He walked into the kitchen to see the same degree of frenetic activity. Griff, putting the finishing black olive on a taco salad, grinned at him over his shoulder. "Can you put on an apron?" he asked. "Jackie's little girl is sick and she had to pick her up at school and take her to her mother's."

"Sure." Rob whipped off his coat and looped a utilitarian white apron over his head as he studied the order wheel. "What do you want me to do? The crepes? The fetuccini? The bordelaise sauce?"

Griff gave him a second look as he placed the salad on the pick-up counter. "The burgers. You went to business school, remember?" He studied his cousin's smile suspiciously. "What's with you?"

"Nothing," Rob said innocently. But he seared three burgers while humming quietly to himself. It was time to do something about Jocelyn.

Chapter Five

"Dorothy from Harbor Florist brought this by *herself* about five-thirty." Mrs. Gustafson, who lived in the apartment across the hall with a cranky peekapoo, handed Jocelyn a cut-crystal vase filled with tight, red rosebuds and snowy white baby's breath. Their fragrance filled the hallway.

Jocelyn gasped and then frowned. "Are you sure they're for me?"

Mrs. Gustafson indicated the card tucked into the flowers. Jocelyn's name and address were written in a bold man's hand.

The Peke darted out of the apartment's open door and ran around Jocelyn's ankles, barking shrilly. Jocelyn didn't mind. She couldn't have moved if she'd wanted to.

Mrs. Gustafson scooped up the dog and kissed the flat, ugly face soundly. "Mama's Biddy is so bad," she scolded affectionately. "Your birthday?" she asked Jocelyn.

Balancing the flowers, Jocelyn groped for her keys. "No."

"Anniversary or something?"

"No."

"Dorothy said they were from a gentleman."

As Jocelyn pushed her door open, Mrs. Gustafson crowded close, obviously hoping for an invitation—and the opportunity to learn the identity of the mysterious gentleman. Biddy barked in Jocelyn's ear.

Jocelyn sidled into the apartment. With an apologetic smile, she closed the door in the disappointed woman's face.

She dropped her purse and jacket on a chair, placed the flowers in the middle of the coffee table and herself in the middle of the sofa. She stared at the bloodred rosebuds whose perfume now filled her small living room.

The only man in Salty Harbor who would have a gift delivered to her was her grandfather, and he'd never think to send flowers. They had to be from . . . No. She wouldn't let herself think it.

She finally removed the small gray envelope and opened it. It held a card and a ticket. The card read, "Roses are red, Robert is blue, 'Cause he's missing you."

Jocelyn giggled, holding the card to her for a moment, then reading it again. The ticket was for the Saturday-night show of the Salty Harbor High School's production of *Steel Magnolias*. She remembered telling him she'd wanted to go last weekend but had been too busy. She examined the single ticket.

She wasn't sure whether to be disappointed or relieved that he hadn't included himself in the gift. He was apparently trying to show her he understood her wish not to become involved. Yet the card said he missed her. Just words. Or a deliberate attempt to confuse her.

There was a perfunctory knock on her door and Phyllis walked in, wearing a fuschia silk raincoat and carrying a large, round tin.

"Hi," she said. "I baked some—" She stopped still three steps inside the living room, her eyes rooted to the bouquet.

"What are those?" she demanded.

Jocelyn dreaded explaining. "They're called roses," she said. "Come in."

Phyllis walked to the sofa as though in a trance, shedding her coat. "They're yours?"

"No, I stole them from Gibson and Gable Mortuary."

Phyllis darted her a glare as she sat beside Jocelyn, then focused on the flowers once more. "Who are they from?"

"Harbor Florist."

"You're very close to having your earlobe twisted," Phyllis threatened. That had been her favorite power tactic as a child, and maturity hadn't blunted its effectiveness.

"Rob Donnelly," Jocelyn tossed over her shoulder as she rose from the couch and went into the kitchen.

"And who is this Rob?" Phyllis asked from the doorway, reaching out to deposit the tin on the corner of the counter.

"Tea?" Jocelyn asked, taking two dark blue mugs off a wall rack. "Cocoa? Café Vienna?"

"Café Vienna," Phyllis replied as she walked into the room, leaning against the molding. "And why did he send you flowers?"

Briefly and without drama, Jocelyn explained how she'd met Robert Donnelly. The kettle whistled and she poured boiling water into the two cups, briskly stirring Phyllis's, then bobbing her cranberry tea bag up and down until the brew was satisfyingly dark and aromatic. She opened the tin Phyllis had brought and found her favorite peanut-butter cookies.

"Thank you, Phyl," she said, putting several on a plate, then she led the way back to the sofa. "He doesn't really like me, he's just doing this for science."

Phyllis grinned. "Biology, I'll bet." She blew daintily into her steaming cup. "What does he look like?"

Jocelyn shrugged a shoulder. "Tall, dark, handsome. Relax. They're just roses."

Phyllis looked horrified. "Just roses? A man who sends them is obviously a romantic and shouldn't be allowed to get

away. Joss—'' Phyllis put her cup down and closed a hand
over Jocelyn's wrist ''—it's time to forgive Jeff and me for
falling in love.''

Jocelyn looked at her in hurt surprise. Was she really that
transparent?

''Oh, I know how you think,'' Phyllis said. ''Jeff married me, and Charlie blossomed into a gorgeous creature
and the middle child syndrome hits you like a ton of bricks.
You put on that silly armor you wear...'' she swept a hand
down Jocelyn's turtleneck and coveralls '' ...and you went
forth to serve the world of service and senior citizens and
retired from the mating game.''

''Because it's foolish.'' Jocelyn saw no point in denying
anything Phyllis thought to be true.

''It's sweet,'' Phyllis corrected. ''If you'd loosen up a little, you'd see that. You'd feel it, too. You'd appreciate a gift
of roses.''

Jocelyn put her cup on the table and patted Phyllis's
hand. ''I love all of you, you know that. I hold no grudges
and don't have to forgive anyone. I'm happy that you're all
happy.'' Changing the subject, Jocelyn said, ''Have you
talked to Charlie in the last few days?''

Phyllis pointed a finger at her. ''We'll talk about Charlie
later. Right now, I want to know when you're seeing Rob
again.''

Jocelyn sighed. ''Next time we have to talk about the bazaar.''

''If you don't call him and thank him gushingly for these
roses and make a date with him, I won't bake one cookie for
Freddie,'' Phyllis threatened.

''Phyl!'' Jocelyn protested. ''One has nothing to do with
the other. Freddie would be hurt and...''

Phyllis retrieved her cup and leaned back. ''You can prevent that from happening. I promised her twelve dozen drop

cookies and a couple of pans of bars. Just promise *me* you'll call Rob."

Jocelyn gasped indignantly. In proportion to the money needed for the Senior Center, the funds the cookies would earn would hardly make a dent, but Freddie's baked goods were the spirited backbone of all of the group's fund-raising projects, if not their financial strength.

"You have not changed one bit," Jocelyn accused, "from the bossy, critical big sister you were twenty years ago."

Phyllis accepted that as a matter of pride. "I haven't, have I?" Then she glanced at Jocelyn over the rim of her cup and asked casually, "What are you going to wear for the auction?"

Jocelyn put a hand to her head and groaned. "Thank you. I wanted to torture myself with thoughts of the auction. Oh, God! I'm going to make a fool of myself."

Phyllis frowned at her. "What made you agree to do that, anyway? You've always declined in the past."

"Must have been the subtlety of Laurel Parker's approach," Jocelyn replied dryly. "Reminds me a lot of yours. She told me if I agreed to auction my services, she'd see that the proceeds went to the Senior Center instead of the benches downtown."

The animosity between Laurel and Jocelyn had been the subject of much discussion and advice among Jocelyn and her sisters when they were growing up.

"She was setting you up," Phyllis observed grimly.

"Tell me. I just didn't think I could deny the center the kind of money the auction usually brings." Jocelyn gave her sister a wry grin. "Promise you'll bid on me if no one else does?"

Phyllis dismissed that possibility with a wave of her hand. "Everyone loves you. You'll have no shortage of takers.

Why don't you buy a new outfit?'' Then she added diplo-
matically, ''I'll come with you.''

Jocelyn made a scornful sound. ''Come on. Clothes don't
make the woman. Either you have it or you don't, and I
don't.''

''No,'' Phyllis corrected. ''Either you *think* you have it or
you *think* you don't. It's not in the buns and the boobs—it's
in the brain. Aren't you the one who's always saying that?''

''But I mean . . .''

''I know what you mean. You think a man should ignore
the way a woman looks and concentrate on what's inside.
That may be true, but to glimpse what's inside, he's got to
be drawn close enough to see it. And you can do a lot with
a very little if you put some savvy behind it.''

Jocelyn stared at her sister in surprise. ''You don't sound
like a married woman.''

Phyllis grinned, put her cup down and stood. ''Inside
every wife and mother is a siren planning what she'd do if
she had Kevin Costner to herself for thirty minutes.'' She
started for the door, then stopped and turned, her expression suddenly grim. ''About Charlie.''

''What?''

''I've been thinking about what she told you. If Chris
comes home late every Monday, Wednesday and Friday, I'm
going to follow him from the office.''

''Phyl . . .''

''Jeff's home to watch the girls. I'm going to tell him I'm
helping you with the bazaar.''

Before Jocelyn could refuse to be part of such a deception, Phyl was standing in the hall, blowing her sister a kiss.
''Don't forget,'' she threatened sweetly. ''By Monday, I
want to hear that you have a date with Rob—or Freddie
loses my cookies. See ya.''

Oh, God. Jocelyn put the cups in the sink and added half
a glass of water to the roses. *She* could bake eleven dozen

drop cookies for Freddie and a couple of pans of bars. They'd burn, but she could do it.

She would call Rob tomorrow to thank him for the flowers and the ticket. Courtesy demanded that she do so. But she wouldn't ask him out. She would tell Phyllis that she had and that he'd refused. Coercive measures justified sneaky retaliation.

Maybe she would consider a new, more traditional outfit for the auction, Jocelyn thought. If she was going to be embarrassed, she might as well go all the way.

She remembered what Phyllis had said about every woman planning what she'd do with thirty minutes alone with Kevin Costner. Jocelyn knew what she'd do. She'd put him in the audience at the auction and make him bid on her.

Eyes closed as she enjoyed that fantasy, she felt herself smile. She'd love to see Laurel's face if that happened.

ON THE TWELFTH RING, Jocelyn hung up the telephone. She was really beginning to worry. Her grandfather hadn't answered her calls all morning and he hadn't been home when she stopped by at lunch. Without a key to let herself in, all she could do was keep calling and entertain horrible images of him lying on the floor, suffering from a broken leg or a heart attack.

She put off her thank-you call to Rob. She wanted her full faculties about her when she spoke to him. She was too worried about her grandfather to think about anything else.

After calling Mary Maloney and John Whittaker and learning that neither had seen or heard from Nathan that day, Jocelyn tried to call her sisters on the chance one of them knew where he was. She was greeted by Phyllis's answering machine and the continuous ring of Charlie's unanswered phone. She canceled an afternoon appointment and drove to Nathan's house.

When there was still no answer to her knock, she tried the two windows reachable from the porch. Locked. She walked around, searching for another way in. The basement windows were securely locked, and the first-floor windows were too high for her to reach.

She was considering driving home to get a ladder when she noticed the pet door. The spoiled Brittany spaniel to whom it had belonged had long since gone to his reward, but Jocelyn suddenly saw it as a means of entry.

Looking left and then right in the midafternoon quiet and seeing no one watching her but a sleepy-eyed tabby cat on the neighboring back-porch steps, Jocelyn wrapped her voluminous denim skirt around her, got down on her stomach and pushed through the rubber door. Her head and shoulders emerged into her grandfather's kitchen. The chrome legs of his kitchen chairs made a complicated pattern at her eye level. Braced for the worst, she looked across the kitchen but saw no trace of Nathan.

Planting her hands on the floor and noting with a trace of shame that it was probably cleaner than hers, she pulled herself inside. Her body slid as far forward as her hips and stopped—firmly. She rolled her eyes at her predicament and the general state of her life at that moment.

"Can't anything be easy?" she demanded of the yellow-and-brown tiles.

She imagined she heard a divine answer. "Easy? Are you kidding?"

Reaching a hand out to grasp the table leg for leverage, she found herself a handspan short. A grimly amused sense of panic tried to take hold of her, but she refused to let it.

"All right," she told herself. "Your choices are, going unnoticed for three days and dying half in and half out of a pet door—or being noticed and having the entire neighborhood collect and wonder what the denim-clad protrusion is in Nathan Foley's back door."

That frank assessment of her situation provided the impetus for a series of determined wiggles. Red-faced and breathless, she spewed into the kitchen a moment later like a dill pickle out of the tight neck of a jar.

She took a moment to collect herself, then scrambled to her feet and went cautiously into the living room, afraid of what she might find.

She found nothing.

She walked into Nathan's den-bedroom where he spent hours at the computer, her eyes half-closed against what she might find, her anxiety increasing. Nothing.

She checked the upstairs bedroom, the bathrooms, even the closets on the wild chance he'd been robbed, bound and gagged, and stuffed away. Still nothing.

She went down to the basement and checked under and behind the storage boxes and old furniture. She noticed the washer was full and the dryer empty. With a sigh that wasn't quite relief because she still didn't know where he was, she transferred the clothes and started the dryer.

She made her way back upstairs and tried her sisters again from her grandfather's phone. Still no answer.

Jocelyn accepted there was nothing to do but let herself out the way she'd come in. The front and back doors locked with a key—the key her grandfather refused to give her. She couldn't let herself out the door and leave it unlocked.

With a prayer that exit would be easier than entry had been, Jocelyn wrapped her skirt around her and pushed herself through the back door. Head and shoulders emerged effortlessly as before.

"All *right*," she congratulated herself. Planting her hands firmly on the concrete path that ran by the back door, Jocelyn dragged herself forward, sucking in her breath. Her waist slipped through, but her hips wedged in and stuck.

She folded her forearms on the concrete and rested her head on them for a moment. "Calm," she told herself. "Just be calm."

"Mrowr!"

Jocelyn looked up in time to have her nose batted by the tabby cat from next door, who now perched in front of her, obviously mistaking her for a large mouse or a rolling toy.

"Now, look," she said reasonably, reaching out to pet him. "I've got enough trouble as it—"

The cat grabbed her hand in both his paws and in the equivalent of a karate toss in reverse, fell onto his back, still holding her. The fact that he and not she had fallen, didn't seem to diminish his pleasure in the game.

"Hey, you silly—"

Then he leapt at her head. She felt his forepaws catch in her hair while his hind feet beat against her in the mode of cat play that mimed the disembowling of prey.

Her eyes screwed shut against his beating feet, she tried to grasp him and pull him off, but couldn't without ripping her scalp. To add insult to injury, he was purring like a Porsche.

She tried to tell herself she was going to wake up in her bed and this absurd dream would be over.

The cat rolled off her head, one paw still tangled in her hair, and proceeded to groom Jocelyn's face. A sandpaper tongue that smelled of tuna licked her nose and cheek.

"Your number's up, kitty!" Jocelyn said, tilting her head to try to free the other paw. It was then that she noticed the shoes.

Inches from her face, a pair of worn, brown leather hiking boots shifted weight from one foot to the other. She recognized them as her grandfather's.

Beside the boots was a pair of black wing tips skimmed by the hem of perfectly creased gray, pin-striped pants. She had a bad feeling about them.

"Jocelyn Cassandra!" Nathan's voice demanded. "What in the hell are you doing?"

"Checking on you!" she returned heatedly, in no mood to be shouted at. "I called and called . . ."

Her diatribe was halted when the owner of the black wing tips squatted in front of her and reached gently into her hair to disengage the now-struggling cat. Jocelyn's scalp prickled, and gooseflesh ran the length of her spine. She remembered those hands in her hair.

She looked up at Rob as best she could from her prone position. "Hi," she said, as though they'd met on a street corner. "Thank you."

"My pleasure." He put the cat aside and beckoned invitingly. "You can come out now."

She propped herself on her elbows and shook her head, her cheeks pink, her eyes avoiding his. "I'm afraid I can't. I'm stuck."

"Good God!" Nathan exclaimed. "What in the hell were you . . . ?"

Jocelyn tried to glare at him, but his arthritic condition didn't allow him to stoop down, and her ensnared condition didn't allow her to look that far up. "You weren't here when I came by at lunch, and I haven't been able to reach you on the phone all afternoon. Nobody knew where you were, and I could just imagine you collapsed somewhere in the house, dead or dying. You won't give me a *key*," she said, a forceful emphasis on the word standing in for the glare she couldn't give him, "so I got in the only way I could. Unfortunately, I had to leave the same way or leave the door unlocked. And now I'm stuck. You may have sixty seconds to laugh, then I want out of here."

"Shall I call the fire department?" Nathan asked in concern.

Great. They'd talk about that for days around the old firehall.

"Maybe that won't be necessary," Rob said, going down on one knee beside her. "Sorry, Joss," he said, reaching a hand through the rubber door. "I'm going to have to get familiar here."

About to make a witty rejoinder, Jocelyn found herself suddenly speechless as his hand swept exploringly across her bottom. Her heart thumped, and all oxygen left her.

"Ah!" he said as his fingers worked on something that kept his knuckles moving against her right hip.

She had to gasp for air.

"Hold on," he said. "Have you out in a minute. I think your skirt's stuck—" there was a faint grunt as he dealt blindly with the problem "—on the inside screw of the pet door."

He reached in with his other hand, flattening it against the swell of her bottom while tugging on the fabric of her skirt with the first. "Now try," he said, putting both hands at her waist.

Jocelyn braced her hands on the concrete and pulled. Rob's hands stopped her propulsion as her knees cleared the door. With a little groan of mortification and relief, she rolled onto her side and drew her feet up.

Hands under her arms, Rob pulled her to a standing position. "Okay?" he asked gently.

She surprised herself as much as the two men staring at her when she burst into tears.

"Jos-sie!" Nathan exclaimed in concerned surprise.

Rob pulled her close and wrapped his arms around her. "You were out of touch a long time, Nathan," Jocelyn heard him say as she wept against his shoulder. "You frightened her. Doesn't it comfort you to know if you had fallen, she was that determined to reach you?"

"My God, I'm not senile," Nathan growled, sounding as upset as she was. "I can go out for a few hours without someone launching a search party."

"Come on," Rob chided quietly. "She worries about you. You owe her a little peace of mind."

As Jocelyn raised her head from Rob's shoulder, her body and her brain suffering hopelessly muddled impulses, Nathan pushed a paper bag under her nose.

"I was out of bran flakes," he said, his voice gentling. "I can tolerate the stuff better since you started buying it fresh for me at Columbia Fruit and Produce. I walked down and met Rob, picking up produce for the restaurant. He invited me back to the restaurant for lunch. I had such a good time in the kitchen with him and Griff that I forgot the time." He put an awkward hand to her cheek. "I'm sorry. I'm not used to being old. At seventy-seven, I should be, I guess, but I'm not."

Jocelyn sniffed, swiped a hand at her eyes and cast a dark look up at Rob. Had she called to thank him first thing that morning as she should have done, she'd have known where her grandfather was. "So, it was your fault," she said.

Rob grinned, apparently not offended by the accusation. "Why did I know you'd think that?"

She smoothed her long skirt, striving vainly for some modicum of dignity. She gave Nathan a quick hug. "Now that I know you're all right, I'll be on my way." She turned to Rob, and said briefly, "Thank you. Goodbye."

She had reached her car when he caught up with her. He put a hand over hers on the door handle. "Thank you for what?" he asked.

She caught a whiff of his spicy scent and stood eye to chin with him in the rare January sun, remembering with alarming, debilitating clarity what it had felt like to be pressed to his shoulder.

The need to be angry and difficult with him rose in her, then she had a fleeting mental image of her beautiful roses and hostility was defeated by confusion, by elusive needs that had gone unidentified so long, she'd been sure they'd atrophied. Then she'd had a broad male hand pressed against her bottom, been gathered in comforting arms and realized her needs were in startlingly good health.

"For saving you from death in a doggie door?" Rob teased. "Or for the flowers?"

She leaned against the car door and folded her arms, frowning up at him. "Why did you send them to me?" she asked.

He put his hands into the pockets of his pants, the tails of his coat thrown back. He smiled into her frown. "Because I thought you should have them. For your collection of data on men."

"Flowers are beautiful," she said, "but roses are... personal."

He nodded. "I know. I'm beginning to feel very personal about you."

She studied his dark eyes, looking for evidence of playful blarney and charming white lies. She could find nothing but honesty. Fear and excitement filled her simultaneously.

She was finally able to look back on what had just happened and allow herself an amused smile. "Don't get any ideas just because you were allowed to...to..." She stopped, embarrassed.

His answering smile told her he knew exactly what she meant. "Conduct a hands-on experiment? That was the most delightful few minutes I've had in a long, long time. However, there's much more to this than that, and you know it."

You know it. He'd said that quietly, scoldingly, as though daring her to deny it. She stared up at him, speechless, her cheeks pink, caught in the snare of his charm. She made herself turn to her car. "Thank you," she said breathlessly, trying desperately to behave as though she were in control. "For the flowers and the ticket. Particularly for just sending one. I'm . . . I'm glad you understand."

He nodded gravely. "I do."

"I have to go back to work," she said, digging in her purse for her keys. She fumbled with the lock and leapt into the car, desperate to escape.

She sketched a wave through the window at her grandfather, watching from the porch with a frown of confusion, and at Rob, who returned her wave with a smile she simply didn't trust.

She pulled away, raced down the street and screeched to a halt at the stop sign. She looked left and right, and raced on, waiting for the feeling of being hunted to leave her. It didn't. She concluded unhappily there was no escaping whatever made her feel this way, because she carried it with her.

THE BRIGHTLY PAINTED OLD church converted into the Salty Harbor Performing Arts Center was three-quarters filled when Jocelyn ran in five minutes before curtain. The lights dimmed as she followed the usher serenely to her seat, prepared to enjoy her solitary evening of cultural enrichment.

The usher stopped at a row with one empty seat in the middle. Jocelyn apologized as she concentrated on her steps, hurdling tucked knees and feet to reach her place. She fell into her seat with a sigh of relief, leaning forward to pull off her coat.

Skillful hands beside her tugged her free and draped her coat backward over her seat. She turned to thank the gentleman beside her and gasped in surprise when she encountered Rob's open grin.

"You!" she whispered, caught between pleasure and dismay. "What are you doing here?"

He pretended perplexity. "Now, think a minute, Joss," he said. "This is a theater, and that's a stage."

She closed her eyes, now caught between impatience and laughter. "I thought I was going to be alone."

He smiled with all apparent innocence. "That's because you haven't been listening to me. I'm after you, Jocelyn."

"I keep telling you I'm not interested," she said in an annoyed undertone. "You don't listen very well, either." The lights dimmed completely. "And if you insist on sitting there—" with a jab of her elbow, she pushed his arm away "—the armrest is mine."

"Of course." He raised his offending arm and dropped it across her shoulders.

She turned to protest, but the curtain rose and the audience began to applaud. Besides, she rather liked the possessive, protective comfort of his arm. She decided that since it was dark and everyone's attention was on the stage, she could enjoy it until intermission.

When the lights went up, Rob did not remove his arm, and Jocelyn couldn't muster the will to insist. As friends and acquaintances walked up and down the aisles, waving and smiling in her direction, she saw their surprised double takes.

Rob had leaned closer, his full attention focused on her as he recounted an amusing near disaster in the Old Cannery's kitchen. She allowed herself to enjoy his attention and her neighbors' speculations.

He pulled her a little closer when the lights went down again, and offered his handkerchief when the plot reduced her to tears near the end.

He put her coat over her shoulders when the lights went up and walked her to her car. She dug nervously for her keys, expecting he would invite her back to his place for coffee or drinks. When he simply stood by quietly, patiently, her nervousness increased and she turned up everything but her keys. The cold January wind whipped around them.

Rob finally put a hand under the large leather pouch she carried so that she could search with both hands. She finally held up the keys with relief. "There! I've *got* to do something about that purse, but I really *need* everything in it. Well, thank you for the ticket. I—"

"Come with me," he said. He took her arm and began to guide her toward the church's dormant garden beyond the parking lot.

She resisted, suspicious. "Why?"

"Because I want to kiss you good-night," he said with a smile that smoldered in the light of an antique street lamp. "And I don't want to do it in a parking lot. I promise not to be long. Unless, of course, you want me to be."

She stared at him, amazed by his candor and his tenacity. She had truly enjoyed his company, his arm around her. But his kiss would require abandonment of her protected position. She was already vulnerable enough that if he didn't enjoy kissing her, she'd be crushed. Better safe than sorry.

"No," she said firmly. "I have to go home."

"You can't," he said pleasantly.

"Why not?"

He took the handles of the pouch purse he still held, yanked until the top gathered closed, then tossed it over his shoulder, letting it dangle there from his index finger. "I have your bag, and probably your license and all those things that, by your own admission, are *so* necessary to you."

She closed her eyes, feeling frustration and a determined excitement that had been building all evening.

"I could report my purse stolen," she said calmly.

He grinned disarmingly. "I could report my heart stolen."

Jocelyn put both hands over her eyes and groaned. "Why are you doing this to me?"

With one hand, he pulled her hands down, and he looked her in the eye, scolding gently. "You know why. Because I want to learn all there is to know about you. I want to teach you about me."

She gave up pretending she didn't want to be kissed and trying to understand why he wanted to kiss her. She simply allowed herself to be led into the dark, fragrant garden and into the arbor laced with the gnarled wild rose vines. The scent of roses lingered, though there were no flowers.

Rob dropped her purse on the grass and took her into his arms.

Jocelyn felt her knees stiffen and her nerves tighten. She hadn't been kissed in years, and she knew that, unlike riding a bike, kissing was not a skill one retained, because it was different with every man, every mood.

Rob cupped her head in one hand with a confidence that communicated itself to her. She might feel out of her depth, but he certainly knew what he was doing.

The warmth and muscle of his chest and thighs engraved her own as his mouth closed over hers. His lips moved on hers gently, coaxingly, experimentally.

Rob was surprised and pleased by her compliance. What had begun when he'd first met her as simple interest had changed to the lure of a challenge and was now subtly something more. He felt the potential for real romance in Jocelyn's arms. She was too honest for deception and too genuine for artifice.

Her soft, trusting mouth opened under his. Her face, her arms lifted to him. He took her with restraint, determined not to frighten her with the feelings coming alive in him. They surprised even him with their intensity.

He stopped analyzing when her fingertips hesitantly stroked the nape of his neck. He felt the sensation up into his scalp and down the length of his spine.

Jocelyn lost identity with herself—or with the woman she thought she was. Wrapped in Rob's strong arms, she felt small, delicate, pretty.

His hands were sure, his mouth artful, and she responded with an eagerness that made her rise on tiptoe to take everything his lips offered.

Her heart was pounding, and she felt his heart thunder against her as he finally dropped his mouth to her ear. "Friday," he whispered, "I'll take you dancing."

"I can't." Her voice was husky and she cleared her throat as she drew back from him. His arms remained around her, letting her back only so far. "I promised to do this auction thing for Laurel."

He nodded and smiled. "I heard about that. Then, when?"

When? The need for an answer brought Jocelyn out of the dream state Rob's kiss had created and back to the middle of the church garden. The distant sounds of car doors slamming and theatergoers calling goodbye came from the parking lot.

"I don't know," she hedged, running a finger under the collar of her shirt because it suddenly felt tight. "I've got a million details to attend to for the ba—"

"Do I have to kidnap you after work one night?"

She looked up into the resolve in his eyes and asked frustratedly, "Why are you so determined?" Then she grinned and answered her own question. "Never mind. It's for science, isn't it?"

He didn't give her the smile she expected, but a surprisingly serious once-over of her features that ended wistfully at her mouth. "I don't think so," he replied gravely.

She now yanked at her collar. "What, then?"

For a moment, he felt at a loss, then he released her and buttoned his jacket, grinning to cover his confusion. "Romance, Jocelyn. It's the season. It's time for cupids and arrows and all the hearts-and-flowers claptrap you so despise. Everyone needs a valentine."

She smiled, strangely displeased with his reply. "I'll just take the chocolates, thank you very much. How about coffee Monday afternoon at the restaurant. I'll catch you up on bazaar plans."

He rolled his eyes. "People who've just kissed in a garen not meet for coffee to talk business. They dance the night away or sip champagne in front of a fire."

She laughed softly. "Get real, Donnelly. This is Salty Harbor and Jocelyn Foley."

He shook his head over her stubbornness. "Romance can live anywhere, under any conditions...." He slipped his fingers inside the collar with which she continued to fuss and pulled her toward him. "And it can turn even the most difficult woman," he said very softly as he leaned over her, "into a willing partner in the game of love." Then he kissed her quickly but soundly and pulled her back toward the parking lot. He put a hand out for her keys, opened her door, then handed them back to her.

He put her inside, grinning at her before closing the door. "Keep your backside covered, Foley," he warned. "The air's full of arrows, and there's one with your name on it."

Chapter Six

"You shouldn't be drinking that. You'll be up all night." Rob indicated the coffee nudge in which Griff drowned a blob of whipped cream with a spoon. They sat alone in the darkened lounge after closing. The quiet sounds of cleanup came from the kitchen.

"The brandy neutralizes the caffeine," Griff said with a sigh. His chef's hat sat on the booth bench beside him, and he ran a hand through tight, curly, dark hair. "Do you ever get sick of this?"

"The rain?"

"The solitude."

Rob closed the order book they'd been checking over and shook his head. "Not when I consider the alternative is a prison, however gilded, of someone else's wants and needs. My own are too demanding to allow that."

Griff turned to him, his eyes tired. "Then what are you doing with Jocelyn Foley?"

Rob smiled. "Same thing you'd like to do with Laurel. I'm romancing her."

Griff frowned. "Doesn't romance lead to prison?"

"Love leads to prison," Rob corrected, downing the last of his wine. "Romance opens doors. How is Laurel?"

Griff shrugged. "She hasn't come looking for you in days. I think you having dinner with Jocelyn bruised her ego."

Rob grinned at him. "Why don't you take the opportunity to soothe it?"

Griff shook his head moodily. "I want a loving little homebody who'll raise my kids and throw her arms around me when I come home from a hard day of slinging pasta. Can you see Laurel doing that?"

Rob couldn't. But then, he'd never imagined he could be attracted to a woman who resisted him at every turn.

"Do you want *everything* to work out the way you planned it?" Rob asked, pulling at his tie.

Griff considered him a moment, then nodded. "Yeah."

Rob laughed grimly. "Then brace yourself for disappointment. I thought Sandy hung the moon. When she walked into my place, I felt like Bogey when he caught his first glimpse of Bergman. She was mine—born for me, meant for me, tied to me for time and all eternity." He raised an eyebrow in a self-deprecating gesture. "And we all know how that turned out. After fourteen months of never having me home at night and putting money back into the restaurant instead of buying a bigger house, she took my restaurant and moved in with a guy who looks like Alfred Hitchcock."

"Sandy was selfish from the beginning," Griff said quietly. "You just never saw it. And anyway..." He hesitated, shook his head and took another sip of spiked coffee.

Rob rested his elbow on the back of the booth and sighed. "Don't stop now. I feel an analysis of my character coming on."

"I just think," Griff said cautiously, "that any woman would have a right to expect more of you. You're so busy trying not to be your father that you don't leave yourself time enough to breathe, except in Jocelyn Foley's direction, and that worries me. Do you think you'll be able to give her any more than you gave Sandy?"

"No," Rob replied honestly. "But neither one of us is looking for that."

"She said that?"

"Not precisely. She insists she doesn't want involvement with a man." He explained briefly about her romance and her sister. "She's hidden this very charming woman under these...these costumes, and I want to uncover her for her."

Griff frowned. "Noble. What'll you do when you present her with her naked self?"

"Depends on her."

Griff exhaled noisily, downed the last of his coffee nudge and grabbed up his hat. "I think you're lowering both of you into the deep-fat fryer, buddy."

"Hey," Rob said, sliding out of the booth with a grin. "Have a little faith. My feelings for her are genuine. I'd never hurt her."

Griff got to his feet with a groan of weariness. "Just remember that what we intend and what results from what we do aren't always the same. I think I'm going to start house hunting."

Rob put the heavy discussion aside. Griff worried about everyone; that was Griff. "The nesting instinct, huh?"

Griff looked out at the rain beating against the wall of windows in the lounge and shook his head. "Would you believe I'm falling in love with this place? I want to buy a piece of its ground and a gingerbready Victorian with a history."

Rob tucked the order book under one arm and put the other around Griff's shoulder. "Now you're talking," he said as he led his cousin toward the kitchen. "You know Marsha Stone, our afternoon-coffee regular from the real-estate office across the street? She was telling me just yesterday about a three-story monstrosity on the water that used to belong to a flock of fallen doves...."

JOCELYN KNELT IN THE middle of her office floor, tracing hearts on a giant piece of pink poster board. The door opened and she looked up into Phyllis's face with a smile of greeting.

"Tell me I didn't imagine this!" Phyllis demanded, stepping over a corner of the poster board and falling into the nearest chair. She put a hand to her heart dramatically. "I have two children under four and an amorous husband. My heart can't take these shocks on a regular basis."

Jocelyn rolled her eyes at her sister's histrionic reaction to the simple message she'd left on her answering machine. She sat back on her heels and arched her back to relieve a painful kink. "You did not imagine it. I asked you for the name of your hairdresser." She'd awakened that morning with a need to buff up her image, to make an effort on the outward appearance she'd ignored for so long. Rob's kiss had...softened her, and she had to find a look to match the way she felt.

Phyllis put the back of her wrist to her forehead and closed her eyes. "I knew it. First the Berlin Wall went down, then *Dark Shadows* came back to television and now you want the name of my hairdresser. Tomorrow, we're going to collide with Mars and it'll be all over for all of us."

Jocelyn nodded. "Well, if it is, I'm going with a loose perm. You could have just called me back."

Phyllis shook her head emphatically. "Not on your life. This I've got to see for myself. Come on. I made you an appointment." She glanced at her watch. "In twenty minutes."

"Phyl, I've got a hundred and fifty hearts to trace and cut out by—"

"The bazaar is still two weeks away."

"I know, but after the hearts, I have to cut out flowers and cupids and arrows—" The mention of the arrows reminded Jocelyn of Rob's parting caution and sent a pleasant little shudder up her spine, and that made her put a reflexively protective hand behind her.

"Aren't the seniors helping with all this?"

"Arthritic hands don't cut very well."

Phyllis stood, carefully picked up the poster board, the pattern, the pencil and scissors, and opened the door. "Come on. I'll do these while I'm waiting for you."

JOCELYN SAT OBEDIENTLY still under a pink-and-purple plastic cape while a very young woman with long spirals of platinum hair combed and cut the straggly wet mess on Jocelyn's head.

Behind them, Phyllis knelt in the middle of a purple carpet, tracing hearts on the poster board. Around the room filled with the roar of dryers and conversation loud enough to be heard over the din, women in various stages of their toilette were cutting out hearts. Jocelyn watched them in the mirror, trying to take her mind off what was happening to her.

Not that the hairdresser wasn't competent. Phyllis's beautifully sculpted, carefully highlighted wedge cut was due to the blonde's skill. Jocelyn watched her turn on the blow dryer and begin a back and forth motion over the stringy red mass. What concerned Jocelyn was that this was her head, not Phyllis's. She couldn't be made to look elegant like her older sister or dramatic like Charlie. What if the haircut didn't make a difference? What if she emerged from all this the same, only curlier? What if... what if Rob Donnelly never kissed her again? The wrong answer to any of those questions would leave the future equally bleak.

It had been twenty-four hours before she'd been able to put his kiss to the back of her mind and function normally.

And it was still with her, tickling her bottom lip, making her lift her shoulder now and then as though a warm breath blew in her ear.

The silence alerted her. She'd absently lost her focus while she thought about Rob. The room had gone suddenly quiet. The blow dryer had been stilled. The hairdresser had stepped back.

Jocelyn forced herself to look in the mirror and take the consequences of what had been a silly idea to begin with. Clothes didn't make a woman. Hair didn't make a woman. She made herself.

Her eyes half-closed, she looked at the glistening red curls rioting at the crown of her head, then falling to the tops of her ears where they met the straight red fringe too short to perm. She drew in a breath that seemed to scream in the quiet room.

She looked like she had when Rob had threaded his fingers in her hair, only more so. Her eyes sparkled brightly, her cheekbones almost had definition, and her chin came to a pretty, soft point.

"Jossie!" Phyllis breathed, coming to stand behind her. Their eyes met in the mirror, and for the first time that either could remember, they glimpsed a family resemblance. Personality made them far too different to look alike, but Phyllis's elegance was there in the tilt of Jocelyn's head. Their mouths were the same, and for the first time in years, Jocelyn's curved with a tentative but present confidence.

"Do her face," Phyllis said with sudden excitement. "Debby, make her up."

"Not too much!" Evelyn, the owner of the shop directed. "Keep it subtle. Let that wonderful coloring show."

"Phylly, I don't know—" Jocelyn began.

Phyllis's hands came down firmly on Jocelyn's shoulders. "It's on me. Hurry, Debby, before we lose her."

When Debby had finished, a small army of purple-caped ladies crowded Jocelyn's chair like uniformed troops in some bizarre operetta, armed with pink hearts and scissors. Some of them were part of the merchant force downtown whom she'd dealt with in her work. Two of them went regularly to the Senior Center. The others were simply interested, caught up in the ever-feminine pursuit of making one of their number more attractive. No one had to ask why. In the tenth century or the closing decade of the twentieth, men ruled their hearts, if not their lives.

The approval of Debby's handiwork was unanimous.

"That little bit of eyebrow pencil softens the width of her face."

"Look at those lashes! Before the mascara, they were invisible."

"Apricot lipstick is perfect. I wonder if I could wear that?"

"You can't. You only have lips when your teeth are in."

"Dangly earrings. Or big round ones. She needs earrings. Anybody got clips we can try on her?"

Evelyn yanked off two quarter-sized gold disks and put them on her. Jocelyn couldn't believe her eyes. The face reflected was hers, and yet it wasn't. The curious thing was that the reflection wasn't completely unfamiliar. *I know you,* Jocelyn thought. *I've lived with you. You were inside me all this time. I knew you were there, but I—I couldn't find you.*

Her lips parted in surprise, she caught Phyllis's glance in the mirror and was startled to see tears running down her sister's cheeks.

Phyllis threw her arms around Jocelyn's neck and hugged her. "Welcome home, Jossie," she said. "Welcome home!"

Chapter Seven

"You should buy an outfit to go with the new do. Then go out to dinner, pick up a man." Phyllis gave Jocelyn a grinning glance as she pulled into a parking spot in front of the building that housed Jocelyn's office. "Or does *Rob* make the latter unnecessary?"

Jocelyn patted her hair affectedly. "Unfortunately, life goes on, even for we knockouts. I have to trace one hundred and fifty cupids. But thanks to you and the ladies at Evelyn's, the hearts are done."

Phyllis turned as far as the steering wheel would allow and fixed her sister with a serious gaze. "Jossie, you look wonderful. Let the change make a difference."

Jocelyn made a face at her. "It's all superficial, Phyl. Cosmetic changes can't make a real difference in someone."

"In your case, they can," Phyllis insisted, "because your defense against the world has been cosmetic. You've shed that skin, Joss. Look at you! Why don't you go show him how you look?"

"Because I have a hundred and fifty—"

Phyllis took Jocelyn's earlobe between thumb and forefinger and applied a gentle-but-threatening twist. "If you don't buy some new clothes and report to me that you have a date with Rob within the week, you're going to have ears like you see in *National Geographic!*"

"Phylly! Geez!" Jocelyn grasped her sister's wrist and yanked herself free. "Will you get off my case? If you need to worry about your little sister, worry about Charlie."

Phyllis drew back gloomily into her corner of the car. "I am worried about her. I followed Chris last night."

Jocelyn felt a stab of alarm. "And?"

"And I didn't see anything we can take to court, but I saw enough to make me think there may be some foundation for Charlie's fears."

"You saw—" Jocelyn was almost afraid to say it aloud "—another woman?"

Phyllis nodded.

Jocelyn's heart sank. "That rat! That snaggletoothed, two-timing son of a snake is lucky he didn't marry me. I'd—"

Phyllis stopped her sister's tirade effectively. "They didn't do anything."

"They didn't? Then why...?"

"I followed him to Burger King, then to the parking lot of the community college," Phyllis explained. "In the parking lot, he met a woman in a chic suit with legs up to her armpits. They talked for a long time, they hugged chastely, but a class had just let out and people were walking to their cars, then he went inside and she left in a little white Toyota. I promised Jeff I'd be home by ten. Chris was still inside."

"Maybe he's taking a class," Jocelyn suggested hopefully.

"I'm going to check that out."

They looked at each other grimly, worriedly, for a moment, then Jocelyn reached into the back of the car for the large plastic bag of cutout hearts. "Thanks for making the appointment, Phyl," she said, opening her door. She paused

in the act of stepping out onto the sidewalk and turned back
to her sister. "Maybe we shouldn't make judgments until we
know for sure."

Phyllis gave a single nod. "But if he doesn't have a damn
good reason for scaring Charlie like this, he's going to find
himself in the cornerstone of some new construction somewhere. Buy some clothes."

"WHATSSA BATTER? My rent shord?"

Rob frowned down at Laurel. At least, he thought it was
Laurel. The brunette glaring at him from behind a stack of
hangered jackets on the counter in the dress shop bore little
resemblance to his tenant, except for the glossy hair, which
was tied back in a nondescript ponytail this morning.

Her dark eyes were soupy and shadowed, her nose was
red, and her lips weren't. She looked as though she hadn't
slept in days. He decided that might account for the foreign
language she was speaking.

"Are you all right?" he asked, watching her fumble with
the simple task of tying a tag onto the hanger. She tried
several times, then gave up, dropping her hand to the
counter with a thump.

"I hab a code, bud I'm find! Ad whadda you care ady-
way?"

Rob took a moment to decipher that, then said gently,
"Of course, I care. We're friends."

Laurel tried to give him a venomous look, but it was di-
luted by the physical misery brimming in her eyes. "Freds,"
she said scornfully. "Whad good are freds? Freds don't stick
by you when you lose evythig!"

He frowned at her, surprised by the outburst, unsure what
it meant.

"Dever mide," she said, picking up the tag again and
working slowly to loop it over the hanger. "Whad is it? I'm
bidzy."

"Are you taking something for it?" Rob asked.

She clicked her tongue against the roof of her mouth in an expression of disgust, but in her state of nasal congestion, the action apparently created a vacuum in her sinuses. Her eyes widened, she swallowed audibly, opening her mouth to gasp for air. Then she sneezed six times into a hastily snatched tissue. Finally emerging, she gave Rob a sarcastic smile.

"Ob course nod. I'b edjoying it too buch."

"Hold on," he said. "I'll get you some soup."

She called something after him, but he ignored her and loped across the court to the restaurant's kitchen. At the stove, Griff stirred a large pot of chicken noodle soup.

Rob clapped him on the shoulder and handed him a tube-shaped to-go carton. "Today, you're not only an extraordinary chef, but a merciful man of medicine. Take some of that wonderful brew to Laurel. She's in a bad way."

"Why?" Griff asked sharply. "What's the matter?"

"We haven't seen her," Rob explained, taking the ladle from Griff when he didn't comply quickly enough. "Because she has a terrible cold. She looks like hell and seems to be blue and crabby."

Griff asked in all seriousness, "How could Laurel ever look like hell?"

Rob ladled the chunky, broad-noodled soup redolent of thyme and parsley into the container and capped it. He handed it to Griff. "Go see for yourself."

Griff looked him in the eye. "I know what you're doing."

"Then what are you waiting for?"

"She doesn't like me. She's got her eye on you."

"I've got *my* eye on Princess Valiant. Go. The man who can turn eggs and sugar into things otherwise civilized women would kill for can certainly turn a spoiled, self-important young woman into a homebody who'd be waiting for him at the end of the day."

Griff sighed, tempted but obviously reluctant. "Don't taunt me with the impossible."

"Nothing," Rob said, quietly emphatic, "is impossible. I'll cover for you. Don't be too long." He grinned over his shoulder as Griff started for the swinging doors, tossing his hat aside. "Unless, of course, she tries to drag you back into the fitting room, in which case you can take all the time you need." His grin widened. "Which, I imagine, would be considerable."

"When I come back," Griff said, pushing at the doors, "you're in tomorrow's stew."

JOCELYN HAD COME TO the pier to feed the sea gulls. She even clutched a bag of day-old bread from the bakery to convince herself or anyone who might ask. How she'd come to find herself in the Old Cannery Mall was beyond her. Either she'd wanted to see Rob Donnelly, or she'd wanted to look at clothes. She discarded the first consideration and perused the window of Laurel's shop to confirm the second. That was it. Clothes.

She caught a glimpse of a pretty young woman reflected in the window and felt the same surprise she'd felt yesterday afternoon in the beauty shop, this morning, when she'd brushed her teeth and, thirty minutes ago, when she'd powdered her nose before leaving her office.

She tried to concentrate on the clothes. In the window was a mannequin frozen in what appeared to be a spasm of pain, but she wore straight-legged gray pants, a gray herringbone blazer over a black sweater accented by a bright yellow scarf. Jocelyn was suddenly filled with covetousness. She sighed and braced herself. Owning the outfit might even be worth dealing with Laurel.

She pushed the door open and heard the overhead bells announce her arrival. She went unnoticed, however, because a man and a woman were arguing loudly in the back. For a moment, she didn't recognize either of them.

"Whad do you know about id?" the woman demanded, waving a plastic spoon at the man. "You hab enough modey to be parders in a restaurad!" Laurel?

"I know more than you might think," the man returned with quiet anger. The back of a curly dark head was to Jocelyn, as was a vaguely familiar back around which an apron was tied. "Because people don't act rude and superior, it doesn't mean they haven't struggled to get where they are." Griff?

He sighed, and even across the distance of the shop, Jocelyn saw his effort to quiet down and be reasonable. "Look, I didn't come to fight with you," he said. "Rob sent me over with the soup to try to help."

"Rob sed you?"

He didn't seem to understand the significance of the question. "Yes."

Laurel pointed the spoon at the door. "Thed you can just go bag. I dod need you!"

"Well, you're welcome for the soup!" Griff shouted.

"You dind even brig crackers."

Halfway out the shop, Griff rounded on her. "You put crackers in *my* soup and that's the last time you'll ever see me!"

Jocelyn tried to step out of his way but succeeded only in colliding with him as he tried to weave around her. He steadied her with both hands on her shoulders and a polite but terse, "Excuse me. I'm sorry."

"It's all right, Griff," she said.

He frowned at her in surprise, and she saw recognition dawn. "Jocelyn?" he asked, releasing her and stepping back to study her.

"By God!" Laurel cried, a tissue to her nose, a paper cup of soup in her other hand.

"What happened?" Griff demanded.

Jocelyn waved a careless hand in the direction of her hair, embarrassed. "Beauty shop."

Griff put a hand to his heart, then extended it in a gesture of speechlessness as he looked her over again. "God!" he finally exclaimed.

"I thod you were leavig," Laurel said.

"Are you okay, Laurel?" Jocelyn asked. Despite their long-standing animosity, she couldn't help but be touched by her nemesis's pitiful appearance.

"She has a cold," Griff said, "and an attitude. Watch yourself." He glanced back at Laurel. "I'll bring a toddy by."

"Dod do be any favors."

"You're welcome," he said. He winked at Jocelyn. "See ya."

Laurel folded her arms and glared at Jocelyn, then sneezed into her tissue. "Cad I help you?"

Jocelyn was determined to be civil. She felt beautiful, inside as well as out, and she refused to let the day be spoiled. "I'd like to try the gray suit in the window with the yellow scarf. Would you like me to get you some cold medicine or some cough drops?"

Laurel looked at her suspiciously. "I hab some." She went to a round rack, reached in and pulled out a pair of slacks. "Sixteen?" she asked.

Jocelyn felt the stab at her pride. It was curious, she thought, that a sudden awareness of one's physical attributes brought with it a painful vulnerability. "Twelve," she said.

Laurel appeared unconvinced, but replaced the slacks and reached in again. She looked at Jocelyn's chest. "Small in the jacket?"

Jocelyn let it roll. "Medium, please."

Laurel added the accessories and hung them up in the fitting room. "Call be if you need be."

As Jocelyn removed her Birkenstocks and wriggled out of her old jeans and the pink silk jacket, she heard the telephone ring. She heard the distress in Laurel's voice even under the effects of her cold and her usual haughtiness.

"I dow I'm late," Laurel said, "but I promise you'll hab it next week. I've boved to a dew location that'll be better for bidzness eventually, bud righd now..."

She was silent a long moment. "I'b trying, but I cad do the imbossible."

Another silence, then the sound of a receiver being slammed into its cradle.

Jocelyn stood silently in the dressing room clad only in her underwear, the black sweater clutched in front of her as she listened. Immediately after the slam, she heard Laurel sobbing as though her heart would break.

ROB WAS STIR-FRYING prawns and vegetables when Griff returned.

"How'd it go?" Rob asked.

Griff took a cup out to the coffee-and-tea station, calling back over his shoulder, "The usual. After a brief discussion that started amiably and somehow turned caustic, she threw me out."

He returned with the cup filled with hot water, added a squirt of lemon juice and rummaged in an open overhead shelf.

"There's something wrong with your approach," Rob said, turning the contents of the pan onto a bed of rice and carrying it to the pick-up counter. "What did you say?"

Griff pulled down a jar of honey and added a large spoonful to the cup. "I told her she should go home and rest. She said she couldn't afford to, that she'd laid off her

part-time girl. I suggested that her health was more important than her shop, and she demanded to know what I knew
about it since I'd had enough money to be your partner in
the restaurant and mall. It went downhill from there."

From the same shelf, he took down a bottle of Cour-
voisier and added a jigger to the cup. He put the plastic lid
on it and handed it to Rob. "Take this to her," he said.

Rob pushed it back at him. "You do it. It'll give you an
opportunity to make amends."

Griff shook his head, staunchly holding back a smile. "I
think you should do it."

"Griff, I've got a million—"

Griff took his hand and placed the warm cup in it. "Now.
Before she's gone."

"Laurel?"

"No, her customer."

Rob was beginning to understand. He looked into the
strained line of Griff's mouth and guessed, "Jocelyn?"

Griff hesitated. "Sort of."

"Sort of?"

"Just go."

Rob pulled off his apron and left with a parting look of
puzzlement for his cousin. It wasn't until he was out the
door that Griff gave in to the grin.

Rob knew Jocelyn instantly, and not because Griff's
strange behavior had alerted him. He knew her because he—
because she— Well, it really didn't matter why. He stopped
in his tracks several steps inside the shop as she turned this
way and that in a three-way mirror, with Laurel tugging,
adjusting, smoothing.

In the subtly colored, sleekly tailored outfit that suggested rather than revealed the shape of her hips and legs,
Jocelyn turned away from the mirror to look over her
shoulder. Where the jacket opened, a black sweater shaped
itself artfully to her chest, a bold slash of yellow scarf fall-

ing across it for impact. Her hair was a wild and curly cap of red. He found the urge to touch it almost overwhelming.

"No need to check," he said, coming toward her. "You look wonderful from every angle."

Her head turned in quick surprise, and he saw pleasure in her eyes when she saw him. She masked it quickly, doing a self-conscious turn. "It's the elegant cut of the clothes," she said, concentrating on the mirror. Her reflected cheeks were pink, her eyes bright. "Do you think the color's too quiet?"

He went closer to look over her shoulder, feeling the pull of her—and the smallest niggle of alarm. Something about her had drawn him when she'd worn outrageous clothes and hair like a medieval page. Now, with hair like a riot of silk ribbon, and in elegant clothes, he felt her pull increase and his resistance diminish. It didn't matter. Any man afraid to explore the possibilities wasn't worthy of the name.

"You have the color," he replied quietly. "The clothes are just a flattering frame for it."

Their eyes held in the mirror. He was to remember later that that had been the moment at which he made the choice. He could have simply told her how wonderful she looked, handed Laurel her toddy and walked away. Instead, he looked back at Jocelyn steadily, letting her see everything he felt.

"More soub?" Laurel asked irritably.

Rob forced himself to shift his attention. Laurel looked worse than she had earlier. He handed her the cup.

"Griff made you a toddy."

"Thak you." She took it from him with cool courtesy, then looked at Jocelyn. Rob was surprised and confused by a glimpse of envy in her eyes.

"I'll take all four pieces," Jocelyn said, tugging the scarf off. "Do you have earrings that would go with it? Clips?"

"I'll cheg." Laurel took the scarf from her and went to the counter. "Do you wad to wear id?"

Jocelyn considered a moment. "Sure. Why not." She reached into the dressing room, scooped up her things and handed them to Jocelyn. "Can you bag these for me?"

"Yes." Laurel said, handing the scarf back to her. She held the pile of clothes away from her body as she went back to the counter, as though afraid of fashion contamination.

Jocelyn pinched the sleeve of Rob's coat and pulled him with her into the concealment of the mirror. The harmless little gesture robbed his breath. A quick glance at the two of them reflected into infinity by the trick of mirrors stalled his heart.

"Do you have a few minutes?" Jocelyn whispered, looking up at him with concerned blue eyes that made him feel like some high-flying bird lost in the sky. She glanced at her watch. "I know it's getting on to lunchtime, but I need to talk to you. I promise to be quick."

"Of course."

"Thank you." She gave him a quick, pleased smile, then dropped the scarf around her neck as she went to the counter to pay for her purchase.

He followed her out of the shop, taking the large bag from her, turning to caution Laurel to take care of herself. Laurel peeled the lid off the cup and toasted him with it, her expression sad. "Sure."

In the court, Jocelyn looped an arm in his and pulled him toward the small hallway that led directly into the restaurant's kitchen. Concealed from shoppers and from the kitchen staff, she backed him up against the wall and faced him with a frown.

"This is absolutely none of my business," she said, "but I think Laurel's illness isn't all physical." She told him what she'd overheard while she'd been in the dressing room.

Rob tried valiantly to concentrate on what she said, but he found himself distracted by the way the dim hallway light made her hair glow like a crown of roses.

"Rob?" She pinched his jacket sleeve again and shook it. "You're her... friend. Should we do something?"

In an effort to make himself focus on the issue, he lowered his eyes to her mouth. Mistake. He stared at the bridge of her nose. "What do you suggest? I mean, probably every business has faced a stop-shipment threat at one time or another. Maybe it isn't as bad as it sounded."

"She cried, Rob," Jocelyn said urgently. "I've known her since the fourth grade. She always lorded it over the rest of us because her parents were wealthy and drove her to school in a Lincoln. She always had the best clothes and clowns at her birthday parties. Then her father went to jail for manipulating stocks or something, and her mom went into a sort of decline. But Laurel still played the role. She would have died before she ever betrayed weakness of any kind, even to herself."

Rob nodded. "Okay. But, I've heard the way she talks to you. Why do you even care?"

Jocelyn sighed and considered that, taking a few steps away from him, allowing him a quick view of an elegant swish of hips. "Several reasons," she said. "On a professional level, there might be a few things I could do for her. She might be entitled to a small business loan—and there's some money in that pot specially earmarked for women in business. I could find her a senior employee so that she could have a day or at least a couple of hours off. I know a few retired ladies looking for part-time work just to have something to do. As the community-development director, it's my job to look out for my people that way. Also...," She looked up at Rob with a cautious smile. "Griff likes her, doesn't he?"

Rob raised an eyebrow in surprise and admiration. "Yes. But I just became aware of that myself. How do you know?"

Her smile widened. "Maybe I'm just quicker than you are."

Her angled glance was openly flirtatious, and Rob had to fold his arms tightly around the bag to keep them to himself. "You said she lorded it over everybody, but why the particular animosity between the two of you?"

Jocelyn shrugged, trying to remember. "I'm not sure. I don't precisely recall how it all started. But all through school, she had the looks and I had the brains, and neither one of us seemed able to reach into the other's territory. But she always had all the boys, and that seemed to be what she wanted most—I don't know why she continued to hate me because I never had any. Of course, as I recall, I didn't go out of my way to be kind to her." She shrugged again. "Who knows why we do the things we do? Anyway, I used to think her taste in men was atrocious...."

Rob frowned, and she laughed suddenly, obviously also remembering Laurel's interest in him.

"Present company excluded, of course. I saw her in action with Griff today, and I think she keeps resisting him because she's interested, too. If she's leaning toward a man with substance, maybe there's hope for her." She took the ends of the scarf around her neck and held them up to Rob. "Maybe there's hope for both of us."

Rob gave up the struggle, put the bag down, and taking the ends of the scarf from her, pulled her toward him. He claimed her mouth with a need that surprised him. It wasn't a physical need, although that was present also, as much as an emotional desperation. He had to communicate to her how beautiful he thought she was in the chic suit, how sharp she was to have noticed what was beginning to happen between Griff and Laurel, how kind she was to want to help Laurel and how compassionate to try to find a sensitive means to do it.

She returned his kiss with a tentative confidence that seemed to define the new Jocelyn. She leaned into him with easy trust, wound her arms around his neck and parted her lips, inviting his invasion.

He accepted with restraint, trying to remember where they were. But he forgot his noble intentions when he tasted the sweet generosity of her and felt the inclination of her body against his that indicated surrender.

He dropped the scarf, wrapped both arms around her and kissed her with all the ardent tenderness of a man determined to turn a woman's thoughts to romance.

Bracing her head against his arm, he leaned over her, determined to kiss her until she was breathless, until there was room for nothing in her mind but thoughts of him.

Jocelyn returned his kiss, losing the sense of restraint she'd always felt around him. She was aware of every texture of the moment—its surprise, its sweetness, its promise—and held fast to the man who'd brought it about.

She felt the wiry crispness of his hair, the smooth warmth of his angular chin, the muscle in the arms that held her, the solidity of the body with which she seemed to be fused. She smelled his spicy cologne and felt the sweep of his eyelashes against her throat when he released her mouth and leaned down to plant a kiss there.

Warmly, lazily content with how that had gone, Rob exhaled slowly and raised his head, his senses filled with her. Then he looked into her eyes and saw a smile begin there. It remained for a moment, swelling until it spilled onto her lips and became soft laughter.

He stared down at her, almost paralyzed with tenderness. "It isn't nice to kiss and laugh," he scolded.

"Then how do you react," she asked, her arms still twined around his neck, "when something feels so wonderful?"

"You do it again."

She glanced over his shoulder toward the sounds of activity in the mall. "We shouldn't have done this in the first place, considering where we are."

"Where we are," he said, leaning closer to her, "is just inches from the kitchen. It's part of my job to taste everything."

Reluctantly but resolutely, Jocelyn wedged a space between them. "There's a lot more to your job, too, that's being ignored at the moment. And mine. I've got to go."

He continued to hold her. "Want to come to my place this weekend?"

She shook her head and grimaced. "The auction, remember? Then I have a million details to work on for the bazaar."

Rob closed his eyes, and admonished quietly, "No, no, no. You're just not getting this. Romance cannot be swept aside until you have time for it. If it's to grow, it needs attention, nurturing..."

"Fertilizer?" Jocelyn put in with a teasing grin when he hesitated.

He uttered a groan of exasperation. "Joss..."

"I'm sorry," she said, trying hard to look apologetic. "But you know how I feel about that stuff."

"Stuff?" he asked, dramatically indignant. "You call that kiss 'stuff'?"

She arched an eyebrow. "You think that kiss was an expression of romance?"

He frowned. "What did you think it was?"

"Attraction, interest—" she gestured with a hand, confused "—I don't know. But I didn't think of it as anything...frivolous."

He rolled his eyes. "You're such a pragmatist! Romance isn't frivolous. It's substantive and supportive." He lowered his voice and tightened his grip, smiling. "And if you'd come to my place this weekend, I'd prove it to you."

She shook her head and firmly removed his arms from around her. "Then, if that's true, it'll survive the demands made on me by the bazaar, and you can extend the invitation again afterward."

Rob folded his arms and accepted that the new Jocelyn would be no easier to deal with than the old one. "Two weeks?"

"We'll see each other many times between now and the bazaar."

"In the presence of the Senior Center committee, and to talk about business."

"You can do it," she challenged.

He looked doubtful. "Maybe if you get back into your old clothes." He reached down for the bag and handed it to her. "Remember what I said about the air being full of arrows."

She nodded. "I know. Keep my backside covered."

"Romantics believe that when the arrow's meant for you," he warned, "there is no armor thick enough."

"But you're dealing with an expert on armor here," she said with a smile, patting the bag that contained a sample of it. She turned serious for a moment. "Think about Laurel, will you, and try to find out what she needs?"

"Right."

She backed away from him with her large bag, sketching a wave and smiling. "See you."

He waved back. "Yeah. See you."

Jocelyn turned away, humming as she went to her car. She had handled that well. She'd let him know she was interested without letting herself be snowed under by romance. After all the confusion she'd experienced since Rob had sent her the roses, it felt good to be in charge again.

Rob walked into the kitchen, deaf to Jackie's greeting and Griff's question about tonight's Greek entrée. He was thinking that if Jocelyn thought she'd effectively put him on the sidelines of her life for the next two weeks, she was in for a surprise.

Chapter Eight

"Why don't *you* go home?" Griff suggested. "I've got a few things I can prepare for tomorrow."

"Because you were here an hour earlier than I was. You go." Rob looked over the swinging doors to the darkened restaurant, closed early because of the quiet Wednesday night and already set up for breakfast. "Everything's under control. Get some rest."

"All right." Griff tossed his apron in the laundry bag, downed the last of a glass of water and crossed the kitchen to take his jacket off a peg. He paused halfway through the swinging doors, looking through the quiet dining room to the windows against which another storm beat furiously. "It's raining again," he reported.

Rob, unloading the last round in the dishwasher, looked up with a grin. "So, what's new? See you in the morning."

"Right."

The doors swung into stillness behind Griff, and Rob went back to his task, only to have his cousin reappear in a matter of seconds. He was frowning. "The lights are still on in Laurel's shop," he said. "She might have just forgotten them, but maybe we'd better check."

Rob dug into his pocket for keys as he followed Griff through the restaurant and across the court. The dress shop was brightly lit, an obviously wrong note in the long, dark bank of stores.

Rob unlocked the door and they stepped inside, Griff calling Laurel's name. There was no reply, but they heard the subtle sound of something falling in the back room.

Rob stopped Griff with a hand on his arm when he would have gone forward to investigate. Griff turned, frowning at him. "There's somebody back there," he whispered.

"I heard it," Rob replied softly. "I'll go."

Griff pulled him back. "I'm the one who was the street fighter."

"I'm the one," Rob reminded, "who saved the street fighter's butt."

He went silently to the drapery that separated the front of the shop from the stockroom, swept the cloth aside with a swift movement and stepped inside, Griff right behind him.

Asleep on a padded bench that usually held piles of things that required mending was Laurel. Her cheeks were pink, her nose red, her breathing noisy with congestion. One hand dangled off the bench near the floor, an empty cup inches away from it on the planks.

"What'd you put in that toddy?" Rob asked as Griff knelt beside her, putting the back of his hand to her cheek.

"Just the usual. I suppose if she hasn't been sleeping, it worked better than I'd anticipated. Laurel. Laurel, it's Griff." He patted her cheek and shook her gently. She smiled, but continued to sleep.

Griff tried again and got the same reaction. He leaned a forearm on his knee and looked up at Rob. "We can't leave her here."

His manner was vaguely defensive, Rob thought, and he held back a smile. Griff had it bad. "She lives alone," he said. "If you take her to her place, there won't be anyone there to look after her."

Griff studied the sleeping woman, who began to stir uneasily, and got to his feet. "I'll take her home with me. I'm sure I'll regret it when she wakes up, but I can't leave her here." He looked around. "She got a coat or something?"

Rob took a fashionable lavender raincoat off of a hanger hooked on an otherwise empty clothes rack. It smelled faintly of her scent. Griff sat her up, and they pulled and teased the garment onto her.

Holding her upright with a knee on the bench propping up her back, Griff dug into his pocket for his car keys and tossed them at Rob. "I'll carry her out if you'll open the car door for me."

"Sure."

Moments later, Rob watched Griff drive away with Laurel's head in his lap. Standing in the pouring rain, it occurred to him that his cousin had no concept of romance. He just wasn't the type. Like his father, he was solid and dependable and hardworking—and he couldn't wait to assume all the little tyrannies of family life.

Rob on the other hand, had tasted that and wanted no part of it. His mother's commitment to his father had only hurt her. His own love for his father had left him bitterly disappointed, and his love for Sandy had wedged itself between him and his restaurant, then finally taken it from him in the divorce settlement.

No. That wasn't for him. People settled into permanent relationships because it was more comfortable, but it had been his experience that it wasn't beneficial. The world was new every day. The earth spun, things died and were reborn, everything changed. Opportunities, personal and otherwise, came along, and it was up to the individual to seize them, to enjoy them as long as they were offered, then move on to other things when it was over. It was all so simple. Trying to hold on only complicated an otherwise satisfactory arrangement.

Hurrying back inside the restaurant, he heard the sharp, resonant bark of a sea lion. From farther out in the channel, probably on the buoy, came an answering bark. He shook his head in sympathy. Even an old sea lion bull could find himself a victim of the trap.

ROB RAPPED ON THE apartment door.

Griff answered it wearing jeans and a white T-shirt, a towel around his neck. With one end of it, he buffed at a headful of tight, dark ringlets. There were circles under his eyes. He lowered the towel in surprise.

"What's the matter?" he demanded.

"Nothing," Rob assured him. "I came to tell you to take your time coming in today. Jackie and I can handle lunch. How's Laurel?"

Griff waved a hand in the direction of the bedroom. "Still asleep." He stepped back to let Rob into the room.

A blanket and a pillow were neatly stacked on the end of the blue-and-beige sofa. Rob smiled sympathetically. "You don't look as though you got much sleep."

Griff balled the towel in his hands. "No. She was pretty sick. Want some breakfast? Coffee?"

Rob sniffed the air. "Irish cream?"

"Yeah." Griff led the way into a small, utilitarian kitchen. He poured coffee into two glass mugs. In the process, his elbow collided with a cupboard door in the narrow space and he growled impatiently. "I can't wait to get out of this place," he said, "and into one with a kitchen I can move around in!"

Rob studied his cousin's uncharacteristically grumpy expression and wondered if it had been caused by having to sleep within feet of the "important" woman he'd talked about a week ago.

"I'd like to take Friday night off," Rob said, leaning against the counter neatly lined with the tools of Griff's trade. "Abby said she'd take my shift, and the kid we're training for days said he'd come in, too, to help out."

Griff hiked up on the counter, nodding over the rim of his cup. "No problem. You're only passable in the kitchen anyway. If the dining room's covered, that's all we have to worry about."

"Friday's a rough night, and I don't want to put you in a bind."

Griff frowned at him. "Rob, it's your restaurant. You've got to learn to throw your weight around. Is that all you came to tell me?"

"Not entirely." Rob repeated quietly what Jocelyn had told him she'd overheard in the dressing room at Laurel's shop. "Joss thinks there are ways to help her, but is afraid Laurel wouldn't appreciate it coming from her. She asked me to help, but maybe you're in a better position to do that."

"Do what?"

Rob and Griff turned to the kitchen doorway to find Laurel standing there in a blanket, her hair hanging limply, but her general appearance considerably healthier than the day before. The pink in her cheeks now appeared to be temper rather than fever.

"Good morning," Griff said calmly. "Want some coffee?"

"Do what?" she asked again, emphasizing the word. She looked around in cranky confusion. "Where am I, anyway?"

"My place," Griff replied.

She lifted her chin in haughty disdain. "Well!" she said. The single word was rife with dark implications. Rob saw his cousin's temper spark.

Griff rolled his eyes. "Don't flatter yourself. You did sleep in my bed, but you were alone. We found you asleep in your stockroom and took pity on you. Rob helped me get you in my car, then I brought you here. You had about as much sexual appeal last night as . . ." Apparently unable to find an appropriate simile, he ended with, "As you do this morning."

Laurel swallowed and kept her chin high with obvious difficulty. "And just what was it the fabulous Ms. Foley wanted you to do for me? Or *to* me?"

Rob admired his cousin's courage. Griff came out with it honestly, telling her what he'd told him. "She thinks she can help you get a business loan," he said at last. "But she'll need some particulars from you. And a willingness to work civilly with her to find a solution to your problem."

Laurel's eyes brimmed with unshed tears, the humiliation she felt apparent in the deep flush that rose from the blanket held tightly around her shoulders. "I'll solve my own problems!" she shouted. "I don't need the two of you—" she looked from Rob to Griff with equal venom "—butting into things that don't concern you."

"We were trying to help," Rob said quietly. "I've been in business long enough to have been in your position a couple of times myself. It's nothing to be ashamed of. You can't control the economy or the vagaries—"

"Don't lecture me!" she shouted. "If I—"

"Hey." Griff's voice stopped her without his raising it a decibel. "This is my home. You don't scream at me or my cousin in my home." He put his cup down with a bang and walked to within inches of her, hands on his hips. "If you had any manners at all, you'd thank us for finding you a place to spend the night and for caring enough about you to try to help. God knows, the way you've treated all of us at one time or another, you haven't earned our concern."

Laurel's lips quivered, a tear spilled over, and she gathered the blanket up and ran back into the bedroom. As the door slammed behind her, Rob put his cup down and observed candidly, "Griff, you're in love with a food processor with all the attachments—dice, chop, slice."

Griff sighed and ran a hand over his face, staring at the spot where Laurel had stood. Then he shook his head. "Something really hurts that woman."

Rob clapped his shoulder consolingly. "Go back to bed. I'll take her home on my way to work."

"YOU OWE HIM AN APOLOGY," Rob said as he drove up the hill toward the row of turn-of-the-century mansions where Laurel lived. "He was worried about you last night. I'm the one who brought up the subject of your business problems."

She glanced at him darkly before turning away again. "After Jocelyn brought it up to you."

"Because she wanted to help. Though the way you treat her, and everyone else, for that matter, God knows why."

"I have my pride," she said stiffly.

"You don't have pride," Rob returned mercilessly, "you have snobbery and disdain. You use it to keep all of us at bay or to try to draw us toward you—whichever suits you. Griff tried to get past it anyway to help you, and this is the thanks he gets."

"He doesn't care," she said, almost to herself. "No one really cares."

He pulled up in front of the yellow-and-white Victorian at the top of the hill. Laurel let herself out of the car and ran inside without a backward glance.

"I WISH I WERE IN New York. No. That isn't far enough. I wish I were in Malta."

"Malta?" Phyllis fluffed Jocelyn's hair with a pick.

"Or Mars," Jocelyn went on, feeling as though she were rapidly losing her grip on sanity. "Mars would be nice. I'll bet there are no auctions on Mars."

Beyond the busy wings of the high school auditorium's stage, hoots and applause could be heard as Marvin Strong, Salty Harbor's mayor, walked the plank of the runway.

"Jossie, you look so wonderful." Charlie, in stirrup pants and an oversize shirt over her protruding tummy, applied blusher to Jocelyn's cheeks. Charlie's hair was caught back in a simple ponytail, and she managed to look both beautiful and tragic. "I can hardly believe it's you!"

"It isn't," Jocelyn said. "An alien has invaded my body." She truly felt as though it had. What did she think she was doing? She couldn't parade down that runway—after Laurel—pretending she had all the confidence in the world in the new her. What new her? She suddenly felt as fear filled and fragile as the old one.

She caught Charlie's wrist and pulled her hand away from her face. "I've changed my mind. I'm not going out there."

Phyllis ignored her and continued to fuss with her hair. "Don't be ridiculous. You—"

She spun on Phyllis, panic rising in her chest. "I'm not. I'm serious. I'm not—"

"Jocelyn!" The imperious sound of Laurel's voice froze all three sisters into silence. She wore a dark blue silk dress that clung everywhere and looked magnificent. Her mass of black hair was caught back in a long, glittery clip that resulted in a mass of curls from the crown of her head to her shoulders. Artful makeup concealed all traces of her cold. Jocelyn forgot their mutual dislike for a moment and stared enviously. "What a dress," she murmured.

"I'd like to speak to you for a moment," Laurel said. She stepped several feet back and behind a fold of curtain, beckoning Jocelyn to follow.

"Don't." Phyllis tried to hold Jocelyn back. "She's on next, and you're right after her. Don't let her upset you."

"It's all right." Jocelyn pulled free of Phyllis and went to Laurel, some sixth sense telling her what the lady wanted to talk about. Laurel looked furious, but as Jocelyn got closer, she saw fear under the anger.

"How dare you," Laurel whispered harshly the moment she was close enough, "eavesdrop on my business conversations, then pass them on to every Tom, Dick and Harry!"

"I told only Rob," Jocelyn replied evenly, "and only because my office can help you, but I didn't think you'd want help from me. As your friend, he seemed the one to suggest it to you."

"Well, you're right!" Laurel snapped under her breath. "I don't want *your* help, and he's no longer my friend, so I don't want his!"

"He was only doing what I asked him to do."

"Really? Did you ask him to tell Griff?"

So that was what this was about. Jocelyn folded her arms. "Griff is his cousin and best friend. And he knows Griff cares about you."

For just a moment, Laurel looked unsettled. Then she tossed the column of curls and glared at Jocelyn. "Just because you suddenly have a *little* style—" she emphasized the word with a half-inch space between her thumb and forefinger "—don't think you can run my life, because under the clothes, you're still plump, brainy Jocelyn, who couldn't get a boy to look at her on a bet."

That was just what she needed to hear, Jocelyn thought, feeling her small reserve of self-confidence plummet to her toes. The need to strike back was swift and urgent. "You won't be happy," she said quietly, "until you alienate everyone. Do you want to be alone, is that it? You look gorgeous tonight, Laurel, but how long do you think that's going to last? We're both pushing thirty. Then what?"

Laurel's face flushed a deep red. "I'll worry about that in ten years. For now—" she pointed in the direction of the stage "—I'm going to go out there and make all kinds of money for your old people. You're going to go out there..."

Her threatening smile was vengefully wide. "And there's going to be silence." She cut the word off, letting the silence she foretold echo about them like a promise.

"Laurel!" the event's director called from the wings. "You're next."

Chin up, a disdainful glance over her shoulder for Jocelyn, Laurel walked seductively onstage. The wolf whistles were loud and immediate. The part of Jocelyn that was dedicated to Salty Harbor's senior citizens knew the audience's reaction meant money in their pockets, or more accurately, on their roof. The part of her that was dedicated to her own fragile, hesitant rebirth knew the ruckus Laurel created on the runway would only accentuate the lack of enthusiasm she, Jocelyn, was bound to generate.

"What did she want?" Phyllis demanded. "What?"

"To tell me no one's going to bid on me," Jocelyn admitted with a wince. Serious terror formed in her chest.

"Don't be ridiculous," Phyllis said, fluffing Jocelyn's hair with her fingertips. "Those are all your friends out there, and you look positively stunning in that suit. And we'll bid on you, won't we Charlie?"

Charlie brushed at the shoulders of Jocelyn's sweater and smiled uncertainly. "Well, I would if had any money. But you know . . ."

Phyllis frowned her into silence. "You look beautiful," she said to Jocelyn. "Don't worry."

Beyond the wings, the auctioneer's voice touted Laurel's expertise as a fashion consultant as the bid for her services rose to several hundred dollars. Jocelyn, Phyllis and Charlie crowded closer.

"For those mothers out there planning weddings, Laurel promises to attend to every little detail, from the bridal gown to the ring bearer's shoes.

"Five hundred dollars!" a shrill female voice shouted from the audience.

"Wow!" Charlie whispered, obviously impressed by the amount. "Who's that?"

"Julia Clayborn Winston," Phyllis whispered, "of the fourth-generation Winstons. If she wins, I wouldn't be Laurel for anything. She has two daughters getting married this summer, and she's as picky as a monkey with fleas."

Jocelyn winced at the simile, but the mental image it created was certainly effective.

The bid rose and rested at six hundred dollars, Julia Winston shrieking with delight when she was declared the winner of Laurel's services.

Laurel, apparently also aware of the woman's reputation, stormed backstage, elbowing her way past Jocelyn and her sisters.

"Joss!" the stage manager whispered. "You're on!"

Phyllis took Jocelyn by the shoulders and gave her one small shake. Her thickly lashed gray eyes looked into hers with big-sister firmness. "Forget everything she said to you. You look wonderful. Your hair was done by the best hairdresser in Salty Harbor, your new outfit looks elegant, and a gorgeous man sent you roses. Think about that and hold your head up."

Jocelyn had no idea what propelled her onstage. It certainly was no impulse from her brain, because it had turned off. She couldn't think.

She heard the auctioneer speaking, though she couldn't understand the words. She could see a thousand faces staring at her—in silence.

Dread trickled down her spine, striking one vertebra at a time with an ominous chill. The audience continued to stare. They weren't bidding. No one would bid!

She tried to remember what Phyllis had told her, but all she remembered was that Rob thought she was special. *You look beautiful from every angle,* he'd said the other day in Laurel's shop. And he'd looked as though he'd meant it.

Her brain clicked on. "...A lifelong resident of Salty Harbor, I'm sure most of you recognize Joss as the community development director who's spent the last two years coordinating the community's needs with commercial and charitable events. The proceeds from this very auction will replace the furnace and the roof in the Senior Center." There was applause.

"Jocelyn brings to this auction expertise as a secretary, an office manager and a PR person. A day with Ms. Foley in your office is bound to double sales, triple efficiency, quadruple..."

"Two hundred dollars!" Jocelyn heard the bid with genuine surprise. It hadn't even been Jeff's voice; it had been a woman's. Janice Reston. Laurel had said Janice wanted her services.

"Take a few steps down the runway, Jossie," the auctioneer said encouragingly. "Let this crowd see what a pretty girl in an office could—"

"Three hundred!"

"Four hundred!"

The bid had doubled in an instant. Thawing out of her frozen paralysis, Jocelyn took several steps toward the end of the stage and the beginning of the runway under the full complement of lights. Everyone was staring at her, openmouthed. The impulse to draw back was almost overwhelming. But the bid kept going up.

Here and there in the audience people stood and began to cheer. Jeff and Nathan whistled, and Mary and Freddie clapped their hands over their heads. Friends and neighbors, clients she worked with on a daily basis, were whistling and shouting. She realized in shock that they offered all-out support for the auction, but it was more than that. This was for her. For the change in her.

The bid had reached seven hundred dollars by the time she stood at the foot of the runway. Charged by the enthusiasm of her friends, Jocelyn felt every sense engage and her brain move into overdrive. She'd made more money than Laurel!

As the applause continued, she did a slow, seductive turn. The cheers rose to a deafening pitch.

"Eight hundred!" Janice Reston shouted.

"Nine!" another voice called from across the auditorium.

"Nine fifty!"

"Two thousand dollars!"

Jocelyn froze in place, and the entire audience fell silent. Even the auctioneer required a moment to compose himself. He cleared his throat.

"Would the bidder identify himself, please."

Everyone turned as a man in a three-piece suit rose from a chair at the far end of the auditorium. "Rob Donnelly," he called. "The Old Cannery Mall."

Across the sea of faces, Jocelyn met his eyes, which were filled with amusement and definite purpose. In front of a considerable portion of the Salty Harbor community, Jocelyn blushed to the roots of her hair.

There was laughter and approving applause, and for a moment, the event seemed to lose its civic purpose and become a forum for a particularly unique romance.

Then the auctioneer cleared his throat again. "We have a bid of two thousand dollars." He shuffled through his papers. "A record, I think, for this event," he said in an aside to this audience. There was more applause. "Do I hear another bid?"

Silence.

The gavel banged. "Sold to Rob Donnelly of the Old Cannery Mall for two thousand dollars!"

The applause was deafening. Jocelyn took a bow, then walked back up the runway to shouts and cheers. When she reached the stage, the auctioneer encouraged her to take another bow. She did—then bravely blew a kiss to the audience and ran backstage as quickly as her legs would allow her.

She was immediately enveloped by her sisters and friends waiting in the wings.

"You did it!" Phyllis shouted. "Two thousand dollars! I have *got* to meet this man."

Jocelyn couldn't speak. She was afraid if she opened her mouth, a wild giggle would erupt. She, Jocelyn Cassandra Foley, had just brought a full auditorium to its feet with applause because of the attentions of a man. And she'd brought in fourteen hundred dollars more than Laurel had.

A little drunk with power, she raised her eyes heavenward and thought, "You can take me now, Lord. It doesn't get any better than this."

Then she saw Laurel's pinched, hurt face and felt instantly guilty. Involuntarily, she'd embarrassed Laurel twice in the past few days—not that making six hundred dollars for the Senior Center should embarrass anyone, but Laurel was used to bringing in the auction's highest bid.

A loud gasp sounded behind Jocelyn, then rippled through the men and women gathered backstage. Jocelyn turned to see Rob making his way toward her. He looked pleased with himself and flatteringly pleased with her.

Instinctively, she reached a hand toward him. She saw the acknowledgement of that small victory in his eyes when he took it. "You look so beautiful," he said, using her hand to hold her away for a moment as his eyes went over her in careful appraisal.

Jocelyn was sharply aware of the envious female glances and the satisfied masculine nods.

Afraid she might slip into a swoon, she drew him into the circle of her sisters. "Rob, these are my sisters, Phyllis and Charlene. Phyl, Charlie, this is Robert Donnelly, owner of the Old Cannery Restaurant and Mall, and benefactor to the Senior Center."

Phyllis shook his hand and nodded approvingly. "You have excellent taste in women, Mr. Donnelly," she said. "They don't come any better than Joss."

Charlie smiled shyly. "It's so nice to meet you."

"And you." Rob smiled from one sister to the other. "Would you excuse me if I steal Joss for a few minutes?"

Phyllis stepped out of his way. "You can have longer than that."

When Charlie continued to stare at him, unconsciously blocking his path, Phyllis drew her and her protruding tummy back.

Rob put an arm around Jocelyn's shoulders and led her to the stage door and out into the parking lot. He removed his jacket and dropped it on her shoulders. She leaned back against the building, pulling the sides of his jacket around her. The shoulders stuck up emptily, and the hem fell to her knees.

He put a hand on the wall beside her head and looked down at her in mild perplexity. He couldn't quite define how he felt. When she'd stepped onstage, he'd been as struck as the rest of the audience by how elegant she looked. When she took the first few hesitant steps down the runway, he'd been snared by her ingenuous humility. Then he'd watched her chin lift with confidence, and when she'd done that sexy little turn, a sharp, full-blown possessiveness had risen in him with startling intensity. He'd have bankrupted himself *and* Griff to win her.

Now, wrapped in his jacket, she inspired tenderness in him and a subtle, quiet passion he'd never experienced before and didn't understand.

Jocelyn's mouth had gone dry and everything inside her had been invaded by an insidious little tremor. She wished he'd say something. When he didn't, she said, "You know, you could have hired a secretary for two months for what you paid for me for a day."

He shook his head. "I wasn't bidding for a secretary."

Her breath left her. "What were you bidding for?"

"A companion for twenty-four hours."

"Eight," she corrected quickly. "You only get me for eight hours."

He considered her a moment, then his smile gleamed wickedly in the darkness. "That ought to be enough time." He leaned closer.

She swallowed. "For what?"

His lips were inches from hers. "To make you believe in romance." He lowered his head the last few inches and kissed her slowly, lingeringly, coaxingly, until she was as reluctant to draw away as he was.

He kissed her cheekbone, her eyelid, her forehead. "Sunday morning," he whispered. "I'll pick you up at six o'clock."

"Okay," she breathed.

"Okay." He gave her a last, quick kiss, opened the door and put her back inside. "I've got to go back to work. See you Sunday. Dress comfortably."

"Where . . . ?" she began to ask.

He shook his head. "Romance requires an element of surprise. Sunday."

"Sunday," she whispered, completely aware of having been caught in his spell, completely unwilling to struggle too hard to be free.

Laurel, her coat over her arm, collided with Jocelyn's arm as she hurried past.

Jocelyn, brought back to reality, caught Laurel's elbow and stopped her. "Laurel, don't be angry," she said reasonably. "I meant to help you by telling Rob what I'd overheard, not hurt you. And about the bidding, I—"

"Forget it." Laurel cut her off. Her dark eyes were still angry, but now they held sadness as well as the fear Jocelyn had seen earlier. "You've always had everything, you just didn't know it. Now that you do, it . . . it just doesn't matter. Good night.''

She hurried off into the parking lot, shrugging into her coat, beautiful and perfect and somehow tragic.

Chapter Nine

Jocelyn wondered how Rob could look so gorgeous at six o'clock in the morning, particularly since he'd probably worked until one or 2:00 a.m. In jeans and a thick navy sweater over a pale blue shirt, he looked dark and... *loose*, she guessed, might describe it. In the suit in which she usually saw him, he seemed always controlled and professional. This morning, he looked rakish.

Standing in the middle of her living room, arms folded, he looked over her slim-legged jeans and the thick, blue-and-gray argyle turtleneck she tugged self-consciously over her hips. The sweater was new, and in deference to self-discovery, she'd resisted the impulse to buy something that fell to her knees. The garment just cleared her hip bone. As he looked at her, all her old insecurities threatened to return.

He brushed her hands away and eased the ribbed hem of the sweater into place. "Quit pulling on it," he said with a grin. "Nice hips shouldn't be hidden."

She rolled her eyes. "They're not nice, they're—"

He put a hand over her mouth. "I think they're nice, and these are my eight hours. Got a raincoat?"

She nodded, pointing to the blue trenchcoat on the sofa. Beyond her living room window, the morning was still dark, and rain fell in torrents.

Rob picked up the coat and held it open for her. She slipped into it, breathlessly conscious of his knuckles grazing her chin as he closed it around her then turned her toward the door. *This is going to be a long day,* she thought. *A very long day.*

The old cottage on a cul-de-sac overlooking the bay surprised Jocelyn. In the predawn shadows, she strained to see the building, discovering that a rickety set of steps and a deep porch had been newly repaired, but the weathered gray paint needed a fresh coat, and the small front lawn and flower beds had been sadly neglected. It looked as though it could be comfortable and cozy, though, and she fell in love with it instantly. It suited the man in the jeans and sweater, but she'd half expected some spiffy condo more appropriate to the man in the three-piece suit.

"What a wonderful place," she said, stepping out of the car, blinking against the rain as she stopped to look up at the peaked roof and the old brick chimney.

Rob came around the car, put an arm around her and led her at a run to the porch. "It has a long way to go to be wonderful," he said, fitting his key into the lock. "And at the rate I'm getting to it, it might fall down around my ears before that."

He pushed the door open and led her through a dark living room to a large, square room beyond that appeared to be a slightly more modern version of the old keeping room. In one corner were kitchen facilities, while the other, lined by wide windows that looked on the bay, had a round oak kitchen table and chairs, an old, brown-plaid sofa and a coffee table strewn with magazines, several books and a folder that looked as though it might contain paperwork from the restaurant.

As Rob took Jocelyn's coat, she went to the windows. Below her, a pine-covered hillside swept down to the water where harbor lights picked out several dozen fishing boats and pleasure craft bobbing at anchor in a small marina. A bridge spanned the gray water, frosted with whitecaps this morning despite the sheltering hills. The far side of the bridge disappeared into fog, like some artistic interpretation of the mysteries of the future or the afterlife. A relentless rain beat at the scene.

"How do you feel about eggs Benedict?" Rob asked.

Jocelyn turned away from the surreal view to find him tossing pots and pans around and adjusting burners with a competence that was impressive. She sat on the arm of the sofa, several feet from the stove. "I don't know," she replied. "I've never had one."

"What?" He looked at her over the refrigerator door, his expression horrified. "Never?"

She shrugged. "Pedestrian, I know, but even when I have breakfast in a restaurant, I order the old, traditional bacon and eggs."

"Then you're in for a treat." He slammed the door and carried a bowl of eggs, a covered plastic bowl and a wedge of ham to the counter. "My hollandaise is better than Griff's." He smiled in her direction as he reached overhead for a package of English muffins. "But don't tell him I said that. He's sensitive and sometimes violent when his reputation as a chef is challenged. We'll start with a mimosa."

"A what?"

"Orange juice and champagne. Never had one of those, either?"

"Sorry."

He shook his head regretfully. "Such deprivation. I walked into your life just in time, young lady."

As she picked up a thin volume of poetry from the coffee table and wandered over to lean against the counter beside him, he couldn't help but wonder if he'd been just in time for her or for himself.

She studied the spine of the book she held in her hand, then looked into his eyes, hers wide with surprise. "Swinburne?" she asked.

He put the ham on a griddle, turned the heat low and inclined his head in a vaguely embarrassed way. "I was a business major with a minor in literature. I did a paper on English poets of the nineteenth century. Swinburne was a flamboyant romantic."

She looked up from paging through the book. "Like yourself?"

He shook his head. "I'm a private romantic."

The ham sizzling lightly, he poured orange juice into two flutes, then added champagne.

She took the glass he offered her, and said with a smile, "You bid two thousand dollars in front of half the residents of Salty Harbor for eight hours of my time. I think that qualifies as flamboyant."

He touched the rim of his glass to hers, his dark eyes darkening further. "So you're admitting at last that you're involved in a romance?"

"I'm not sure I'm involved yet," she hedged.

He turned the ham and glanced from his watch to her with a grin. "I still have seven hours and forty minutes. Want to set the table?" He pulled open a drawer. "Utensils are in here, place mats in the drawer underneath."

JOCELYN'S PLATE WAS EMPTY before she realized what she'd done. She'd intended to pick politely at one of the two fragrant but calorie-laden mounds and rely on the coffee to dilute the mimosa. But somehow, while a gray and gloomy day dawned outside, she and Rob had pursued a warm and cozy discussion of Rossetti and the Brownings inside—and she'd eaten every bite. She looked up at him in self-deprecation.

He frowned. "You didn't like it?"

She made a face and indicated her empty plate. "You're lucky I left the gold trim. I've consumed two days' calories at breakfast."

He picked up their plates and carried them to the counter. "You're going to need your strength. I've got a big day planned."

She scooped up glasses and cups. "But it's still pouring."

"Afraid of a little rain?" he teased, taking the things from her and putting them in the dishwasher.

"Of course not," she replied righteously, "but being soaking wet doesn't really produce the romantic atmosphere you're after, does it?"

He closed the door on the dirty dishes and gave her his full attention. "Rain can be an important element in romance," he said.

"How so?" she challenged.

He put an arm around her and led her toward the coat closet, asking quietly, "Have you ever spent hours with someone you cared about under an umbrella?"

"No."

"Well, you're about to."

"THIS UMBRELLA IS SMALL," Jocelyn noted as they stood at the very top of the Salty Harbor Tower, a stone structure built on the highest hill in honor of the generations of fishermen lost at sea. They'd climbed a spiral staircase in the center of the tower to reach the narrow gallery on which they stood. Rain pounded on the stretched silk over their heads.

Rob, holding the umbrella, stood behind her and held her under its shelter with an arm across her chest. "Is that a complaint?" he asked.

Jocelyn turned her head to look up at him. Suddenly, the pose of polite interest she'd tried to affect this morning was difficult to maintain. She was isolated with Rob hundreds of feet in the air, above a town barely awake, under the spare diameter of his umbrella. For an instant, nothing else existed but the inch of space between their faces. "Just an observation," she replied finally, quietly.

"You're beginning to feel it, aren't you?" he asked, his breath tickling her ear as he spoke.

"What?" she asked, pretending innocence.

"The romance of the moment."

She did. She felt as though it had a grip on her and was pulling her inexorably toward something she didn't want to confront again. She tossed her head.

"I feel the spray of the rain and the bite of a northerly wind," she said, refusing to be drawn.

"Hold this." He took one of her hands and wrapped it around the handle of the umbrella. Then he opened his parka and wrapped the sides of it around her, pulling her into the radiant warmth of his chest and arms.

The sensation of being inside his coat with him stole Jocelyn's every breath and thought. Even through her raincoat, she felt every muscle in contact with her body, his smooth, cool cheek against hers, his strong legs bracketing hers, braced to support both of them as the wind blew across their high perch.

"Better?" he asked.

She couldn't decide on what level to answer that question. Physically, she felt infinitely better. Emotionally, she was in trouble. She nodded, unable to form words.

The wind stirred the shroud of fog and revealed the town of Salty Harbor, an undulation of turn-of-the-century houses following the swell of hills down to the water. Part of the bridge was visible, a tall hotel, the port. To their left was the sheltered bay Lewis and Clark had explored and which Jocelyn had studied from Rob's kitchen window. Sea gulls cried, and sea lions barked.

Jocelyn felt Rob's sigh. "What a beautiful place this is," he said. "Griff's completely taken with it."

"So am I." Jocelyn felt herself relax, caught in the grip of a curious rightness. She'd loved this place from the time she was young enough to be aware of her surroundings. She could remember playing on the front lawn when she'd been three or four and stopping to breathe in the smell of river and ocean, and to look down the hill and watch a freighter glide upriver. She recalled awaking on a dark night with all the normal fears of a child and being comforted by the hum of ships and barges going about their work and the warning bleat of foghorns.

"When I graduated from high school," she said with a little sigh, "my friends couldn't wait to move away, to get a taste of life in the big city. Not me."

Rob felt her lean her weight against him, accepting his embrace. The small movement filled him with a swell of satisfaction out of all proportion to the simple action. But she continued to talk, and he directed his attention to her words.

"It's my theory," she said, "that certain people belong in certain places. Mine is here."

He took advantage of the softness of her mood and nuzzled her ear. "That's a romantic notion, yet you claim to be a nonbeliever."

"No, it's practical," she corrected, hunching her shoulder against his touch and gently pushing his head up. "I wouldn't be able to function where I wasn't happy. Just like you need to be inside a restaurant."

That was true. Although at this moment, out-of-doors with the rain beating mercilessly and the wind whipping around him, he felt curiously content with Jocelyn in his arms. He breathed a little sigh of satisfaction. She could continue to deny it, but romance could brighten any moment, and he vowed to convince her of that before the day was over.

He pushed her back inside the tower toward the steps, then closed the umbrella and followed her.

"Where to now?" she asked, leading the way down the stairs.

"The harbor," he said, coming around ahead of her to give her a helping hand down.

She giggled. "You are determined to drown us, aren't you?"

He stopped a step below her to grin threateningly. "The more you resist, the harder I'll work at changing your mind. And the more dramatic my tactics will become."

He saw real concern cross her eyes for an instant and was surprised to be able to identify with it. A vague little something hovered on the fringes of his thoughts, beyond detection, something that took the casual edge off his mood every time he looked at her. And she was so beautiful today with her confusion of curls and that cautious-but-anxious look in her eyes.

Without removing his gaze from hers, he took her face in his hands and pulled it down the inch or so that separated them. He kissed her thoroughly, then swept her up in his arms.

"Rob!" With a squeal of surprise and concern, Jocelyn wrapped her arms around his neck. No man in her life had ever carried her in his arms, except her father and grandfather, and only when she'd been very small. She felt cosseted and helpless, thrilled and frightened. "There are one hundred and fifty-seven steps in this thing. I'm no featherweight. You'll fall."

He started down steadily. "I won't fall if you don't struggle."

"You'll get a hernia."

"Such a romantic thought." He kissed her cheek as he continued to descend. "I knew I could convert you."

Jocelyn tried to take the umbrella from the hand under her knees. "At least let me carry that."

"I'm carrying you, so even if you carry it, I carry it," he said. After several steps down they looked at each other, registering the confusion in that sentence. Then he shook his head. "Anyway, I'm going to hit you over the head with it when we reach the bottom."

"Ah," she said as she dropped her head against his shoulder. "The romantic caveman approach."

"Something's got to work with you."

He carried her through the door, called a polite "Good morning" as they passed the smiling caretaker in coveralls wandering through a dormant rose garden, and proceeded down the fog-shrouded walk to the parking lot.

"For this to be truly romantic," she said, "there should be a horse waiting, not a car."

He set her on her feet, opened the passenger-side door, then wanged her lightly on her bottom with the umbrella when she got inside. Ignoring her scolding glance, he dropped the umbrella onto her lap, leaned in to kiss her, then closed her door.

ARM IN ARM, ROB HOLDING the open umbrella, they followed a footpath that rimmed the harbor. It was midmorning, and the small fleet of boats was alive with activity, some returning from a night of fishing, some going out, yellow-slickered deckhands handling lines and nets. The air smelled of fish and diesel oil and storm. It was perfume to Jocelyn, but she felt obliged to tease Rob. She sniffed the air and coughed.

"I suppose you see romance here, too," she said.

He looked down into her eyes and she knew he saw through her, but he seemed willing to play the game. "Of

course, I do.'' He stopped her on a knoll overlooking a
spindly pier that pointed out into the harbor. Next to it, a
charter boat strained against the line that secured it to the
dock. The boat was named the *Mary Rose.*

"Imagine," he said in a quiet, narrative tone, "the sail-
ors and fishermen who've said goodbye to wives and sweet-
hearts on this very spot—who've made wild promises and
spun beautiful dreams."

For practical, pragmatic Jocelyn, his voice erased the
scene her eyes saw and evoked a picture of the past. The
charter boat became a square-rigged freighter, and on the
pier, she saw a nineteenth-century sailor with a seabag over
his shoulder sweep off his cap and capture a weeping, bon-
neted woman in his arms.

"Imagine them returning," Rob's voice went on, "to
keep those promises and make all those dreams come true."

Her mind held the same picture, but added laughter to the
woman's tears. She expelled a ragged little sigh of which she
was unaware. Rob heard it and smiled.

"Come on." He pulled her close and led her down to the
pier.

"Where are we going?" she asked.

"To lunch," he replied. At the end of the pier he called
out to the boat. "Hello the *Mary Rose!*"

A black beard and mustache under a black watch cap
emerged from below decks with a forbidding frown. Jocelyn took a step back.

Then the frown was replaced by a broad grin as the man
hoisted himself on deck. "Hey, Rob!" he called. "Just delivered Griff the best crab you ever tasted. This the little
lady?"

Little lady? Jocelyn enjoyed the title. Of course, after
having been carried down one hundred and fifty steps without apparent effort on Rob's part, she could almost believe
it was true.

"Joss, do you know Gabe Wisdom?" Rob pulled her to the very edge of the dock.

Before she could answer, the big man braced a foot on the rail of his boat, reached up two ham-sized hands, pinched her waist in them and swept her onto the deck. He doffed his hat and offered his hand with a kind courtesy that took all the menace out of his size. His hand swallowed her smaller one.

"Pleased to meet you, Mr. Wisdom," she said breathlessly.

Rob landed lightly beside her. "Food get here?" he asked.

The skipper swept a hand toward the shelter of the cabin. "It's all waiting for you." He reached just inside to a row of pegs and handed out two slickers. He took the umbrella from Rob and hung it on an empty peg. "When you're ready to eat, we'll find a quiet spot. Until then, find a comfy place at the rail, and we'll cruise through this poor excuse for a nor'easter."

Rob watched the Salty Harbor riverfront slip by as Gabe followed a slow course that hugged the shore. As a man who'd spent most of his life in major metropolitan centers, Rob had been surprised to find this little town tug at something inside him he hadn't known was there. He still wasn't sure what it was, but seeing it from the river seemed to intensify his feeling. Had he been a man who believed in the permanence of anything, he might have identified it as a sense of belonging. He put the fanciful thought down to the romantic quality of this dramatic day and the woman with whom he shared it. When she looped her arm in his and leaned her hooded head against his shoulder, he stopped thinking altogether.

They passed the skeletons of long-dead canneries and the low, simple structures of those that still functioned. Sea lions swam nearby, drawn by the waste. The boat glided past the hulk of an old barge that had run aground in a storm decades before, and past a refueling dock where a trawler prepared for a day of hard work. The trawler's captain called a greeting to Gabe.

Gabe guided the *Mary Rose* past the radio tower, an automobile agency, several picturesque but empty warehouses, a condominium with its wind socks flying and stalwart green plants on the verandas.

"There's my office window!" Joss pointed upward to the decrepit back of the Stoveman Building. The third window from the left on the second floor had white curtains drawn back and a pink poster board heart in the middle.

Rob looked down at her. "A heart?" he teased.

. "I put it up to inspire me to think romantically for the bazaar," she explained defensively, then she laughed and tightened her grip on his arm. "It's working, so don't spoil the mood by haranguing me about it."

"'Course not." He tried not to look too pleased. It was working. They drifted slowly past the rough-wood structure of the Old Cannery Mall.

"Look!" Jocelyn said excitedly. "There's Griff. And Laurel's with... Oh-oh." She'd started to wave at Rob's cousin in his kitchen whites, apparently taking a coffee break under the awning on the deck that ran around the water side of the restaurant. Then she noticed Laurel standing beside him, arms wrapped around herself against the cold. They appeared to be arguing. Jocelyn pulled her hand back and sighed.

Rob turned to study the arguing pair worriedly as the boat moved on. "He's in love, but she's not at all what he needs in a wife. I'm worried about him."

"He strikes me as the kind of man who can take care of himself," Jocelyn said. "And Laurel's never had to be real for any man before. If he can make her do that, she might turn out to be just what he needs."

Rob looked down at Jocelyn with an apologetic smile. "I'm sorry I didn't handle the question of her business problems very well. She overheard me talking to Griff and got furious. I understand she took it out on you at the auction."

Jocelyn shrugged, leaning her forearms on the rail as they passed the maritime museum. "I'm used to it. Sometimes, I think she dislikes me so much because maybe she doesn't really."

Rob leaned beside her. "Women. Aren't any of you born uncomplicated?"

She smiled into his eyes. "If we were, then we'd arrive unequipped to deal with men and their clever efforts to lure us into romance."

He returned her smile. "Maybe that would be better. You'd bend to the inevitable instead of fighting it. Or are you like Laurel at heart, fighting to cover a need to surrender?"

Jocelyn looked into his eyes and felt the strong grip of that nameless something—and herself slipping into it.

"Men," she said softly. "You always confuse love with war. In love, surrender can be victory because love is all about giving, not gaining. If I surrendered to you, I'd win anyway."

She delivered that combustible little package of truth, then turned her pretty profile to him and smiled as they passed a mooring basin and a breakwater on which half a dozen sea lions barked noisily. He felt a jolt of panic as he realized she described a battle he wouldn't mind losing.

Chapter Ten

Gabe anchored in a small cove several miles beyond Salty Harbor. Mallards, grebes and canvasbacks swam lazily in the tall grass along the bank, unconcerned with the inclement weather.

"You're welcome to join us for lunch," Rob called to the skipper.

Gabe stuck his head around the wheelhouse and waved a battered paperback. "Three's a crowd. And I'm on the last chapter of *Patriot Games*. But if Griff sent some of those Parisian tea cakes, save me one."

Rob laughed. "Deal," he said, drawing Jocelyn to the hatch. He stepped halfway down the small ladder, then offered up his hand.

"If Griff did send tea cakes," she said, moving cautiously onto the top step, "Gabe's come out of your half."

"Selfish, selfish," Rob scolded, flipping the overhead light on, revealing a comfortable oak cabin. A table opened out between two denim-covered bunks. In the middle were a picnic basket and a thermos.

"Is that coffee?" Jocelyn asked in anticipation as she pulled her slicker off. She stood it up in a corner along with Rob's. He poured her a cup and handed it to her.

"What can I do to help?" she asked, hovering near as he peered into a small oven. She gasped as she spotted two skewers on a broiling pan. "Brochette?" she asked. "At sea?"

Rob grinned as he took two plates from the picnic basket. "This is hardly blue-water sailing, Jossie," he said, transferring one of the skewers to a plate. "We're about two miles from the restaurant."

The coffee cup she held balanced on the palm of her hand, she gave him a moue of disapproval. "Now *you're* taking romance for granted."

He handed her the plate and raised an eyebrow. "So you do appreciate that it's precious and special."

She put the plate and her mug on the table. "I never denied that it was," she replied reasonably, placing the picnic basket on the floor. "Just that it didn't . . . appeal to me."

He reached into a small refrigerator and pulled out two salads. "Still?" he asked, his dark eyes daring her to deny that her attitude might have changed this morning.

"Well, maybe just a little," she conceded quietly as he placed the salads on the table and took his place opposite her. More than just a little, she admitted to herself.

Rob stretched out on the bunk and ate propped up on his elbow like some ancient Roman aristocrat. Jocelyn sat in a corner of her bunk, her shoes off, her legs curled under her.

He marveled at how different she looked from the woman he'd met a few weeks ago at a corner table of the restaurant. The awkwardness had left her, though some of the wariness remained. He felt partly responsible for the former, and found himself wanting to do something about the latter.

"I understand the Church Women United's fund-raiser for the seniors," he said, "is a Valentine's dance the night of the bazaar."

She nodded enthusiastically, innocently playing into his hands. "Isn't that wonderful? The band has volunteered its services, and the Scandinavian Club is letting us use its hall free of charge. I can't believe how well this is coming together.''

"What time shall I pick you up?" he asked. He'd phrased the question carefully. A simple "Would you come with me?" would have left her too many options.

She looked startled, then cornered. "I don't dance."

"Yes, you do."

She looked up from a struggle to remove the last cube of beef from the skewer. He took it from her and forked the piece onto her plate. "Phyllis told me," he said.

Her eyes widened. "When did you see Phyllis?"

"She had lunch at the restaurant yesterday with Jeff," he replied, carefully nonchalant.

Jocelyn frowned. "How did the subject of my dancing come up?"

He poured more coffee. "She's on the tickets committee. I bought four."

"Four?"

"Us. Griff and Laurel."

Jocelyn rolled her eyes. "You might have consulted me first."

He smiled into her mutinous expression. "You'd have only said no."

"That's irresponsible."

"It's expedient."

"Well, I'm not going." Concentrating on the last bite of beef, she gave him a superior, victorious glance.

He did not look vanquished. "How're you going to explain it to Phyllis when we leave her house after dinner and you go home while the rest of us go to the dance?"

Jocelyn sighed, defeat closing in on all sides. "Phyl invited us to dinner?"

He nodded. "And Griff and Laurel. Charlene and... what's his name?"

"Chris."

"Right. And your grandfather and Mary Maloney."

Jocelyn groaned. That was the situation that always made her the most uncomfortable—being in the company of her sisters and their husbands in a chummy, family atmosphere. She acted her part well, but it was never easy.

"You'll have me this time," Rob said, a quiet, knowing glance from him telling her he had read her mind.

"You have no idea what you're in for," she warned. "They'll want a wedding date from you before the evening's over."

He smiled wickedly. "You can tell them that you're just toying with me until some practical attorney comes along."

He was only half teasing. When she looked into his eyes and he saw that she recognized his casual hedge, he felt guilt rise up to blunt his smile.

She looked at him levelly. "Maybe I'll just set a date," she said, "and watch you squirm."

He pretended horror, hoping he didn't betray real concern. Because he felt it. "That sounds like a tactic more worthy of Laurel than you."

She shrugged a graceful shoulder. "We all do what we have to do. Maybe we're paired off into the wrong twosomes, here. Laurel did have her eye on you to begin with, and Griff sounds more like my type than hers."

Rob shook his head. "Marriages dissolve because it all becomes so predictable. We lose the romance. I imagine a relationship with someone a little dangerous to your peace of mind is more hectic, but less dull."

He delved into the picnic basket and straightened with a round, flower-patterned tin balanced on the flat of his hand. "Dessert," he said, offering it to her.

She tugged at the lid, dutifully allowing herself to be distracted. Two dozen round cookies dusted with powdered sugar rested on a paper doily. The tantalizing aroma of butter and almond rose to fill the small cabin.

She looked across the table at Rob, holding the tin possessively to her so that he couldn't see its contents. "Parisian tea cakes. Eighteen for me, and six for you and Gabe."

"Greedy," he accused. "Hand over my share." When she continued to withhold them, he leaned toward her. "I could take them away from you," he threatened softly.

Her mind filled with a dozen images, each more exciting and alarming than the last. She took one cookie and handed the tin across the table, unwilling at the moment to explore that potential.

Grinning at her cowardice, Rob filled a third mug with coffee, put several cookies in a sandwich bag and made a delivery to Gabe.

"GIVE ME THAT. I'll build a fire." Rob tugged at Jocelyn's sodden coat. They stood in the middle of his living room, completely drenched. When Gabe dropped them off at the pier, they'd run to the parking lot, forgetting the umbrella. Then Rob had driven them home. He'd said very little, and Jocelyn had half expected to be dropped at her apartment.

She kept a firm grip on the lapels of her coat. "I should go home," she said, her voice and her conviction flimsy. She knew she should, because she was succumbing to his charm. Though there was a new Jocelyn Foley growing, she hoped she was at least as smart as her predecessor.

He looked genuinely distressed. "Why?"

She had a hundred reasons, none of which made sense when she looked into his eyes. She glanced at her watch with a businesslike twist of her wrist. "Your eight hours are up," she said.

They stared at each other for a long moment, he trying desperately to read what she tried unsuccessfully to conceal. The rain continued, and the house was filled with long winter-afternoon shadows. Trusting instinct, Rob closed a hand around the back of her neck and pulled her to him. He parted his lips over hers and rid both of them of the playful sparring that had kept them at a careful distance all morning and during lunch.

He dipped his tongue into her mouth, demanding honesty. She gave it with an intensity that would have made him draw back if he were thinking straight. But he wasn't. He was filled with her and the way she made him feel. He'd never known this simple sweetness before, this down-deep well-being he felt when she was within reach.

He raised his head, his left hand still woven in her hair. "Tell me," he dared, "that today really had anything to do with the auction."

For a moment, her brain was still too filled with sensation to put a meaning to his words. Then she got a grip, pulled herself back. "Tell me," she challenged, "what it did have to do with."

Still too drunk with her to be remotely intimidating, he gave her a scolding glance as he hung her coat in the service porch, then settled her on the sofa while he knelt to build a fire in a deep, brick fireplace. "Us," he replied. "Do we have to know more than that right now?"

She couldn't dispel the feeling that it would be wise. Still, the day had proceeded beautifully, and she'd had a wonderful time without understanding or even trying to analyze what precisely was happening. Maybe there was something to be said for Rob's "romantic" approach.

A fire bloomed in the tepee of alder branches behind the grate, and Rob got to his feet. "Can I get you anything?" he asked. "More coffee? A glass of wine?"

Jocelyn groaned feelingly and put a hand to her stomach. "Nothing, please."

He sat beside her. "That's what you get for eating all your cookies and half of mine."

"That's what you get," she said, leaning her head back, unrepentant, "for leaving them."

"I hadn't left them. I went up on deck to give some to Gabe."

"Well, you should have explained you were coming back."

"We were on a thirty-foot boat," he said, hooking the underside of the coffee table with his toe and pulling it closer. He reached down for her crossed ankles and propped them on the edge of the table. "Where was I going to go?"

She closed her eyes and grinned. "I'm sure a romantic like yourself would have thought of something. A swim to Washington across the river on such a day would be a story you could tell for years. Or you could have dumped Gabe overboard in a life vest and kidnapped me for a slow cruise to Bora Bora."

She felt his feet thump onto the table beside hers and his arm come around her. He took the point of her shoulder in one hand and angled her slightly so she rested against him.

"You're wasted as a pragmatist," he said, kissing her hair. "I know you've got dreams hidden away, Jossie. What are they?"

"Dreams." She repeated the word, realizing with some surprise that all the old ones came rushing to the fore. She'd had them when she'd been in love with Jeff, but when he'd married Phyllis, she'd thought she'd killed the dreams, or at least buried them so deep, they'd surely suffocated.

From the shelter of Rob's arm, it was easy to let the dreams take shape again.

"I'd like a loving husband," she said. "A house with a view of the river, just like the one where I grew up. A passel of beautiful children..." She sighed and spread her arms expansively, then wrapped them around herself again. "And a long life like my grandmother had in which to enjoy them. What about you?" She turned her head to look up at Rob. "A successful chain of restaurants?"

He smiled. "No. Just one that does well and keeps Griff and me solvent." He pointed to the worn kitchen cabinets. "Then I'd like someone to wave a wand and finish this cottage."

"This room is wonderful," she said, turning her head to watch the fire dance. Warmth and the fragrance of alder surrounded them. "If I lived here, I'd never leave the kitchen."

"I don't know that this room alone could accommodate a *passel* of children." He emphasized her word by giving her a gentle squeeze. "How many are in a passel, anyway?"

"Four or five at least." She measured the wisdom of asking the question, then did it anyway. "Do you want children?"

There was a moment's silence. "I used to think I did," he said finally. "But they should come with a mother, and I saw firsthand how bitter a relationship can become. Kids shouldn't have to live with that."

"I suppose it would be stating the obvious to say that all relationships aren't like that."

"For me, they probably would be," he said. "I have to have a restaurant, and restaurants take a lot of time. Most women like a man to be around and share the burden of raising that passel of kids."

"That's why God made work shifts."

He made a scornful sound. "When food and hospitality are served in your name, you'd better be on hand to make certain it's done the way you want it."

"There are ways around that."

"None that work." He was silent a moment, then he added, "My father did all the glad-handing at The Brahmin, and delegated all the real responsibility to the rest of the family. I vowed I'd never be like that."

She reached up to rub her knuckles along his chin. "Then why are you here with me today instead of hard at work?"

He caught her wrist and lightly bit a knuckle. "Because you're bad for my resolve."

She delighted in the little intimacy and felt herself slipping further into danger. "What time are you going in to work this afternoon?"

"I'm not," he said. "I'll go in tomorrow morning after I take you home."

It took her a moment to realize what he implied. She didn't turn to look at him, afraid he'd see how much appeal the prospect of spending the night with him held for her. He was teasing her, baiting her to react, but on a moody, rainy afternoon in his arms, she found it difficult not to surprise him by falling in with his playful plan.

"Tell me about the restaurant where you grew up," she said, seeking to distract herself as well as him. She sat on her knees and turned to lean into him, resting her forearm on his shoulder. She smiled. "Were you always so responsible, even as a child?"

He nodded, returning her smile. "I think so. I've loved everything about the business for as long as I can remember. I never had the magic touch in the kitchen Griff has, but I developed a skill for purchasing and planning and understanding what people want in a good restaurant besides food." His smile was warm with reminiscences. "For a while, our lives were almost perfect—or so it seemed to me. My father was always laughing and full of big ideas, and I thought he was the greatest man on earth. I didn't understand then that he was carefree because everyone else did the work and he just...talked."

She rubbed his shoulder in silent comfort. "What was your mom like?"

He laughed, shaking his head. "Short, round, warm and happy." His smile took on a hard edge and disappeared. "Until my father got tired of everything and left. She was never herself after that. She and my uncle held things together for a couple of years, but he was already in poor health. When he died, we had to sell."

Jocelyn hooked her arm around his neck, sensing pain he hadn't expressed.

"How old were you when your father left?"

"Fourteen."

She winced. Her childhood had been so full of loving people who were always there—parents, grandparents, sisters, friends. She could only imagine how Rob must have been hurt.

"Who took care of your mother and Griff and you when your uncle died?"

He shrugged, as though it had been a simple matter. "I did. Anger generates a lot of energy. I felt betrayed by my father, and it became critical to me that I succeed and show him we could do just fine without him."

"Does he know how well you've done?" she asked gently.

Rob shook his head. "We never heard from him again. But I showed *myself* I could do without him. I suppose that was more important than showing him."

He came out of his thoughts and focused on her with sudden concentration. He snaked an arm around her waist and pulled her into his lap. "This was supposed to be a day dedicated to romance. Let's talk about something else."

She wanted to remind him that confidences shared between friends were important, too. But he seemed determined to let the past be for the moment.

"Okay," she said lightly, "let's talk about how holding me in your lap is going to stop your circulation."

He shook his head. "I work out every day. My legs are indestructible." He ran a hand lightly, caressingly up her back. "You're gorgeous, you know," he said with sudden seriousness. "I wouldn't want an ounce of you moved or removed."

She felt so beautiful in Rob's arms. Every fiber of her being in contact with his seemed to generate a kind of music she heard in her brain. Every sense was sharpened by his nearness, every emotion amplified.

She had to struggle to remain coherent when his lips traced kisses along her jaw. "The woman you met the day I came to ask to use your center court didn't believe in romance."

He worked down her throat. "You did. You just tucked that part of you away because it's gotten you hurt."

She frowned as she realized she was losing the argument. "You should understand that," she said distractedly. "You don't want to be married again because your wife hurt you."

"Yes," he admitted huskily, his lips moving up to nip the lobe of her ear.

She gasped at the touch of his tongue. "Then why are you... pursuing me?"

He dragged himself out of the delicious languor beginning to overtake him and looked into her eyes. He had to be careful here; it was going to take his full attention. "Because... marriage doesn't have to be the point of every relationship."

"Then what would be the point of this one?" Her eyes were wide and steady. They made him suspicious. "Romance?"

"Very good," he praised. "You're catching on."

She leaned back against his arm, tracing a finger along the pattern on his sweater. "But romance has to be applied to something, doesn't it?" she asked.

"What do you mean?"

"Well, it can't exist in and of itself. You can have a romantic marriage or a romantic afternoon or a romantic movie... but you can't just have romance."

He got the point. "You can have a romantic relationship."

She leaned an elbow on his shoulder and smiled. "That's kind of nebulous."

He acknowledged the truth of that with a grin and a tilt of his head. "Sometimes, clearly defining something hems it in. It can't grow beyond the parameters you've set for it."

There had to be a good answer for that, but she couldn't come up with it. "I'm just not sure," she said softly, "that I could cope in such an unreal situation."

"It's not unreal," he insisted. "It's done all the time."

She nodded. It was a fact of life today. "We have a world full of significant others." She gave a little shudder. "If I took up with a man, even if he couldn't define the relationship, he'd damn well better be able to define *me*. I could be girlfriend, lover, even roommate, but I could never be a significant other. Talk about fuzzy parameters."

Rob wrapped both arms around her and laughed.

Jocelyn pointed to the book of poetry on the coffee table. "Of course, your friend Swinburne had no such problems. In his day, they called love what it was."

"They were no more sure how to deal with it, though," Rob argued. "The angst of being confused by love was most of what the romantic poets wrote about."

Jocelyn reached out for the book, Rob lacing his fingers around her waist to prevent her from overbalancing. The book in hand, she leaned against him again, paging through the thin, yellowed volume.

"You must have a favorite," she said.

"I do. Page 61."

She found the page and perused the poem, reading aloud a particularly beautiful verse.

"If love were what the rose is,
    And I were like the leaf,
Our lives would grow together
    In sad or singing weather

Blown fields or flowerful closes,
   Green pleasure or gray grief,
If love were what the rose is,
   And I were like the leaf.''

Concentrating, she reread the last line. '''If love were what the rose is,/And I were like the leaf.''' She held the open book against her breast. ''Wow.''

''Call *that* claptrap,'' he challenged.

''Well, that isn't romance,'' she said. ''That's just reality beautifully put.''

He pinched the backside perched on his knee.

She jumped and squealed in protest. ''Rob!''

''A hardheaded woman,'' he said sternly, ''has to be approached through other means. Come on. I'm taking you dancing.''

He turned her unceremoniously onto the sofa and got to his feet.

''Like this?'' she asked dryly, propped on her elbows and raising a jeans-clad leg for his inspection. ''Unless they have a dance floor at Barbeque Heaven, we're not dressed appropriately.''

He reached down for her hand and pulled her up beside him. ''I'll change and then we'll stop at your place.''

She shook her head. ''Even at home, I don't have anything to wear dancing.''

''Can you borrow something from one of your sisters?''

She folded her arms mulishly. ''Phyllis is two sizes smaller than I am, and Charlie is smaller than that.''

He folded his arms, his eyes steady. ''I'm not letting you go until the wee hours of the morning, and if we don't go dancing, I'm taking you upstairs.''

She didn't have to ask what was up there. She crossed the room to the wall telephone. ''You change. I'll call Phyl.''

"PERFECT." PHYLLIS stepped back to look at Jocelyn and spread both hands in helpless wonder. "Perfect. I can't believe it. This man is a magician."

Rob sat in Phyllis's living room with Jeff and Lindsay.

Jocelyn looked at the reflection of herself dressed in the cap-sleeved black tent dress covered in sequins. Despite the disparity in Phyllis's and her sizes, the full cut of the dress made it flare flatteringly just above her knees as though it had been made for her. A common shoe size allowed her to borrow Phyllis's black satin pumps.

"I'll bring it back first thing in the morning," Jocelyn promised.

Phyllis put a tiny black mesh bag into her hands. "Like I'm going to a black-tie affair before lunch. Don't worry about it. I won't need it until the Valentine's dance. You know everyone's coming here for dinner first?"

Jocelyn frowned at her. "Yes. Plans were made without anyone consulting yours truly."

Phyllis patted her cheek and pushed her toward the bedroom door. "Yours truly isn't always very smart. Sometimes, it's easier to work around her. Have a good time."

They tiptoed past the night-lighted nursery where Robin slept and into the living room.

Jeff, sitting back in a cordovan recliner, shouted and pointed at the television screen. "Geez! Did you... God...? Did you see that?"

The question was directed at Rob, who sat in the middle of the sofa, also in major distress. Lindsay, settled on his knee in banana-colored footed sleepers, a bear in her arms, shouted, "Wimp! Blockhead!" at the television.

Jeff and Rob exchanged a grin over her head. Phyllis shrieked, "Lindsay Marie!"

Lindsay shrank back against Rob. "Well, that's what Daddy said."

Phyllis turned her ire on Jeff. "Now that makes a wonderful impression on Rob, I'm sure."

Rob stood and put Lindsay in her father's arms. "Please. I've spent all day in Joss's company. This is all very tame." He straightened to give Jocelyn a slow once-over with lazy, dark eyes.

She held a blush back, waiting for him to make a comment that Phyllis would tease her about tomorrow, repeat to Charlie and probably write to their mother. It was almost worse when he said nothing.

"Auntie Jossie, you look beautiful," Lindsay said in wonder. "You have hair like Annie."

Joss raised an eyebrow. "Annie?"

"Little Orphan Annie," Phyllis explained. She pushed Jocelyn toward Rob. "You and Daddy Warbucks have a good time."

THE MOMENT ROB TOOK HER in his arms on the dance floor, he knew it was a mistake. Jocelyn was pliant and just a little dreamy, and they came together like two ends of a jeweled clasp, perfectly fitted, honed to lock. Trepidation was instant, but for the moment, need overrode it. After the long, delicious day with her, he could no more have put her away from him than he could have flown.

Violins and a haunting saxophone wove a melody that wrapped around him, invaded him and settled in like an ache.

Jocelyn, relaxed and happy, wrapped her arms around his neck, rested her head on his shoulder and swayed with him on the small dance floor.

The dress made her feel pretty, and a day spent in Rob's company had made her feel—romantic. There, she'd admitted it. Serenity settled over her. Looking it full in the face was cleansing. Of course, she knew her concept of romance differed from Rob's, but at least it was something they almost held in common, a place to start.

She heaved a deep sigh against him as excitement fluttered in her breast. She was falling in love again—and she wanted to. She felt like Cinderella, except that the fairy godmother's wand had transformed her emotionally as well as outwardly.

Jocelyn leaned back to look up into Rob's eyes. "I've had a wonderful day," she said softly. She gave him a rueful little smile. "I hope you enjoyed it, even though it cost you two thousand dollars."

He looked into her eyes and saw the fragile beginnings of love there. Panic and passion fought for his attention. "You are priceless," he whispered.

The last vestige of caution Jocelyn held fell away and she forgot, for a moment, their earlier conversation. She was satiated with food and wine and his gallant attention. She stopped dancing and looked into his eyes, her own brimming with emotion and wonder. The erratic pattern of light from a rotating mirrored ball played across her face and hair and the shoulders of her dress. She glowed like a star plucked from the sky. The music from the saxophone rose on a lighthearted trill as she caught her breath, gave a startled little shake of her head, and admitted, her eyes wide with romance, "I love you, Rob."

For a startled moment, Rob stared at her. Then he pulled her to him before she could see any reaction in his eyes. He knew it had to be there—an unwillingness to become involved on that level coupled with a niggling little fear he didn't entirely understand himself. He knew only that he'd wanted to romance her, but he didn't want to love her, and he didn't want her to expect love from him. He'd thought he'd explained all that this afternoon.

He held her tightly through the next two numbers, moving to music he didn't hear. Then he told her it was late, went for their coats and led her through the dark parking lot to his car, keeping just a little ahead of her to avoid her eyes.

He had to find a way to tell her. He had to explain it all over again. He didn't love her. He wouldn't love her.

He put her into the car and walked around to slip in behind the wheel. His brain was feverishly formulating explanations, excuses, justifications as he fitted the key into the ignition.

"I could take it back," she said into the stillness that surrounded them.

He turned to her in surprise, startled by the weary, knowing expression in her eyes. While he'd been hiding his gaze from her, she'd done a good job of concealing hers from him. Their dark blue depths told him now that he wasn't fooling anyone. She'd read him clearly on the dance floor.

"Of course, it wouldn't change anything," she added quietly, her hair and her dress glittering in the darkness of the car. "I would still love you. How many days like today do you think a couple can string together in a lifetime with just casual affection between them?"

He struggled to remain honest and calm. She couldn't know that his need to hold her was as desperate as his unwillingness to love her. "As many as they want," he said, "if they're careful not to bog them down with the drudgery of commitment. I explained this afternoon that—"

She stopped him with a raised hand, her voice still quiet. "Yes, I know. That stuff about a romantic relationship and significant others."

Impatience rose in him, though he wasn't sure why or with whom—her or himself. "You brought up the significant-other stuff. Those weren't my words."

She fiddled with the little bag on her lap. "It occurs to me," she said, "that a strange thing has happened here."

"What's that?" he asked warily.

She looked up at him, the expression in her eyes difficult to read—except that he could clearly see there was no love in it as there had been on the dance floor. He found himself wishing urgently that he could be different.

"We've crossed over," she said.

He frowned. "Pardon me?"

"We've crossed over," she repeated. "And we're still on opposite sides. You turned me into a romantic, but you've become a pragmatist."

He couldn't see that at all. "I don't understand."

"You've opened my life," she said with unabashed sincerity. "You've convinced me that I'm pretty, that a little attention to the soft side of life isn't foolish but wise. That seeing things with a rosier eye lends an added dimension of drama to everything. Every day has a texture I was never aware of before. Today—" She closed her eyes for a moment, then opened them and sighed. "I'll never feel the rain on my face again without remembering today. But now, you're the realist. I was willing to be swept away with it, to let it work its magic on me, but you aren't. I said the wrong words, and you brought everything to a screeching halt. Wasn't it you who told me just this afternoon that clearly defining something hems it in? That setting parameters—"

"Because you're talking about love, Joss."

A vaguely pitying expression entered her eyes. "Do you really think romance can be anything without it?"

He thought about the relationships he'd had since Sandy. They'd been brief whirlwind affairs. He couldn't remember having been affected in any way by the women he had been involved with. But a day with Jocelyn had turned him inside out.

"You're running from something," she said, "that's part of you. Love blossoms and grows in all of us because of our need for someone beside us to make the trip through life worthwhile. Romance might brighten the journey, but what happens to romance when you fall into a pothole or get hit by a truck?"

He opened his mouth, but before he could answer, she told him. "It's shot to hell, is what it is. But that someone beside you filled with love for you will pull you out of the hole and get the license number of the truck."

Rob put a hand to his thudding head. "The truck got me on its last pass, Joss. Maybe that's the problem. Are you telling me you want out?"

"No," she said, her voice rising. "I want in. *You* want out. Okay. Okay." She straightened in her seat and snapped her seat belt in place. "Let's test the theory. Take me home with you."

He raised an eyebrow at her.

"Take me home," she said again, turning the key for him. The engine purred, and she gave him a smile he didn't like and didn't trust. "Make love to me as you've been suggesting all day, then drive me back to my place in the morning. Let's see how romantic it is to lie in each other's arms all night, then go our separate ways. Come on." She made a get-going gesture in the direction of the gas pedal. "Let's do it. If you're wrong and I'm right, then I'm still the only one with something to lose. Put it in gear, Donnelly. I know you've only paid for eight hours, but what the heck."

He pulled out of the parking lot with a squeal of tires and a deadly determination.

Chapter Eleven

Jocelyn was not surprised when Rob braked in front of her apartment with a jolt that rocked both of them forward. She was depressed, discouraged and even faintly disappointed, but not surprised.

Without a word, he got out of the car, walked around the front to the passenger door and opened it. She stepped out and he slammed the door. She extended her hand. "I presume this is where we say—"

"Be quiet." He took her arm in the biting fingers of his right hand and led the way to the door, then up the inside stairs.

At the door to her apartment, he put his hand out for her key. She slapped it as though she'd just slam-dunked a wild ball and he'd offered congratulations.

"All *right!*" she said. "Gimme five! It's all a game anyway, isn't it. I—"

He pushed her back against the door frame, one hand over her mouth, his angry eyes daring her to say another word. The other hand took the key from her and opened the door.

Mrs. Gustafson opened her apartment door and poked her head out. Her gray hair was covered with pink rollers all askew, and Biddy barked furiously from the crook of her arm. Her mouth fell open as she took in the scene.

Jocelyn glared at Rob, who lowered his hand with obvious reluctance. She smiled at her neighbor and pointed a thumb at her companion. "Just teasing," she said. "He likes to think he's the forceful type."

Mrs. Gustafson nodded with lack of conviction.

"Excuse us," Rob said, and ushered Jocelyn inside. He pushed the door closed behind them, snatched Jocelyn's purse from her, replaced the key, then tossed the bag onto the sofa.

"She's probably calling the police right now," Jocelyn said in a whisper, sure Mrs. Gustafson would be on the other side of her keyhole the moment she replaced the receiver.

"I'll be gone before they arrive," he said, snaking an arm around Jocelyn's waist and pulling her against him so that she felt every plane and hollow of his body from the vicinity of his third rib to his toes. Heat flared the length of her. Fear and excitement welled up side by side.

His other hand went into her hair and applied the barest pressure to make her tilt her head back.

"When you wake up tomorrow," he said softly, deliberately, "and you realize that you're alone and you feel like the lonely morning after, but without the memories of the night before, I want you to remember what you could have had."

And he kissed her, but not like he'd ever kissed her before. His tongue invaded deeply into her mouth and his hand closed over a sequin-covered breast, kneading with the possessive quality of a hand that knew her body—or thought it should. Then it slid down her back to her hip and applied one slow revolution of its palm there. It put them in intimate contact—and gave her one brief but sharp glimpse of what a night with him would be like.

Her spine and her resolve went limp. As he drew away, she looked into his eyes, prepared to capitulate. Then she saw the careful neutrality there, and every vertebra snapped back into place.

He took a step back, said, "You'd have no promises from me, but you'd have everything else," and turned to leave.

But he couldn't. She'd caught his arm, and when he turned, an arrogant eyebrow raised, she caught hold of his tie and pulled him down until they were nose to nose. "When you wake up in the middle of the night and feel the empty place beside you," she said, every soft word enunciated distinctly, "I want you to remember that I offered to be there, but that you—*you*—made the decision to bring me home. Try to analyze why you did that, and please be honest with yourself. And while you're at it, tell me that simple romance ever did this for you."

She caught a fistful of the thick, wiry hair at the crown of his head and did her best to put everything into the kiss as he had. She toyed with his tongue, traced his teeth, nipped at his lip, and when she freed his hair and his tie and allowed him to straighten, she didn't budge an inch, letting every now-quaking muscle in his body slide against hers.

She took a step back. "You'd have every promise I could make you," she whispered. "And you'd still have everything else." Then she walked around him and opened the door. His car roared out of the parking lot before she closed it again.

ROB DIDN'T REMEMBER driving home. He came to awareness in the middle of his kitchen when the cold emptiness of it hit him like a blast of tundra air. He was trembling with anger.

He tossed his jacket off and threw it at a chair. He poured a glass of wine and downed it in a swallow, but he continued to tremble. He had to admit to himself that the anger contained a considerable measure of frustration. He poured another glass and drank it down.

He fell onto his sofa and yanked at his tie. He caught her scent on it and held it a moment as his body remembered the touch of her as she freed the tie and he had straightened, his chest rubbing over the delicate swell of her breasts. He threw the tie aside and crossed his feet on the coffee table.

But that brought back memories of sitting with her in his lap. He leaned forward impatiently, wondering if he'd ever have a clear thought in his head again that didn't involve her.

He stretched out full length on the sofa and closed his eyes. Her pretty, guileless face bloomed instantly in his mind. How dare she hold herself primly away from him when he'd done so much for her, when he'd made a large donation and planned a special day just to be in her company, when he was so... so trapped in her web of warmth and charm, when she promised everything a romantic soul could ever hope for.

He shifted edgily onto his side, his arm dropping off the sofa, his hand brushing something on the floor. He raised his head to see his volume of Swineburne open on the carpet. He picked it up and turned it over.

It was open to the verse he loved, the verse she'd read him while sitting in his lap. ''...Our lives would grow together/In sad or singing weather,/...If love were what the rose is,/And I were like the leaf.''

He stormed into the kitchen, book in hand, looking for a place to put it out of sight. He tossed it into the corner cabinet he'd found too inconvenient to use and slammed the door closed. He wondered crossly why that verse had once appealed to him. It said nothing about what to do with the thorn.

ROB HAD BEEN RIGHT ABOUT the morning after. Jocelyn showered, put on the pants she'd bought at Laurel's and paired them with a new white sweater.

She sliced a banana into her bowlful of Nutri-Grain, downed a glass of orange juice and a cup of coffee, then reached for her jacket.

Congratulating herself on her maturity, on her ability to get on with her life despite a second dumping, she snatched up her purse and the plastic-shrouded black dress she'd borrowed from Phyllis. The sequins caught the frail morning light from her living room window and sparkled as they had the night before on the dance floor. She burst into tears and buried her face in the plastic.

"HAVE YOU SET THE MENU for the Business and Professional Women's banquet?" Rob pulled out a chair opposite Griff at a corner table in the back of the restaurant. Griff pored over recipes, stabbed at a pocket calculator, then made notes on a steno pad.

He glanced at Rob. "Could you move back a little bit?" he asked, returning his attention to the recipes. "My tetanus shot isn't current."

Rob picked up the thermal carafe at Griff's elbow and poured coffee into his cousin's empty cup. "I apologized for shouting at you. It looked like too much basil until I tasted it."

Griff punched figures into the calculator. "'So, I was wrong, so sue me,' does not constitute an apology."

Rob sighed heavily and went to the waitress's station in the opposite corner of the room and pulled a cup and saucer out of the rack. He carried it back to the table and poured himself some coffee. He took a swallow and waited for the caffeine to rev his system. It didn't. He took another.

"Griff, I'm sorry," Rob said, putting the cup aside. "I..." He wanted to explain, but didn't know how. He wasn't sure himself what had happened between him and Jocelyn. He only knew he hadn't won the encounter.

Griff made some notations on the pad, then put the pencil down and leaned back in his chair. "You blew it with Jossie, didn't you?"

Rob sighed impatiently. He really didn't want to get into it. "Nice of you to presume it was my fault."

"The way you've been acting the last few days," Griff said, "we could blame the tides on you. You're pulling us all down like bad gravity."

"That—" Rob turned the pad around so that he could read Griff's notes "—is her fault."

"Said no to you?"

Deeply offended, primarily because it was true, Rob glared across the table at his cousin. "As a matter of fact, she said yes. *I* said no."

Griff studied him suspiciously. "Why don't I believe that?"

Rob flipped a page back and studied a menu without really seeing it. "Because you're nuts. I've always said that." Then he looked up with all apparent innocence. "And how're you doing with Laurel?"

Griff shrugged a shoulder. "She hates me. But then, she's always hated me. I haven't really lost any ground. What happened to you?"

Rob pushed the pad aside and looked out at the beautiful day. Somehow, the arrival of February had brought a string of sharp, clear weather—as though in mockery of his dreary mood. The river stretched out smooth and clear to the hills of Washington on the other side. A rusty, blue-and-white fishing boat angled toward the fuel dock.

Rob leaned his elbow on the wide windowsill and ran a hand over his face. "She told me she loved me," he said flatly.

Griff shook his head and said with irony, "Poor you. How devastating. Don't tell me. Your reply was, 'So what, so sue me.'"

Rob scraped his chair back and stood, but Griff reached across the table and caught his arm. Rob closed a bruising hand over Griff's wrist. The muscle under his hand only swelled as Griff strengthened his grip. Rob could have freed himself, but the violence he would have to use he simply couldn't direct at his cousin. So he stood, mutely angry and momentarily powerless.

Griff's expression softened. "Okay, this time, *I'm* sorry. That was uncalled for. But you need to hear a few truths about yourself. Sit down."

"Griff..."

"Sit down." Griff said firmly. Then he grinned. "Do you really want to see me look like an idiot when I try to make you do it and you cream me?"

Rob sank reluctantly into a chair. "That has a certain appeal, yes. All right, what? And please, be careful."

"Okay. I'll even be brief." Griff sat down, put his hat on the windowsill and joined his hands on the table. His eyes grew serious. "No brother could mean more to me than you do, or do more for me. That's why I kept my mouth shut when you married Sandy."

Rob bristled, and Griff said quietly, "Let me finish. She was selfish. She didn't care about you. She cared about the fact that you owned a restaurant that celebrities flocked to and that you made a lot of money. It wasn't tedium that killed your marriage, or the fact that you spent too much time working. It was the faulty half of the equation. So now your personal life skims the surface in the name of freedom and romance. You find girls who want nothing from you but party time. You know why?"

"Go ahead and tell me."

"I'm sure you've figured it out very carefully. You don't want to get hurt again, but what you've forgotten is that you'll never be loved again, either. You push Jocelyn away,

Rob, and you'll be miserable for a lifetime. I'll even help make you that way if you hurt her."

Rob frowned at him. "It's a good thing you went into food service and not psychiatry. You have no idea what's going on in my mind."

Griff sighed and shrugged. "Then why don't you tell me, because the way you've decided to live doesn't make sense. What *are* you thinking?"

Rob expelled a long breath. "It's very simple. I have to have a restaurant, and Sandy proved to me that that pretty much precludes my having a wife. A relationship with a woman who wants marriage would just be setting both of us up for a breakup."

"Joss is nothing like Sandy."

"Griff," Rob said with forced patience, "she said she loves me."

Griff studied him a long moment, as though trying to see the problem. Then he asked, "Don't you want to be loved?"

Rob had had enough of this. He stood. "I want to be free to give all my time to the restaurant. Otherwise, a couple of months down the road, you and I are going to find ourselves wearing knee-high rubber boots and working in the cannery at the other end of the pier."

"If we were any more successful," Griff said, getting to his feet and gathering up his hat and the pad and pot, "we'd have to expand into the jewelry store next door."

Rob picked up their cups and saucers and dropped them on the busing cart before pushing the kitchen door open with his shoulder. "Attention to business is what's put us in this position. That's the only thing that'll keep us there."

"Crazy me. I thought it might have something to do with my cooking."

"Maybe a little."

Griff shoved the pad he held at Rob's midsection. "Here's your BPW menu. Call Mrs. Sullivan and try to help her make a decision."

"I suppose you're responsible for this?"

The angry feminine voice coming from the corner of the kitchen turned both men in that direction in surprise. Laurel, in a clinging gray wool dress, her hair piled into an elegant stream of curls, leapt off a stool and waved a sheaf of papers at them.

Rob and Griff looked at each other in puzzlement.

Laurel stopped within inches of them and looked from one to the other with a peevish frown. "It's the small-business loan package from the Bank of Salty Harbor. Apparently, I was referred to them by some anonymous benefactor who's willing to cosign."

"You told me to stay out of it, and I did," Griff said, raising his right hand. "I swear."

Laurel's gaze swung to Rob. He shook his head. "Wasn't me."

"Too bad." Her expression changed from anger to cautious optimism as she looked over the papers. "There are some good ideas in here that just might save my shop." She smiled from one to the other as she walked between them, then turned to add silkily over her shoulder. "I was looking forward to thanking someone."

She disappeared through the swinging doors with a casual wave.

Griff turned to Rob with a look of total dejection. "Didn't she say don't get involved? Didn't she de—"

Rob put an arm around his shoulder. "She did. I heard her. It's just a tactic to keep you off balance. Don't let it throw you."

"But she wanted to *thank* somebody. That somebody could have been me. Me!"

"Forget it. The game is set up so you can't win."

Griff sighed. "Well, I'm a poor loser. A real poor loser."

Rob rubbed absently at an ache in his midsection. "Yeah. Me, too."

"THE *SALTY HARBOR SENTINEL* promised to have a reporter at the bazaar," Mary said reading from her notes. "The radio station will do live interviews with patrons. The high school choir will sing for fifteen minutes every hour. And we've been promised enough prizes by participating merchants that we can hold a drawing every thirty minutes from ten o'clock until four." She put her yellow pad down and smiled at the small group assembled in Freddie's tiny housing-authority apartment.

Nathan, John, Freddie and Jocelyn applauded. Jocelyn delighted in how well the project was going. It helped distract her from how completely her personal life had fallen apart.

"We owe it all to Jossie, you know," Freddie said, leaning out of her rocker to put an arm around Jocelyn, seated beside her on a kitchen chair. "She's charmed everyone into working for us."

"And personally raised two thousand dollars," Nathan reminded. He smiled slyly. "Want to tell us how that day went?"

A cold fist gripped Jocelyn's insides. She smiled shyly, knowing he'd misinterpret her reticence and drop the subject. He was becoming Rob's most devoted champion.

"I'd rather not, thank you," she said. She dropped a cutout pink cupid onto the pile on the floor and picked up a traced one from the pile in her lap. "Do you have the list of booths firmed up?"

He raised his clipboard. "Right here."

"How many outlets do we need?"

"Only three. Rob says he can easily accommodate that many."

"Good. And all the cookies are guaranteed, Freddie?"

"Yes. Two hundred dozen." She pushed herself laboriously to her feet, Nathan reaching out to give her a helping hand. "And speaking of food, I made an apple kuchen."

There was a unanimous groan of appreciation.

"How many want it with ice cream?"

The show of hands was also unanimous. Mary followed her into the kitchen.

John leaned over to the television and switched it on, winking at Nathan. "Maybe we can catch the end of the Blazer game."

With everyone occupied, Jocelyn dropped her scissors for a moment and flexed her fingers. They were blistered and cramped and she found herself thinking bitterly that she'd be happy when this hearts-and-flowers claptrap was over.

She immediately regretted the thought. Despite her acute disappointment in the early death of her relationship with Rob, she'd learned something from it. It hadn't killed her — it had hurt like the devil, but she was still alive. She was the object of second looks on the street now, and even an occasional wolf whistle. There'd been times when she'd been sure those little thrills would never be hers.

And, paradoxically, exposing her soft side had strengthened it. She wasn't going to hide again because she'd been dumped a second time.

She flexed her hands and went back to work on the cupid. Maybe she wouldn't take it all so seriously next time. Maybe permanence just wasn't in the cards for her. Maybe she should just live her life from day to day and be grateful for the little pleasures that came her way.

That rhetoric played over in her mind and she dropped the scissors and the cupid to her lap in horror, all her brave resolve dissipating. She'd just quoted Rob's philosophy.

The peal of Freddie's doorbell startled her out of her thoughts.

"Would somebody get that?" Freddie called from the kitchen.

Nathan and John were completely engrossed in the outcome of a free throw. Jocelyn put her project aside and went to the door. She was surprised to find Laurel standing on the doorstep. She was also surprised to find the woman smiling. It was a genuine smile—not the wry or cynical variety she usually dispensed.

"Laurel," Jocelyn said, continuing to stare at her.

"Hi, Joss." Laurel shifted her weight and the large grocery bag in her arms. "May I come in?"

"Ah...sure." Jocelyn stepped aside to let her into the tiny living room crowded with chairs and the memorabilia of Freddie's active lifetime. Knickknacks and photos covered every surface. Crocheted doilies draped the back and arms of every upholstered chair.

Nathan and John looked up with brief greetings and turned back to the television screen.

Jocelyn couldn't imagine what Laurel was doing there—unless she'd tracked her down and come to tell her what she thought of her interference regarding the business loan. She was sure by now Laurel had received the packet from the bank and figured out who'd prompted its delivery. She looked at her warily. "Did you want to talk to me?" she asked.

Laurel took a pair of dressmaker's shears out of her purse.

"Oh, God," Jocelyn thought. She imagined the following morning's headlines—Infuriated Merchant Shear Murders Community Development Director.

"Sure, if you want to talk," Laurel said, working the scissors. "But I came to help you cut out decorations. Mary was in to buy a dress for the dance and she told me your committee was a little shorthanded."

Jocelyn could not have been more surprised if Laurel had, indeed, stabbed her.

Laurel reached to the pile of traced cupids on Jocelyn's chair. "Are these the ones?"

"Yes," Jocelyn said vaguely.

"Good. Here." Laurel put the grocery bag in her arms. "I had some pink-and-white silk roses I used in the shop last year for a wedding promotion. They've been stored in plastic, so they're in beautiful shape. I thought you might be able to use them."

Jocelyn peered into the bag. Dozens of perfect silk rosebuds wrapped with florist's wire looked back at her.

"Thank you," Jocelyn said, her voice still reflecting her confusion.

"Sure." Laurel was already cutting.

Freddie and Mary emerged from the kitchen with kuchen and coffee.

"Laurel," Mary said, leaning over her to give her a hug, "I'm so glad you made it. We need all the help we can get."

Laurel looked from Mary to Jocelyn with a quick smile that might have been Jocelyn's imagination. "Don't we all," she said.

When the pastries had been eaten, the meeting's details wrapped up and the Blazers' coach second-guessed, the group helped Freddie replace her chairs and clean up her kitchen.

"Would you mind giving me a ride home, Joss?" Laurel asked, handing her a pile of neatly cut out cupids. "My car's in the shop and I walked here from the mall."

Here it comes, Jocelyn thought. But she smiled intrepidly. "Of course." She gathered up the bag of cutouts, the bag of silk flowers, and her copy of Mary's report, shouldered her purse and tossed her coat over everything.

"Let me help you with that." Laurel took the coat and one of the bags, and followed her out to the car.

In the privacy of the car, Jocelyn waited for Laurel to turn back to the critical, acerbic rival with whom she'd lived most of her life. But she was digging into the bags Jocelyn had put in the bag seat and emerged with one cupid and one silk flower. "Maybe you could put a flower in the cupid's quiver." She placed the flower at the cupid's back, then brought it forward. "Or on his bow. That would be cute. What do you think?"

Jocelyn glanced at the decorations in Laurel's hands, then quickly at her face before turning up the hill that led to Laurel's home. "I think," Jocelyn said, "that you've either mistaken me for someone else, or that you want something from me."

Laurel dropped the cupid and the rose onto the seat between them and sighed, her cheerful demeanor slipping and growing uncertain.

"I know precisely who you are," Laurel said, "and you're right. I do want something from you."

Jocelyn sighed, relieved and vaguely disappointed. "You have a clear field with Rob," she said, shifting down. "You don't have to threaten me or cajole me or buy me off."

"Really." It wasn't a question, but an expression of doubt. "I might be in a good position to buy you off in a couple of days," Laurel went on, "according to the loan officer at the bank. If that was what I wanted."

Jocelyn crested the hill and turned onto the road that crowned it. "It would be foolish to refuse to consider the loan simply because I instigated it," she said reasonably. "Yours is the only dress shop in town specializing in up-scale fashion. Our economy and our women need you. And don't be angry with Rob and Griff. Their involvement was my fault. I thought you'd take the suggestion better from them than you would from me."

"I didn't turn down the loan," Laurel said.

Jocelyn pulled into Laurel's driveway, turned off the engine, then looked at her passenger in surprise and confusion. "Then what are we talking about?"

"You. Me." Laurel discarded her seat belt and turned to face Jocelyn. She rested an elbow on the back of the upholstery and leaned her head wearily on her hand. "Look, I don't know how to be humble. I was raised by parents who convinced me that we were better than everyone else. I believed my father when he told me we were successful because he worked hard at it."

Jocelyn shifted uncomfortably, discovering in surprise that she might not know how to accept humility from Laurel. Her life had been too full of changes lately. Laurel had been an irritant, but at least she'd been constant.

"Laurel, you don't have—"

"Please." Laurel gripped her curly bangs in a fist. "Let me go on before I lose my nerve. I've been working up to this all day. You know what happened to my father when we were in high school."

"Sort of," Jocelyn replied carefully.

"He was arrested for stock fraud," Laurel said flatly. "He used information he gained secretly to build his own portfolio and that of friends who paid him handsomely for the service." She looked at Jocelyn with wide, injured eyes—something of the disillusioned girl she'd never let anyone see apparently still alive in her.

"Well, you know..." Jocelyn said, groping for words of comfort. "That's all sort of a gray area. Men have probably been doing that for—"

"He took advantage of his position to steal from others and fatten his own pocket." Laurel sat up and folded her arms. "Apparently, he'd been doing it for years. The success for which he applauded himself had been achieved not by hard work, but by theft. He lied to everyone he dealt with—" she swallowed loudly "—and he lied to me. I remember feeling everything I thought I was just fall off of me like somebody with beriberi or something."

Her dark joke had a note of anguish in it. "It dawned on me that we weren't better at all. In fact, we weren't even as good. And everybody I'd enjoyed lording it over knew that. My father was taken away, and my mother hid in the house. But I had to go to school." She sighed and squared her shoulders. Jocelyn caught just a glimpse in her eyes of what the simple act of getting onto the school bus must have cost her.

"So I did what Laurel Parker always did best," she said, raising her chin even higher and giving Jocelyn one of the superior glances for which she was famous even today. "I played the bitch. Parents might talk about me and kids could say things on the bus, but they'd never have the satisfaction of knowing how much I hurt or how very small I felt."

Jocelyn's eyes brimmed in sympathy.

Laurel noted the tears and shook her head commiseratingly. She took a tissue out of her purse and handed it to Jocelyn.

"And you. You know what I always hated about you?"

Jocelyn dabbed at her eyes and laughed. "My hair, my clothes, my grades, my..."

"Those, too. But mostly, the fact that you ignored all the things I thought were important and were gung ho about everything I thought was stupid. I was jealous of you because I thought you were a nerd, yet you had everything I wanted. You had friends."

Jocelyn grimaced. "You had all the boyfriends."

Laurel sobered and shook her head. "No. I had all the boys looking for an easy tumble. You knew boys who were your friends. Do you know what it's like to be convinced you're worthless and have one boy after another anxious to make it fact? I let them—" she shrugged, her chin quivering and her voice faltering for the first time since the difficult confidence had begun "—I let them because they were the only company I had."

Jocelyn dug a tissue out of Laurel's purse and handed it to her. "You know, that was all an awfully long time ago. We're both different now...."

"You are, anyway," Laurel said. She dabbed at her nose, sniffed, then balled the tissue in her hand. "Anyway, I brought that all up because I wanted you to know that you laying the groundwork for the loan was the first gesture of friendship anyone's offered me in a long time. After the way I've treated you, I don't understand why you did it, but I'm grateful for it."

"It was only good business," Jocelyn insisted. "Anyway, you weren't the only one who was jealous. I would have sold my straight-A average and my Oregon Scholarship Federation membership to look like you. I thought you were a snot," Jocelyn said with an apologetic laugh, "but you had a lot of things *I* wanted."

Laurel rubbed her knuckles against her chest in a gesture of self-congratulations. "I prided myself on being a snot. Goes to show you how stupid kids can be." Her expression altered suddenly and she offered her hand across the front seat. "Friends?"

Jocelyn took her hand with a sense of unreality. She was making a pact to be friends with Laurel Parker. Her life was moving in strange directions. "Friends," she said. "If you need help with the loan stuff or you have trouble with your creditors before it goes through, call me. The association has an attorney who can give you advice."

"Thanks. I will." Laurel opened her door, then turned back. "One more thing."

"Yeah?"

"Why is the Rob field free and clear?"

Jocelyn had hoped that part of the conversation had been lost in the drama of the rest of it. She put a hand palm up to indicate lack of an answer.

"It just didn't have the promise we thought it might."

Laurel frowned. "Why?"

"I don't know," Jocelyn replied sharply, then sighed and closed her eyes. "I'm sorry. I can't really explain it. I think I was out of my league all along, anyway."

Jocelyn half hoped Laurel would dispute that claim. Instead, she settled quietly into her corner of the car, suddenly grim and thoughtful. "I know what you mean. That's how I feel about...about Griff."

"What do you mean?"

Laurel plucked at the clasp on her purse. "He's been very nice to me."

"I think it's more than that," Jocelyn said.

Laurel looked at once hopeful and doubtful. "What would a nice guy like that want with a woman who's...been around and given him nothing but grief?"

"Why don't you ask him?"

"Because I'm afraid it's all in my imagination." She smiled sadly and stepped out of the car, then she ducked down and grinned. "Anyway, thanks for the lift—and the friendship."

Jocelyn waved as Laurel pushed the door closed. She drove away, feeling as though she'd crossed into a Salvador Dalí painting.

Chapter Twelve

Jocelyn peered into the Old Cannery's kitchen, relieved to find it empty of everyone but Griff in the midafternoon quiet.

"Hi," she called cheerfully, going to the stove where he poked a turner at something in a small fry pan.

He looked up and smiled warmly. "Hi, Joss," he said. "I was afraid we wouldn't see you any... I mean... Rob's..." He winced and stammered, "T-that is, he hasn't said much, but I gather..." He stopped and sighed. "Can I start over?"

She gave him a hug and handed him a paper-wrapped package. "No need. I just came by to give you this plaque from the Community Development Association."

Griff ignored the package and turned quickly to the sizzling omelet. He took a waiting plate, tipped the pan forward until the perfect half-moon shape, bulging with broccoli and cheese, slipped onto it, then he put the plate into the warm oven.

"Rob's the one who should receive that," he said. "He's in the lounge."

She smiled stubbornly. "He can receive it from you."

Griff looked at her closely and grinned. "Come on. You aren't going to let him get away with this?"

"Oh, yes, I am," she replied. "I have no time for someone who doesn't trust me."

Griff shook his head and pulled her down onto a nearby stool. "It's love he doesn't trust," he said. "He loved his father, who let us all down. He loved my father, who died. He loved Sandy, his ex-wife, and she took him for all he had, including his restaurant." Griff lifted a shoulder, his eyes dark with compassion. "He thinks he doesn't have love left to give."

"He's probably right," Jocelyn said evenly. "If you can't trust, you can't love."

Griff shook his finger. "Actually, he loves very well. When my father died, I was twelve and Rob was sixteen. He took better care of his mother and me than a grown man could have. And a few years later, when I got involved with a street gang out of—I don't know...a need to feel big, I guess, because sometimes life was so scary...he came to the basement where we hung out and dragged me home."

He shook his head, a smile that was half affection, half reflection, growing, then subsiding. "Three of the guys tried to fight him, but he was like a wild man." Griff looked into Jocelyn's eyes and said heavily, "Because he loved me. He got cut and bruised and kicked, but he got me out of there. I'll never forget the feel of his hand clutching the collar of my jacket. I really think he'd have died before he let me go back." He sighed and smiled. "It isn't that he can't love, it's just that he's given his love in a few unfortunate places. It's been thrown back in his face so many times, I think maybe he doesn't even know what it is anymore."

Jocelyn was startled by that glimpse into Rob's past. He'd apparently left out a lot of details when he'd told her about his family that rainy afternoon. She hurt for him, but she hurt for herself, too. "He knows I'm not Sandy," she said.

"Go prove it," Griff challenged, turning her toward the lounge.

JOCELYN ENTERED THE DARK, quiet bar with a confident smile manufactured out of a deep need to hide how much she'd missed Rob.

"There you are."

Rob looked up with a start at the sound of Jocelyn's voice. He'd spent most of the afternoon going over the month's receipts and thinking if he didn't find a place to shelter some of their income, the IRS would hang Griff and him up to dry. He'd come down to the lounge to look out at the water and think. It jarred him to face the monotone gray of river and sky one moment, then curly sunset-colored hair, bright blue eyes and a sunny smile the next.

Jocelyn's wide smile was like a gulp of stream water to a parched soul. He absorbed it, enjoyed it, felt dazzled by it. Then annoyance crept in. What was she so happy about? He hadn't had a peaceful thought in six days, and there she stood in an oyster-colored skirt and jacket, her pink-cheeked face framed in the cowl neckline of a fuzzy wool sweater in a shade of mauve that seemed to color the gloomy landscape.

He stepped out of the booth, trying to rid his face of all expression. "Hi, Joss," he said easily. "What can I do for you?"

He'd been pleased to see her; Jocelyn would have sworn it. But the glimpse of pleasure in his dark eyes had been so swift, so quickly shuttered that she couldn't be sure. She'd give him the damned plaque and let him see that if he wanted to be skimpy with his affections, she would be fine without him. Conceiving the thought and accomplishing the deed, though, were two very different things. Still, she smiled valiantly.

She handed him the package.

"What's this?" he asked.

She hunched a shoulder, still smiling. "It's your plaque from the Community Development Association. I know you're busy, but protocol requires that I deliver them all in person and tell you how much we value your participation.''

She might have lost her composure then, but his remoteness was turning the brave give-him-one-more-chance attitude with which she'd taken Griff's advice to simmering anger.

He nodded. "We'll put it up in the reception area. Thank you.'' He slipped back into the booth in a gesture of dismissal.

Spurred by a vindictiveness Jocelyn had been unaware she'd possessed until that moment, she stood her ground. "So, how was the morning after the night that never was for you?''

He'd once found her candor refreshing. Today, it irritated the hell out of him. He indicated his comfortable surroundings without a change of expression. "You can see that I've survived and continue to function. How was it for you?''

"Much as you predicted," she replied with a gusty little sigh that seemed part philosophy, part theatrics. "Cold and lonely. Enough to make me wonder for the first few minutes if some lofty ideal of love could be worth that.''

Those words would have given him a small surge of hope if he'd been dealing with any other woman. Instead, he waited for the other shoe to drop. "And?" he asked, as though it made no difference to him.

She adjusted the shoulder strap of her purse. "And I remembered that love *is* lofty—we don't make it that way. How we treat it doesn't change what it is. And I'm just not willing to share what I feel with someone who doesn't value it as highly.''

This was considerably more difficult than she'd expected. The sigh she heaved this time was genuine and ragged. "But there's no reason we can't maintain a civilized business relationship, is there? I mean, that'll be easy for you, won't it, since you always did have a certain... distance in this relationship from the very beginning?''

He felt the sting of that—for himself and for her. But before he could reply, her eyes widened as she looked somewhere beyond his shoulder. She put a quick hand to her face in a gesture obviously intended to conceal her identity. She slipped into the booth he'd occupied and snapped in a whisper, "Sit down!"

"What—?"

"Sssh!"

From somewhere behind him came the rich sound of a woman's laughter and the deep bass of a man's. The bartender's voice rumbled in greeting. Jocelyn scooted to the inside corner of the booth, leaning into it while straining to watch the bar.

"Who is it?" Rob whispered.

"My brother-in-law," she whispered in reply.

"Phyllis's husband?"

"Charlie's!" When he looked puzzled, she added, "There's another woman with him."

"Ah." He shook his head at her. "Maybe he's just talking business over a drink."

Hunkered down in the booth but still watching the bar, Jocelyn gave Rob a lethal glance. "Yeah. Right. Next you're going to try to sell me the Salty Harbor Bridge."

He toyed with the mineral water in front of him and said with grave innocence, "I thought, believing in love like you do, you'd have more faith in his dedication to his marriage."

Jocelyn didn't have an answer for that, so she gave Rob another withering look for having made the statement.

"There you are." Laurel appeared beside the booth with a plastic-wrapped garment over her arm. She smiled from

Rob to Jocelyn. "I saw you come into the mall and wanted—"

"Sssh!" Jocelyn pleaded, trying to look around her. Rob grabbed Laurel's wrist and yanked her into the booth beside him.

"What's going on?" Laurel demanded in a whisper. Noticing Jocelyn's strange demeanor, she turned to Rob. "What's she doing?"

"A little P.I. work," he replied.

"What?"

"Never mind. I'll explain later."

"Oh, great!" Jocelyn whispered in distress. "They're ordering lunch with their drinks!"

Rob raised an eyebrow. "That's good for business."

"How am I going to get out of this booth without being seen?"

"Don't you want to stay and observe?"

She watched Chris lean intimately across the small table toward the long-legged brunette in the chic suit. She thought of her sister ripe with his baby and felt sadness as well as anger. Didn't anything work out for anyone?

She shook her head mutely, her eyes wide with distress.

"Then come on," he said with weary reluctance. "I'll get you out."

"How?"

"Don't ask, just cooperate, or you'll get his attention for certain." Rob nudged Laurel out of the booth. "Spread the dress out like you're studying it. Hold it in front of us."

Laurel rolled her eyes, but complied. "I thought you might model this in my spring show Jo—Joanna," she said, catching her near gaffe quickly, pinching one end of a red chiffon skirt so that yards of the fabric fell from her fingers, forming a screen.

Rob helped Jocelyn out of the booth, pulled her closely into his shoulder and walked toward the door to the restaurant, shielding her face with what must have appeared to anyone looking to be an ardent hug. Laurel walked beside them, carrying on about the dress.

Jocelyn's heart and head went into an instant reggae rhythm. His touch reminded her sharply of all the times he'd held and kissed her during that wonderful rainy day, of the brief time on the dance floor when she'd fallen hard for the hearts and flowers she'd wisely scorned before. Despite the hindsight that made her realize she'd been foolish, she felt a painful loss for the sweetness she'd felt in that short time, for the rosy hopes she'd entertained, for the romance that had filled her world.

In the small vestibule between the lounge and the restaurant that also led off into the kitchen, she pushed herself out of Rob's arms as though he'd been a bear and she a hapless camper.

They stared at each other, the width of the corridor between them. Laurel dropped the skirt and looked uncertainly from one to the other.

Jocelyn pulled herself together. She straightened her jacket and smoothed her hair. "Thank you," she said, clearing her throat. "I...that was awkward. I appreciate your help."

"Sure," he said succinctly. He didn't have the breath for anything else. The moment he'd felt her breasts against his chest and smelled her hair, he'd come close to losing it. When she'd wrapped an arm around him for balance, he'd been tempted to take her up to his office then and there and plead with her for the opportunity to start over.

Then she'd pushed him away as though he were poison, and he came to his senses. They were toxic to each other. Neither could offer what the other needed.

"Hi!" Griff appeared in the kitchen doorway, wiping his hands on his apron. "The party break up already?" he asked, a note of disappointment in his voice. "I was just going to join you guys." He held up a bottle of Evian water.

Jocelyn smiled apologetically, uncomfortably. "I...have twenty more clients to call on this afternoon. Maybe another time."

"I'm expecting a call from our attorney," Rob said, less apologetic, but more uncomfortable. With a quiet "bye" sent vaguely in Jocelyn's direction, he headed for the stairs to his office.

Laurel smiled at an obviously confused Griff. "I've got another few minutes to spare."

His confusion deepened. "You do?"

"Yes." She handed the plastic-wrapped garment to Jocelyn with a smile. "Here. I thought you might like to try this. Let me know how it fits."

Griff looked from one woman to the other, his confusion turning to outright abashment.

Laurel tucked her arm in his. "Come on. We need to talk."

He tore his hat off, tossed it into the kitchen and let her lead him away like a man in a trance.

Jocelyn sighed and turned in the other direction. "Ain't love grand," she mumbled, "for some people."

SHE THOUGHT LATER THAT Murphy's Law must have been in effect that afternoon. She arrived back at her office just after five o'clock and leapt for the ringing telephone.

"Community Development," she answered breathlessly, dropping purse and yards of chiffon into her chair.

"Jossie?"

The panicky sound of Charlie's voice filled her with sudden dread. Somehow, she'd found out about Chris meeting that woman in the Old Cannery's lounge.

"Jossie, can you come to the hospital?" Charlie asked, her voice high and thin.

Jocelyn's frown turned to a smile. "Is it the baby?" she asked.

"No, it's Grandpa."

With cold rapidity, Jocelyn's smile became a frown again. She clutched the phone. "What happened?"

"He was visiting John Whittaker and slipped on his front steps. I don't know if anything's broken yet. Phyl's with him in the emergency room."

"I'll be right there," Jocelyn promised, digging her purse out from under yards of dress. "Find a chair, Charlie, and sit down. We don't need to upset the baby, okay?"

"Okay."

"NOTHING BROKEN," a bespectacled young doctor assured them in the soft blue waiting room. "Got a good bruising, though, and he'll be very stiff and find it hard to get around for a couple of days." The doctor smiled. "He tells me he lives alone and likes it that way, but he's going to need help for at least a week. Is that possible?"

"Of course," Jocelyn and Phyllis said at once.

John, who'd been there since he'd accompanied Nathan in the ambulance, shook his head. "He's not going to like that."

"Like it or not," Phyllis said firmly, "he has to be looked after for a few days." She turned to Jocelyn. "You can't take him. Your apartment is up a long flight of stairs."

"You have two little children," Jocelyn pointed out. "He won't get any rest, and neither will you. I'll move into his place."

"Should we call Mom and Dad?" Charlie asked.

Phyllis shook her head. "They'll worry unnecessarily. We can take care of this. Joss, You'll still need help getting him up the front porch steps."

"If we can rent a wheelchair, we can take him in through the back door."

"Harbor Hospital Equipment Rentals is right next door," the doctor said. "You can use the phone in my office."

JOCELYN, PHYLLIS AND JOHN managed to transfer a moaning Nathan from the wheelchair to his bed while Charlie moved the chair out of the way. For a moment, the bed had four breathless occupants.

"I'm supposed to be left alone," Nathan said querulously, "to rest."

"Don't be an ingrate, Nathan," John said gently, his usually defensive nature softened by his friend's obvious pain.

"You can all go home now," Nathan said.

Phyllis helped Jocelyn pull the covers over him. "Jossie's staying with you, Gramps," Phyllis said. "And if I hear you've given her a bad time, you'll answer to me."

Nathan turned to glower at Jocelyn. "You are not staying with me."

"As though you could stop me," she said.

He sat up as though he intended to make every effort to do so, then fell back against the pillows with a wince of pain.

Jocelyn shooed everyone from the room and followed them into the hall.

"Are you sure you're going to be okay?" Phyllis asked doubtfully. "You know how he can be. Maybe I'd better stay the night with you until..."

"Absolutely not." Jocelyn pushed Phyllis and John firmly toward the living room and the front door. "He doesn't scare me. Go home. If I need your help, I'll call."

"Promise?"

"Promise."

Charlie lingered a moment after Phyllis and John had left. "I could come and fix breakfast," she offered. She looked even more pale than usual and was rubbing a fist absently in the small of her back.

"Thanks, Charlie, but I can manage. I'm always up early anyway, and you need your rest." Jocelyn put an arm around her sister and walked her onto the porch. "Have you talked to Chris?" she asked, her tone carefully casual.

Charlie nodded, her eyes brimming. "He insists nothing's wrong. I guess I just have to wait. He'll trip himself up eventually, then I'll have something to fight him with."

Jocelyn hugged her. "Try to think about the baby," she advised. "And just be calm. I'll call you in the morning and tell you how Grandpa's doing."

Charlie wrapped both arms around Jocelyn and held her for an extra moment. "I don't know what we'd do without you. I wish I was competent like you are. I wish I didn't fall apart when things don't go the way I think they should."

"You're eight and a half months pregnant," Jocelyn said, patting her sister's back. "You're not supposed to have to think about anyone but yourself at this time. And I've never known you to fall apart."

"You and Phyl have always taken care of me."

"We're your big sisters. That's our job." Jocelyn walked Charlie down to the car and helped her in behind the wheel.

"Who's driving?" she teased. "You or the baby?"

Charlie smiled thinly and drove away with a wave.

"Jossie! Jocelyn!"

Jocelyn raced up the porch steps and across the living room to her grandfather's side, certain by the sound of his voice that he'd fallen out of bed or was in the throes of some excruciating pain.

"What is it?"

He sighed deeply, looked toward the wall, then back at her. He cleared his throat. "I have to go to the bathroom."

That was a relief. "No problem," she said, running out to the living room and the large bag of things she'd rented in addition to the wheelchair. She returned with a urinal.

Nathan looked horrified, then folded his arms on top of the covers. "I'm not using that," he said flatly.

Jocelyn struggled to remain patient. "Then what do you intend to do?"

He pushed himself up on his elbows. "You're going to help me up and I'm going to walk into the bathroom."

Jocelyn shook her head adamantly. "Gramps, I'm not strong enough to hold you. You'll fall down again, and this time, you'll break something."

He threw the covers back and swung his legs over the side of the bed, grimacing. "You are not handling my bedpans."

"Gramps, this is no time to be proud," she said, trying to push him back onto the bed as he struggled to get up by bracing himself against the bedside table. He resisted her with a strength that belied his years and his injury.

"I'm walking to the bathroom," he insisted. "You can lend me a hand, or you can watch me struggle."

Grumbling, Jocelyn put her shoulder under his right arm and valiantly tried to support the injured side of his two hundred pounds. "If this is the way you're going to be," she said, grunting as they took a laborious step forward, "I'm going to hire a nurse, whether you like it or— Ah!"

They went down together, falling harmlessly against the edge of the mattress and sliding against it to the carpet, Jocelyn doing her best to cushion Nathan's landing.

"See! See?" she said, close to tears with the thought of what might have happened. Then her scolding turned to concern as she saw his white face. "Are you all right, Gramps? Did you hurt something else?"

He shook his head, drawing a deep breath. "No, I'm okay. Are you okay?"

"No!" she replied, seriously concerned about how she was going to get him off the floor. "I think I separated every rib trying to cushion your fall. I'm going to tie your *Hunt for Red October* tape in knots!"

Nathan turned to her dispassionately. "You're getting hysterical. Call Rob."

"I'm going to call Jeff," she said, pulling herself to her feet.

"Jeff's in Portland today," he said. "Phylly told me."

"Then I'll call Chris."

He gave her a knowing look that startled her. "Hasn't he spent the last few months working late?"

"How did you know that?" she asked in amazement.

He leaned wearily against the side of the bed. "You think I got to be this old by being unaware of what's going on around me? Just because you girls don't tell me doesn't mean I don't learn things. It's getting cold down here."

Jocelyn called Rob because he was the only logical solution and because her grandfather's needs came before her own. He cut off her disjointed explanation with a promise to be there in five minutes.

He was there in four, reassuringly large and calm and smiling as he shed his jacket, leaned over her grandfather, wrapped his arms around him, back muscles rippling under his white shirt, and lifted him slowly, but with complete control, to his feet.

"I was on my way to the bathroom," Nathan said with a sigh of relief and a very masculine grin. "Jossie dropped me."

"Not hard enough," she said as Rob started to move slowly toward the bathroom. She went to the kitchen in search of something to prepare for dinner—and something to do to calm her nerves.

She might be a new Jocelyn Foley, she told herself as she stared at a freezer full of "light" frozen dinners, but she wasn't much smarter than the old one had been. One sight of the man she'd repeatedly told herself was dangerous to her peace of mind and her pulse was racing. Time and distance might cure her, but she couldn't hope for either until the Valentine project was over.

She finally settled on soup and crackers and cheese, thinking her grandfather should probably eat lightly anyway, given the shock to his system. Tomorrow, she could shop for groceries.

The soup was warming and she was slicing cheese when Rob walked into the kitchen. He had rolled up his sleeves and pulled his tie away from his throat. He looked darkly gorgeous and disarmingly disheveled. She tried to think of him encircled in red with a line crossed through him.

She turned away from the counter to give him her full attention. "Thank you for coming so quickly," she said. "I tried to get him to use the . . ." She waved in the direction of the bedroom, thinking how silly it was that the word was hard to say.

Rob nodded. "He's just proud. It's hard for him to have his granddaughter taking care of him." His eyes ran the length of her. "You're sure you didn't get hurt?"

The glance had been quick and analytical, but she felt it like a caress. "I'm sure," she said lightly. "The mattress cushioned our fall." She indicated the pot of soup. "I realize this is a comedown from Griff's wonderful concoctions, but would you like to join us?"

He shook his head, shifting his weight with sudden discomfort. He glanced away from her, then back again and jammed his hands into his pockets. "Nathan asked me to stay for a few days," he blurted suddenly. The words hung heavily in the silence of the out-of-date kitchen.

Rob watched her reaction edgily. With Jocelyn here, this was the last place he wanted to be at the moment—and the only place. He wanted to hold her and he wanted to walk away from her. He couldn't remember ever being ambivalent about anything in his life, but Jocelyn was tearing him in two.

But this wasn't about them. This was about a nice old man who was too stubborn and proud to have a nurse, but didn't want to subject his granddaughter to the indignities of looking after him.

She looked at him, her expression guarded. "You mean move in?"

He nodded.

She frowned. "You can't do that and see to the restaurant, too."

He pulled a kitchen chair out and sat on it, squaring one leg on the other and leaning his elbow on the table. "I can for a few days. I suppose—" he grinned dryly "—if you disregard our personal antagonism, it's the perfect solution. I'll be here with him after you've gone to work, and you'll come back shortly after I've left. Then I'll be back in time to help him in the night. He'll spend very little time alone. And if we work it right, we'll keep missing each other."

"I don't like it," she said honestly.

"I'm not wild about it, either. But he'd be more comfortable with a man around, and you won't break your back trying to help him when he refuses to stay in bed."

Jocelyn poured soup into a mug, placing it and a plate of crackers on a tray. She was going to hate this, but she had to admit, it was in her grandfather's best interest.

"You can have the bedroom upstairs," she said, retrieving a spoon and a napkin. "I'll take the sofa."

"I'll take the sofa," he said. "That way, I won't wake you when I come in at one in the morning, and I'll be close by him during the night."

She walked by with the tray. "Fine."

Jocelyn found her grandfather staring at the ceiling. She put the tray on the bedside table and propped his pillows up.

"Well?" he asked her defensively.

She hadn't told him she and Rob had spent a beautiful day together, although he'd been present at the auction and knew Rob had outbid everyone else for her. And she hadn't told him that their very brief relationship was over. But she suspected he knew. As he'd said, he hadn't gotten to be his age without learning a few things.

"Well, what?" she asked, helping him sit up.

"Is he staying?"

She put the tray on his lap. "Yes. I'll have to have your key. He'll need it to let himself in at one in the morning."

Nathan looked reluctant for a moment, then sighed as though he were relinquishing his last freedom. "In my jacket pocket." He gave the tray a cursory glance, then looked back at her uncertainly. "Are *you* going to stay?"

She met his eyes in surprise. "Of course. Did you think I'd refuse to stay just because you're a manipulative old codger with a mean disposition?"

"Yes," he admitted.

She went to the chair to get his key. "Well, it just goes to show you. Some of us can rise above our problems. Want the TV on?"

He looked vaguely sheepish, but also vaguely pleased with himself. "Yes, thank you." Then he seemed to notice for the first time what was on his tray. "Soup?" he asked.

Jocelyn went toward the door. "That was all I could find."

"Well, what about the Salisbury Supreme with potatoes and carrots, or the Rib Roundup with Texas beans, or the Cheese and Eggplant Lasagne with—"

She turned in the doorway, at the end of her rope. "If you want that instead of the soup, you'll have to get up and fix it yourself, then we'll have to pick you up with the dustpan. I suggest you eat the soup.''

He looked so crestfallen that she added more gently, ''Tomorrow, when I've had a chance to do some shopping, I'll fix you potato pancakes and sausage.''

And eyebrow went up hopefully. ''Really?''

''Really.''

With a resigned sigh, he dipped into the soup. Jocelyn left the room. She was halfway to the kitchen when she heard him shout after her, ''Will you be bringing dessert?''

''I'LL BE IN ABOUT one-fifteen,'' Rob said as Jocelyn walked him to the door. ''I'll try not to wake you.''

''Then you'll need this.'' She held up the key, then dropped it onto his palm with a wry smile. ''Unless you want to try the pet door. I wouldn't recommend it.''

He laughed softly, remembering the afternoon he'd found her in that predicament. Then he frowned, remembering also that it had been the first time he'd held her. ''Want me to bring you back anything from the restaurant? Croissants for breakfast, maybe? A couple of seconds in the microwave and a day old one isn't bad.''

She nodded. ''Please. You might bring one for yourself. I checked the cupboards and it's that or bran cereal until I do some shopping.''

''Anything else?''

''I'll leave blankets and a pillow on the sofa.''

''Thank you.'' He stepped onto the porch, then turned to face her.

Suddenly, without warning, her mind superimposed a dream image on this little moment of reality. Rob was dressed just as he was, but he was carrying a briefcase. She wore a lavender silk peignoir and a look of satiated drowsiness. Their eyes met, and she saw things in his for which there were no words. He put the briefcase down, took her in his arms and kissed her.

"Think about that," he whispered against her lips, "until tonight."

"Joss? Jocelyn?"

Rob's voice dissolved the dream. She dropped back into reality with a crash. "Yes?" she asked guiltily.

He frowned. "You'll wait for what?"

She blinked. "Excuse me?"

"You just said, 'I'll wait.' Have I slipped a cog? Am I supposed to do something or send something you'll be waiting for?"

Oh, God. "Until tonight," the Rob in her dream had said. She'd apparently responded, "I'll wait."

"No," she said stiffly, waving him off. "Just talking to myself. See you later."

She closed the door behind him, then leaned against it and closed her eyes, thinking things had come to a sorry pass when Jocelyn Foley didn't know dreams from reality.

Chapter Thirteen

It worked. Three days into Jocelyn and Rob's shift arrangement for care of Nathan, everything proceeded as though planned by an efficiency expert.

Jocelyn made breakfast for herself and Nathan, gathered up laundry for the three of them and put it in the washer before leaving for work, tiptoeing by the sofa where Rob slept.

Rob awoke midmorning, fixed Nathan a snack and himself breakfast, transferred the clothes from the washer to the dryer, then sat with the older man while he patiently tried to teach Rob the mysteries of Soviet submariner tactics.

He prepared lunch. John arrived midafternoon as Rob left for work. He sat with Nathan and caught him up on the latest gossip until Jocelyn arrived home in time to fix dinner.

One morning, Jocelyn opened the refrigerator for orange juice and found a carry-out box with her name on it. Investigation revealed a slice of grasshopper pie Rob had apparently brought home from the restaurant the night before.

Another morning, there was a colorful bouquet of flowers in the middle of the kitchen table. On the third morning, a sinfully fragrant bag of freshly ground raspberry-hazelnut coffee.

In return, Jocelyn stoked the fire in the fireplace before she went to bed after eleven so that it would burn until Rob came home. She repaired a three-corner rent in one of his shirts and replaced the old pillow she'd put on the sofa for him with one of the down pillows from her apartment.

Jocelyn walked into the kitchen on the fourth morning to find a folded note propped up in front of the flowers.

Phyllis and Jeff had dinner at the restaurant last night. She wants you to call her when you have time to talk. Something about Lindsay's birthday.

Also—thanks for fixing my shirt and for the new pillow. Want to have a pillow fight sometime?

Rob

The really innocuous but subtly suggestive notion brought a flutter to her heartbeat. She turned to look into the living room where Rob still slept soundly, and she had another fantasy vision. The sofa turned into a bed, and he rose to his knees on it, bare-chested, and swung a pillow at her. She was wearing her lavender peignoir. She collapsed, laughing and not even pretending to fend him off.

Jocelyn closed her eyes on the image and went to the refrigerator for the orange juice. In the past three days, she'd seen nothing of Rob but his sleeping form on the sofa when she left for work. Yet, somehow, everything she'd felt for him on that beautiful rainy day had blossomed into something that threatened to overpower her.

Reminding herself that he wanted only romance and not love had little effect on her common sense. It seemed to have fled before her other, more demanding senses.

When she came home after work and went into the downstairs bathroom to wash her hands before preparing dinner, she could smell the lingering fragrance of Rob's cologne.

She heard him arrive home in the middle of the night, moving quietly as he checked on her grandfather. Occasionally, the low rumble of his laughter mingled with Nathan's.

She saw the back of his head when he slept, his face pressed into the pillow, one brawny arm hooked over the arm of the sofa as though he needed freedom and space.

Only taste and touch hadn't been indulged—and that thought alone was enough to make her down her juice, jump into a lukewarm shower and hurry to work.

THE MOMENT THE DOOR closed behind her, Rob opened his eyes and groaned. He wasn't sure how much more of this he could stand. He'd come within a heartbeat of grabbing her wrist as she'd walked past him and pulling her down on top of him.

He didn't want to think about commitments or consequences, he just wanted her. He ran a hand over his face, thinking grimly that he was more his father's son than he wanted to be.

"You keep on groaning like that," Nathan shouted from the other room, "and maybe *you* should see my doctor."

"You kept me up until 3:00 with that subversive game," Rob called back. "Can't blame me for groaning."

"That sounded like heartache to me, not headache."

Rob laughed to himself. It was amazing what the man grasped from the confinement of his bed. "You need some coffee, Nathan?"

"I'm fine. Get a few more hours' sleep."

Rob closed his eyes, but knew that wasn't going to be a possibility this morning; Jocelyn lived behind his eyes. Though he hadn't really seen her in three days, he couldn't make a move, form a thought, laugh or sigh without his mind being filled with her.

He was probably fortunate, he thought, throwing his blankets aside, that their relationship hadn't become physical. He was already besotted beyond redemption. He hated to think what a night with Jocelyn in his arms could do to his sanity.

"PHYL," JOCELYN EXPLAINED patiently, the phone cradled on her shoulder, her crossed feet propped on her office windowsill, "Rob isn't going to want to come to a family party. He's very..."

"Handsome."

"No, very..."

"Intelligent."

"Yes, but no. I mean, he's..."

"In love with you."

Jocelyn's feet came down with a thud. She made herself remember that her older sister really was a very kind and loving woman even if she was an incurable buttinsky.

"Phyllis, he is not in love with me." Her voice was quiet and controlled. Even she hadn't known she was such a good actress. "We spent one day together because he bought me at an auction—hardly cause to smell orange blossoms. I told you I didn't want to talk about it, and I meant it. Now, I'm not bringing him to Lindsay's birthday party."

"All right," Phyllis said reasonably. There was a brief pause. "It's just that Lindsay will be very disappointed."

Since the day Lindsay had been born, and later Robin, it had become a family policy that neither child should ever be disappointed. Jocelyn adhered to it as firmly as anyone.

"Why?" she asked.

"Because she specifically asked me to invite him. She said, 'Tell Aunt Jossie to bring her boyfriend. I like him. He said when I grow up I can be a waitress in his restaurant.'"

Jocelyn sighed. "He is not my boyfriend."

"Explain that to Lindsay. And anyway, you'll need him to help you get Gramps in and out of the car."

"Couldn't Jeff come for us?"

"Jeff will be busy barbecuing."

"In February?"

"It's what Lindsay wanted. We'll cook on the covered patio and eat inside."

"Okay, okay." Jocelyn closed her eyes and shook her head. This was not going to be easy. "I'll ask him. Phyl?"

"Yes?"

Jocelyn twisted the curly cord around her index finger. She hated to bring up the subject of Chris and Charlie, but since her emotions were on a downswing anyway, she may as well.

"With Grandpa getting hurt and everything, I forgot to mention this, but that afternoon, I saw Chris and another woman together in the lounge at the Old Cannery. Maybe Charlie isn't imagining things."

"Glossy dark hair, elegant suit, legs like Julia Roberts?"

"Yes."

"That's her." Phyllis sighed. "Maybe we'll be able to tell by how he acts at the party if he's guilty."

A POST-IT NOTE WAS attached to a sandwich bag filled with half a dozen cookies. Rob found it propped up against the flowers when he walked quietly into the dark kitchen and flipped on the light. He reached for it anxiously.

Hi, Rob,
Lindsay has invited you to her birthday party Sunday. Can you come? Just family, lots of talk and good barbecue. Cookies are samples from Freddie's bazaar table.

Joss

Rob smiled. He felt as though he'd been invited to the Riviera, all expenses paid. God, he was in bad shape.

He parted the top of the bag and pulled out a cookie. The smell was tantalizing. He poured a cup of decaf Jocelyn always left in the coffee maker for him and bit into the cookie. It snapped crisply and dissolved on his tongue. He took a sip of coffee, another bite of cookie, and contemplated an afternoon with Jocelyn and her family with an eagerness that alarmed even him.

PHYLLIS, STARING OUT THE kitchen window at the men at work around the barbecue, narrowed her eyes in concentration. She held a fat, red tomato in one hand and a knife in the other.

"Either I'm a poor reader of faces," she said softly to Jocelyn, "or Chris is a damn good actor. I don't see a hint of remorse, guilt-masking cheer or anything. What do you think?"

Jocelyn glanced at Charlie, who sat at the other end of the long kitchen, feeding Robin. The baby opened her mouth wide, like the baby bird that was her namesake.

Satisfied that Charlie was absorbed in her task, Jocelyn studied the men beyond the window.

Jeff, wearing a jacket and gloves, moved hamburgers and steaks around on the grill with the tip of a long-handled turner while regaling his companions with a tale about three clergymen, the details of which weren't clear through the window. A bamboo shade intended to protect patio sitters from the sun had been lowered today to protect them from a spitting rain and a driving wind.

Beside Jeff, Chris, in a down vest, placed hamburger buns around the rim of the grill, laughing heartily as his brother-in-law apparently concluded the story.

Rob, leaning against a patio post, shared their laughter with Nathan, wrapped in a blanket in his wheelchair. In

Nathan's lap sat the birthday girl in a little yellow slicker with eyes and a duckbill painted on the cap.

At some point, Lindsay had reached out of the chair and captured Rob's hand.

There was nothing about the scene to indicate that anyone was unhappy—or that anyone, Chris and Rob included, preferred to be anywhere else.

Jocelyn sighed and resumed her task of transferring condiments from their jars and bottles into the wedge-shaped bowls in a lazy Susan. "I don't see anything, but men are very good at hiding what they feel."

Phyllis studied her narrowly. "Don't you dare give up on him." They were no longer talking about Chris.

"He had a bad marriage," Jocelyn explained briefly. "He doesn't want to get into that again."

Phyllis swirled the tomato slices in an arc around the edges of the plate with an expert swipe of her hand. "All men think they're destined for long lives of freedom and happy promiscuity." She smiled cheerfully at Jocelyn. "It's our job to straighten them out."

Jocelyn bit the end off an enormous dill pickle. "I'm just getting myself straightened out. He's on his own."

"You said he wouldn't want to come but he did."

"Probably because I told him Lindsay invited him specifically."

Phyllis smiled out the window at Rob and her daughter hand in hand. "She's really taken to him. You will ask her to be your flower girl, won't you?"

Jocelyn dropped a mustard jar on the counter with a bang and glowered threateningly at her sister. "Gramps is going to be out of that wheelchair in a couple of days. Would you like to be in it?"

Phyllis frowned at her. "Testy, testy."

"Come on you two, play nice." Charlie reached between them to the roll of paper towels, tearing off several yards.

She smiled thinly at Phyllis, her face and the front of her pink-and-white smock spattered with purple flecks. "Your daughter isn't into beets. That is, she's physically into them. They're in her hair, in her ears, in my ears. But I think that's because she's not into the taste." Charlie dampened the towels under the cold-water faucet and gave Phyllis another dry smile. "When my baby comes, *you* can feed her her first taste of beets."

"Her?" Jocelyn asked.

"In two generations, this family has not produced a boy—so far." Phyllis put an arm around Jocelyn's shoulder. "That'll be Joss's job."

Charlie's eyes widened. "Are you . . . ?" She pointed out the window in Rob's direction.

"No," Jocelyn said firmly. She took one of the towels from Charlie and dabbed at the spots on her sister's face. "Big sister has a big mouth and, as usual, idiocy comes out of it."

"Bide your time," Charlie said, standing stoically under Jocelyn's ministrations. "You may not be the only one single."

"Oh, really!" Phyllis said angrily, dropping her paring knife into the sink with a clatter. "What a thing to say! I'm getting tired of both of you! 'Poor me! Pity me!' That's all I ever hear."

"Phyl!" Jocelyn said.

"Oh, let her rave," Charlie said, her face filling with hectic color, her eyes brimming with emotion long suppressed. "She thinks she can just order us to be the way she wants us, like when we were little. You want us to be perfect like you. Well, we're not! My marriage is falling apart, and Joss doesn't want to get married. You'll have to live with it, Phyl. You can't organize everything!"

Charlie waddled hurriedly to the bathroom, sobbing. Robin screeched in her high chair, apparently upset by the raised voices.

Jocelyn lifted the baby into her arms, ignoring the purple goo her niece wore from head to foot. She bounced the child gently as she turned back to Phyllis, who stood with her mouth open.

"I don't do that," she denied hotly, then asked doubtfully, "Do I?"

Jocelyn nodded, smiling. "Consistently. Because you love us, I'm sure, and not because you're still the martinet you were at eight years old. Charlie's just an emotional mess at the moment."

Phyllis's startled expression turned to a thoughtful smile. "Do you think she's finally getting some spunk?"

"If she is, you'd better watch yourself," Jocelyn advised. "I'll have help putting you in that wheelchair."

LINDSAY, WEARING A PAPER crown, drew in a noisy breath, then blew out the four candles on her birthday cake. The feat was met with cheers and applause.

In a living room strewn with toys, gift wrap, tissue and ribbon, everyone ate cake and ice cream off Mickey Mouse paper plates.

While Jeff told a funny story about Phyllis, which she continually interrupted with defensive commentary, Rob studied Chris. Charlie sat passively in his arm, forcing a smile, but looking decidedly miserable.

Rob looked into the boyishly handsome blond good looks and couldn't find a trace of guile. When they'd all been on the patio while Jeff barbecued, Chris had been unfailingly cheerful and polite to him, attentive to Nathan, fraternally abusive to Jeff and affectionately teasing to Lindsay. He did not behave like a man with anything to hide.

He'd also observed Jeff, trying to imagine him married to Jocelyn. He couldn't. He was the perfect host and by all appearances, a kind and caring husband and father, but Rob suspected he was in need of Phyllis's confident direction.

Jocelyn needed someone at least as strong as she was, who would appreciate and assist her in her mission to help everyone rather than use up all her energies on himself. She needed someone who could shield her from harm. He realized with a jolt that she needed him.

In the nights he'd spent at Nathan's, he'd come to realize how desperately he needed her. And not because he wanted to romance her, but because he loved her.

"So, how's the Valentine thing coming?" Jeff asked. Robin lay fast asleep in his left arm, her little bow mouth open, while he deftly ate cake with his right.

Jocelyn swallowed and nodded. "Good. The way things are going, we may be able to build the seniors the Taj Mahal."

Jeff grinned at Nathan. "Make sure it has a wheelchair ramp."

Nathan shook his head. "Come Monday, I'm trading this thing for a cane."

"If the doctor says so," Jocelyn cautioned.

Nathan shook his head at Rob. "I didn't ask her anything. Did you hear me ask her anything?"

"She's bossy," Jeff said. "Takes after her big sister."

"Amen!" Charlie said feelingly.

There was an instant's tension while Phyllis and Charlie looked at each other, Phyllis uncertain whether the earlier upset remained between them. Then Charlie smiled and added with a giggle, "Rob, did Jossie tell you that they once convinced me that if I gave them my allowance, they would invest in chocolate bars for me?"

Phyllis and Jocelyn exchanged a look of innocence.

Rob laughed. "You didn't fall for it?"

Phyllis shook her head pityingly. "We just told her we'd invest in chocolate, and we did."

"We bought chocolate and ate it," Jocelyn said, laughing as she remembered their youthful deception. "Those were the days."

"You have to feel sorry for someone who'd trust the two of you," Nathan laughed.

Chris turned to Charlie to share the joke, then frowned over her suddenly remote expression. "You're looking tired, honey," he said. "Ready to go?"

"Yes, I am."

Jeff helped Chris raise her inflexible body off the sofa while Phyllis went for coats. Lindsay thanked them politely for her gifts and gave messy, chocolate-cake kisses.

Chris shook Rob's hand. "I enjoyed meeting you. Welcome to the Foley Funny Farm. Every one of them is a little weird, but so far, Jeff and I have survived all right."

Jocelyn opened her mouth to correct Chris's mistaken impression, but Rob replied before she could speak. "Thank you," he said. "Drive carefully."

When the door closed behind them, Phyllis instructed Lindsay to give thank-yous and kisses to Jocelyn and Rob and to say her good-nights. Then she went to put Robin into her crib.

Lindsay hugged Jocelyn with dramatic ferocity. "Thanks for the dress and the doll, Aunt Jossie. When you have your baby, are you going to get fat like Aunt Charlie?"

Jocelyn was surprised into silence for a moment. "Lindsay, I'm not having a baby," she said.

Lindsay, wide-eyed and earnest, waved her little hand in a gesture that expressed the inevitable. "When you marry Uncle Rob, you'll have a baby. Everybody does, you know."

"No, I didn't know that," Jocelyn said, careful not to look at Rob. She was also careful not to argue with Lindsay. She'd been there before and knew it was futile. "But I suppose if the day ever comes when I have a baby, I will get fat." She hugged her again. "Happy Birthday, sweetie."

Lindsay went to Rob. "When you're really my uncle," she said, "you can come here for dinner all the time. Even when it's not my birthday. And you can bring the baby."

Rob hugged her, glancing over her shoulder to grin at Jocelyn, who quickly looked away. "Thank you, princess." He straightened her crown, which had fallen askew. "Good night."

Lindsay gave a dozing Nathan a kiss and a hug, which he roused long enough to return, then she went to her father, who picked her up and carried her toward the bedrooms. "There's wine in the fridge, Rob," he said quietly as Nathan nodded off again. "And glasses in the cupboard over it."

Nathan was snoring comfortably by the time they'd finished their wine and discussed Chris's behavior.

"He *is* taking a class," Phyllis said in response to Jeff's suggestion that it was all Charlie's imagination, "but that doesn't explain the brunette."

"A professor?" Rob suggested.

Jocelyn's and Phyllis's expressions told him to get real.

"Don't try to find a reasonable explanation," Jeff warned Rob. "They don't understand the concept. They've got him on the mat, and they won't be happy until he's shark food."

"Oh, stop," Phyllis scolded. "We hope we're wrong, but we've both seen evidence that suggests we aren't." She disappeared into the bedroom and returned with a blanket that she wrapped around Nathan. He continued to snore.

"Don't get him too comfortable," Jocelyn said, gathering up glasses. "We'll never get him in the car."

"Why don't you leave him here tonight?" Phyllis asked, taking the glasses from her. "You could probably use a break, and I'll bring him back in the morning in time for you to take him to his doctor's appointment.''

Jocelyn caught Rob's eye and tried desperately not to react to what she saw there. They glowed with suggestion. No, it was more than suggestion, she decided, looking away. It was a picture in sharp detail. She closed her eyes for an instant, then smiled brightly at Phyllis. "If you're sure you can cope with the kids and—"

"Phyllis?" Jeff asked, going to the guest closet. "Unable to cope? Not in this lifetime. You guys go home and...and..."

Phyllis elbowed him before he could voice an opinion on what they should do.

He looked at her in exasperation. "I was going to suggest they go home and have a rousing game of canasta. See? Now, aren't you ashamed?"

Rolling her eyes, Phyllis hugged Jocelyn while Jeff shook hands with Rob and grinned, wordlessly making the suggestion that was really on his mind.

IN THE CAR, ROB AND Jocelyn waved as they drove away. Rob stopped at the corner, which was free of any traffic at that hour, and pulled Jocelyn into his arms.

Jocelyn went into them, trembling. Something over which she had no control was overtaking her body. It was almost as though it prepared for something inevitable.

"Rob, I..." She tried to hold him away for a moment. She had to know what was behind that look in his eyes. She'd been watching it for the past several hours in her sister's living room. It was more than romantic affection. It was love.

But was it the forever stuff that she felt? She had to go slowly here. She had to consider what might happen from every angle. She had to think!

Just as she tried to force herself to engage her brain, another dream materialized in her mind—this once complete with animation.

Over Rob's shoulder, a plump little cherub fluttered, nocked an arrow in his bow, drew the bow back, narrowed his eye at her to take aim, then let the arrow fly. The twang of the bow brought her back with a blink. Breath and any semblance of competence seemed to leave her.

"Did you hear that?" she whispered.

"What?" Rob whispered back, his smile indulgent. She was wide-eyed and looked a little scared.

"An arrow," she whispered, lost in his eyes, "with my name on it."

Rob didn't entirely understand what she meant, but he was close enough to her to feel the stiffening go out of her and to see something melt in her eyes when she looked at him.

Suddenly, nothing else mattered a damn but Jocelyn and that he needed her and needed to give to her. He shaped the back of her head in one hand and she raised her face to him eagerly. He took her mouth slowly and tenderly, trying to make up for all the senseless things he'd said and all the thoughtless things he'd done. And to let her know how deeply—and God help him—how permanently he loved her. He heard himself say the words aloud. "I love you, Joss. I love you."

He felt her tremble and held her closer.

She wound her arms around his neck, afraid to let him go, afraid the words she'd heard had been another dream. "I love you," she whispered against his lips. "God, how I love you." She kissed him with a depth of emotion that made her tremble even more.

He rubbed her back and raised his head to look into her eyes. "Are you all right?" he asked.

She uttered a shaky laugh. "Yes. Just a little overwhelmed, I guess. I thought . . . you convinced me this was impossible."

"Shows you what I know," he said wryly but without rancor. He looked into her eyes, a frown of concentration forming on his brow, and saw nothing but love there—endless, unconditional love. It entangled him, captured him. "So . . ." he asked softly, his gaze moving slowly over her face, "what are you doing with the rest of your life?"

His arms were a delicious prison. *As though I have a choice,* she thought with happy acceptance.

"Loving," she replied.

"Loving me," he said. It was half question, half correction.

She nodded. "Yes. Please let me."

In an instant, they were speeding through the night on their way to Rob's cottage overlooking the bay.

Chapter Fourteen

Rob lay Jocelyn atop his sleigh bed tucked under the eaves. In the cold darkness, he looked down at her. He wanted her so much, but he also felt something deeper, more complicated and infinitely dangerous.

He wasn't afraid because he'd already admitted that he loved her, but he didn't think he'd grasped until that moment, when she reached for him in the dark with a need he felt in her hands, just how much of him loving her was going to require—everything he had and everything he was.

Jocelyn half expected to feel hesitance in him. This couldn't be real. He would come to his senses any moment and push her away. But he didn't. In the chilly blackness, he splayed a hand under her back and brought her up into his embrace and held her.

She leaned into him, feeling unutterably precious.

Rob reached under her sweater and stroked a path of warmth from the back of her waist to one shoulder, then across to the other. Her skin felt like the petal of a flower.

At the first touch of his warm palm against her bare skin, Jocelyn felt every nerve ending with which he came into contact come to life. And every nerve everywhere else waited.

He pulled the sweater up, and she raised her arms to help him pull it off. He reached around her for the hooks of her bra. She leaned lazily against his shoulder as he tossed it aside.

Then she turned to him and he saw her ivory torso, like a sculpture on a pedestal. She tugged at the buttons of his shirt as he closed his hands over her small breasts. He explored their contour, ran a thumb over her nipples, and felt her hands still as she expelled a gusty little breath. Her head fell forward, and his nostrils were filled with the floral scent of her hair.

He pulled the sides of his shirt from her fingers and drew it off, throwing his T-shirt after it. With two hands at her waist, he lifted her to her knees and brought her against him, burying his face between her breasts.

Jocelyn felt his bristled jaw against one sensitized nipple, then the other, and felt everything in her world flip over. He nipped, kissed and stroked, and her spine lost all ability to support her.

He eased her back against the pillows, tossed her flats away and tugged her jeans and panties off. He dropped his clothes with hers and felt the chill air ripple across his skin. But it was just an absent observation. A fire burned inside him and warmed him everywhere.

Jocelyn felt the heat emanating from him. It stole around and into her, seeming to create a hum inside her. He placed a warm hand at her waist, his long fingers spread to the jut of her ribs. She felt him sigh, as though something passed from her to him, something he'd needed desperately.

His hand moved downward over her hipbone and down her thigh with such disarming tenderness, that for a moment, she was speechless and paralyzed.

Rob had not been prepared for this. His first sight of her ivory body in the darkness, his first touch of satin skin, jolted him like a live-wire shock. Everything that worked his brain and his body was melted and useless. Only feeling was functional and for a man who danced along the top of emotion, the depth of it was unsettling.

He felt in hyperbole. He craved, he hungered, he desired—until she raised a small, gentle hand to his chest. Then he turned to mush and put his destiny in her hands.

Jocelyn had never gloried in what she was. As a girl, she'd been reasonably satisfied with herself. Then she'd encountered boys, learned painfully that they preferred pretty girls, and she chose to hide herself rather than suffer rejection another time.

Rob had come along and helped her accept herself. New clothes and a new hairstyle had even boosted her confidence and helped her see what a little attention to herself could produce. But she'd never loved the woman she was. Until this moment. And, curiously, her feelings had nothing to do with how her womanhood affected her, but everything to do with how Rob reacted to it.

He lay down beside her, gathering her in his arms and pulling the blankets up over them. He kissed her and stroked her like a man thirsting for what she offered. His lips and his hands explored and revered every inch of her from her hairline to her toes, then he cradled her against his shoulder, swept a hand up her thigh and gently stole inside her.

That first possessive touch made her feel as though her blood had effervesced. A layer of tiny bubbles burst under her skin, spiking up against every already frayed nerve ending.

His fingers moved in a subtle, mind-bending pattern, and she could no longer analyze how she felt, but simply hold on as feeling overrode her, burst over her, consumed her.

Rob moved over her and entered her, reaching under her to hold her to him as he thrust deeply, like a man coming home.

Her body welcomed his like the part of her that had always been lost. For a moment, they simply clung together, each absorbing the wonder of their oneness. Rob felt as though he breathed her air. Jocelyn felt his heartbeat in her own chest.

Then they began to move, following the path of the circle, the pattern of infinity. It wound them closer together, tightening their pleasure until they climaxed together, suddenly spun from the eye of the circle. But still not free of its delicious tyranny, they clung to each other, no longer one and one, but two in one, now composing something one could not be without the other.

Her face pressed in Rob's shoulder, Jocelyn held him while the world seemed to tumble on and on. Though powerless to control or even direct what was happening to her, she trusted the arms around her to keep her safe.

As Rob surfaced out of the whirlwind, Jocelyn wrapped in his arms, he closed his eyes for a moment to assimilate the enormity of what he'd just done. What he'd just experienced with Jocelyn reminded him sharply why he'd sworn never to involve himself in love again and, paradoxically, made him wonder how he'd ever convinced himself he could exist without it.

Then she shifted lazily against him, uttering a languorous little moan, and he didn't need reasons or answers. He needed only her.

She kissed his throat. "See?" she said with a soft sigh. "I was right."

He kissed her hair and tucked the blanket up around her shoulder. "Of course, you were," he said.

She was quiet a moment, then she asked, "Don't you want to know what I was right about?"

"No," he replied. "The way I feel now, you were right about everything."

She propped up on an elbow and frowned down at him. "But don't you want to know specifically?"

He toyed with the red curls over her ear. "No. It doesn't matter."

"Yes, it does," she insisted, feigning a frown, "because I want to tell you."

He grinned. "You mean you want to gloat."

"Yes," she replied, apparently unashamed.

He laughed. "Then by all means, tell me what it is you were right about. Specifically."

She folded her arms on his chest and looked into his eyes, hers as clear to him as though it were daylight. They shone with love and sudden gravity.

"That love is stronger than anything else," she said. "I suppose we could have made love in the name of romance, but it would never have been like that, Rob. Never."

"I know." He pulled her head down to his shoulder. "It was all just a defense mechanism. After losing my father and Sandy, I guess I was trying to protect myself."

He felt her lips against his breastbone. "I wouldn't hurt you, Rob," she whispered.

He held her tighter; he couldn't seem to get close enough. "I know that. Just took me a while to let you close enough to show me."

She wriggled tauntingly against him. "Now, you'll have to do everything with me permanently attached to you. We can tell everyone we're preparing for a three-legged race."

"Or the Valentine's dance," he said.

"Mmm. Wait till you see my dress."

He turned her onto her back, her head cupped in his hands. "The thought of you clothed," he said, "holds no appeal at all for me at the moment." Then he kissed her senseless.

"It's cut really low..." she said breathlessly, determined to give him a full description.

He nibbled lovingly on just what a low cut would reveal.

"Ah!" she breathed. "And...lace..."

He blew a warm breath down the center of her body, lingering at the apex of her thighs.

"And . . . and . . . that filmy stuff . . ."

"Chiffon," he said helpfully as his hand followed the path his breath had taken.

"Yes. It's . . . ah . . . you know . . ."

"Red," he said, gently invading. "Red for passion."

With another gasp of pleasure, she succumbed to his seduction, abandoning all thought, except one. "Red for love," she whispered.

THE SHRILL RINGING WOKE Jocelyn out of an eiderdown dream involving her and Rob around a kitchen table that looked out on a bay, and three little children spooning up cereal.

She elbowed Rob. "Turn the alarm off," she mumbled grumpily.

"It's not the alarm," he said, straining to reach across her. "It's the phone."

"What? Ouch!" She tried to sit up and collided with his shoulder. She fell back onto the pillow with a hand to her forehead. "It feels like we just went to sleep."

"We did," he replied, groping for the receiver. "It's only three-fifteen. Hello? Who?"

Oh, God. She came sharply awake. Phyllis knew where to find her. Something had happened to one of her parents! Or Nathan! Charlie! Charlie was having her baby!

She tried to grab the phone from Rob, but he caught her wrist in a grip that would have broken it had she struggled. She knew instantly that the call was for him. And that it was bad news.

His side of the conversation did nothing to dispel her conclusion. "How bad is he?" he asked. The voice on the other end spoke, then Rob asked, "Where are you?" His question was answered, and he replied abruptly, "I'll be right there."

He was off the bed before he'd hung up the phone. Jocelyn reached to the bedside table for the light. Rob was already pulling on jeans and yanking his shirt off the floor.

"What is it?" she demanded, leaping off the bed and instinctively pulling her clothes on, too.

"Fire at the restaurant," he said, sitting down to pull on socks and shoes. "Griff's been hurt. That was Laurel."

Jocelyn gasped as she pulled her sweater over her head and stepped into her shoes, ignoring stockings. "Badly?"

"She doesn't think so. But he's in a lot of pain." Rob glanced at Jocelyn as he tied his shoes. "You'd better stay here," he said.

"No," she insisted, reaching to the chair for her jacket and purse. "I'm coming with you."

LAUREL SAT ALONE IN THE corner of a blue vinyl sofa in the hospital waiting room, sobbing hysterically.

Rob took one look at her, and muttering, "Oh, my God," burst through a door marked Emergency.

Jocelyn, her heart sinking to her feet, went to put an arm around her new friend.

"Laurel, what happened?" she asked gently. "Is it bad? Is he..."

Laurel raised tear-filled eyes to her, her usually perfect makeup wept away and nonexistent. Her face was white and puffy, her hair a dark tangle around her head and shoulders.

"His hands are burned," she sobbed, "and...and his right arm."

"That's all?" Jocelyn asked, then at Laurel's horrified expression, added quickly, "I mean, the way you were crying I thought..." She pointed to the door through which

Rob had disappeared. Loud voices came from beyond it. "Rob thought..."

"He'll be fine," Laurel sniffed, dabbing at her nose with a wad of tissue. Then she put a hand over her face and dissolved into tears again. "I—I just wish I could say the same a-about me."

Jocelyn patted her shoulder and rocked her gently, taking the first even breath she'd drawn in fifteen minutes. "Laurel, try to calm down," she advised quietly. "You're going to make yourself sick. If it's just his hands, I'm sure he'll—"

"He called me," Laurel interrupted, dabbing at her nose again and drawing a ragged breath.

"Griff?"

Laurel nodded. "When he got here and they asked him who they should call..." Her face crumpled again, but she drew another breath and steadied herself. "He told them to call me." She pointed a finger at herself and repeated in a tone of surprise, "Me."

"Why does that surprise you?" Jocelyn asked. "I knew he cared for you. I told you."

She nodded and pushed back an unruly hank of hair. "I know," she said. Her voice was steady but strained. "I just couldn't believe it. I mean... I've been disliked, tolerated and used, but I've never been needed before." She put a hand to her chest and winced as though she felt pain. "It came as a... as a shock."

The door burst open and a nurse half Rob's size and twice his age led him to the sofa where Jocelyn sat with Laurel. She indicated he should sit, and he did.

"You will wait here until we send for you," she said firmly. "If you haven't completely infected ER with germs and rudeness, your cousin should be free to leave in just a few minutes." She looked down at Jocelyn and asked sharply, "Are you with him?"

"Yes," she replied, thoroughly intimidated.

"Then keep him here. If he bursts into Emergency again, they'll have to find a bed for *him* in orthopedics." With a final glare at Rob, the nurse turned on her heel.

Jocelyn, feeling lighthearted because Griff's injuries were far less serious than she'd expected, and fascinated by Rob's completely cowed expression, smiled at him and patted his knee.

"I think she likes you," she said.

Rob rubbed a hand over his face and leaned back against the wall, apparently not amused by her witticism. He stretched his legs out, crossed his ankles, then drew his legs back in again and stood. Jocelyn caught the hem of his jacket.

"Don't go in there," she warned. "I'm not sure General Schwarzkopf could bring you out alive."

He folded his arms and expelled a breath, giving her a scolding glance. "Don't try to cheer me up when I'm intent on murder, okay?"

"Me or the nurse?"

"Both of you," he replied. "Right after I throttle Griff."

"Why?" Laurel demanded.

Rob paced across the small room, then back again, six feet, two inches of tension ready to snap. "What in the hell was he doing there at that hour, anyway? And what in the hell does he think the fire department is for? God, he's half olive oil. He could have gone up like a witch at the stake."

Laurel uttered a little cry and put the tissue to her mouth.

"Rob, stop it!" Jocelyn caught his arm as he paced by and yanked him down beside her. "You're upsetting Laurel, and she's already had a bad scare. Now, pull yourself together."

Rob raised an eyebrow at her tone.

She put an arm around his neck and kissed his cheek. "You don't scare me, so don't try. I've tangled with Phyllis and lived. So, how was Griff when you went in there?"

Rob propped his elbows on his knees and leaned forward wearily. "Okay, I guess. I don't know. He was bandaged up to both armpits. Napoleon Nightingale didn't let me stay very long."

Jocelyn rubbed between his shoulder blades, feeling the tension there. Only hours before, that ridge of muscle had rippled sinuously under her hands. That memory rose forcefully and filled her with a startling sense of unreality. That had happened, hadn't it?

She forced herself back to the here and now as the tiny nurse wheeled Griff out to them. He looked pale and exhausted, but his smile was genuine. Both arms mummified in bandages rested uselessly on the arms of the wheelchair.

Laurel went to put her arms around him. "How do you feel?" she asked softly. Her eyes, locked with his, said so much more than that.

"Braised, thank you," he replied, raising his stiff arms to bracket her while he kissed her cheek. He studied her puffy face in concern. "How are you?"

She shrugged a shoulder. "Okay."

"He should take it easy for a few days," the nurse said as she pushed his chair in the direction of the door that led onto the parking lot. "And see his doctor on Tuesday. His burns are minor, but they should be watched closely."

Rob opened the door and pointed to his car. The nurse wheeled Griff in that direction. Rob helped him into the front seat and buckled him in. With a wry smile, he turned to thank the nurse.

"My job," she replied, returning his smile. "Yours is to assist, but not coddle. Try to remember that." Pushing the chair, she disappeared inside the building.

Rob opened the back and gestured Laurel inside. "Come on," he said, "we'll take you home."

She pointed to the little Sprint several spots over. "I've got my..."

"You're too upset to drive."

"And I'll need a nurse tonight," Griff said weakly.

Laurel climbed into the back, Jocelyn following.

"I DON'T KNOW WHAT happened," Griff said as Rob drove to his apartment through the dark, quiet night. "I know I turned everything off. I was especially careful because you weren't there to double-check. Then I went upstairs to try to put the daily receipts together for you so you wouldn't have a mess when you came in tomorrow...." He shook his head, his voice deepening. "Then I smelled smoke. By the time I got downstairs, the whole south wall of the kitchen was involved. I called the fire department right away, then I went back to try to save Fanny—"

"Fanny?" Laurel asked.

"The computer system," Griff explained. "The waitresses punch their orders into the terminal at their station, and it prints out the order in the kitchen. It replaces written tickets. Anyway, a copy of every transaction for the day is printed out in a terminal we keep in the back of the kitchen."

Jocelyn's good humor was suddenly deflated. In her concern about Griff, Jocelyn had forgotten there'd been damage to the restaurant.

"That was stupid," Rob said brutally.

"But the setup cost you—"

"A couple of thousand dollars," Rob interrupted Griff's explanation with a quick, angry glance. "Against your life, Griff? Did smoke inhalation leave you brain-dead?"

Griff returned his cousin's angry look for a moment, then he grinned. "That's the nicest thing you've ever said to me."

"I've got a few more things to say to you," Rob said, with a brief glance in the mirror at his back seat passengers. "When we're alone."

Griff sobered suddenly. "You might want to have a stiff drink before you go over there. It was still burning when the firemen put me in the ambulance. It's got to be bad."

Rob simply nodded.

"I'm sorry."

Rob turned to Griff. "You should be. If you'd tried a little harder to save it, you could have flambéed parts of you that wouldn't heal. Don't worry about it. This part's my job."

Griff resisted Rob's efforts to help him to his apartment. He leaned a muffed arm on Laurel's shoulders and smiled. "I've got a nurse here, and some pills to take somewhere . . ."

"I've got them," Laurel said, patting her purse.

"See?" Griff kissed her forehead. "She knows what she's doing. I'll be fine. I'll call you in the morning."

Laurel pointed to his wrapped hand. "Better let me dial," she said.

Laurel looked radiant, Jocelyn thought. Exhausted, but radiant. Rob and Jocelyn watched as Griff and Laurel disappeared inside the building.

"I'm taking you home," Rob said, as he closed the passenger door of his car.

"I'm going with you," she insisted as he slipped in behind the wheel.

"No. It might not be safe."

"*You're* going," she pointed out.

"It's *my* restaurant."

"And the setting for *my* Valentine extravaganza."

Rob was too tired to argue, and he knew he was going to need all his strength to face the mess. He drove to the restaurant.

A mop-up crew was still there, the engine of the red fire truck running loudly in the quiet night, its light bright and garish. The acrid smell of smoke was a weird addition to the odors of fish and diesel.

A yellow warning tape had been stretched the length of the restaurant side of the mall as far as the jeweler's. He stepped over it, pointing at Jocelyn to stay on the other side.

A fireman in full gear came forward to stop him, then he recognized Rob. He and his family were Saturday lunch regulars.

"Floor's solid," he said. "Roof's secure, but there's debris and water everywhere, so watch yourself."

The front half of the dining room was dark with smoke, and the carpeting was muddy. Troublesome, Rob estimated, but easily taken care of. So far, so good.

He stepped into the kitchen and felt his dream disintegrate. The right side was completely destroyed, cupboards and contents gone, grill and hood and counters charred into something indistinguishable. The other side was covered in soot, and everything was under several inches of water.

The computer system that Griff had carried until it grew too hot to hold lay on its side in the water several yards from the door.

Two thoughts occurred to him simultaneously. Had he been here where he was supposed to have been, instead of with Joss, chasing a dream that had always been out of his reach, this might not have happened. He'd have been around to help Griff through the step-by-step clean-up and close-up they followed religiously every night to avoid just such a disaster.

Secondly, had Griff not stayed late to catch up on Rob's work and had not been there to smell the smoke, the entire mall might have been a total loss.

The feeling that settled over Rob was the same cold clutch at his heart he'd felt when he'd stood in the middle of The Brahmin's kitchen the day he'd said goodbye to it.

With one arm around his mother and the other around Griff, he'd looked around the room that had been more of a home for twelve years than the small house in the North End. The three of them had scrubbed everything spotless, but the aroma of onions sautéing, of crusty bread, and strong wine and cheese had still hung in the air, as though another Saturday night's clientele waited in the dining room.

But the kitchen had been still. All the pots and pans, usually in use, hung on the rack on the wall, and the counters, usually full of ingredients being prepared, were clear and pristine. Never before or since had he felt such a sense of loss—until this moment.

Even when he'd lost his restaurant to Sandy, it hadn't hurt like this. Perhaps because Griff hadn't been involved then. The Old Cannery Restaurant was a family venture, like the Boston restaurant had been.

The restaurant was what Rob was. Home had always been there. It had been the source and the target of his talents. Its artful blend of creativity and order defined him in a way nothing else ever could.

This wasn't permanent, of course. Insurance would cover the damage and repairs, and they'd be open again in a couple of weeks. But this had been *his* fault. *His.* He'd been romancing Jocelyn when he should have been on the job. Some things just weren't meant to be.

He felt arms come around his waist, a head lean into his back.

SEEING THE DAMAGE, Jocelyn thought, was far worse than hearing it described. The charred, twisted, sodden interior was a painful shock to her, and she didn't have Rob's close connection with the restaurant. She could only imagine what he was feeling. She knew that all his dreams and energies had gone into this place, and that it meant even more to him than that. The kid who'd grown up in the back of a Boston restaurant was still trying to find what he'd once known there.

She wrapped her arms around Rob and held him.

"I told you to wait outside," he said, his hands remaining in his pockets.

Jocelyn felt the rigidity in his muscles, heard the remoteness in his tone. She refused to be held away by it. She moved around to stand in front of him.

"I'm sorry, Rob," she said, putting her hands at his waist. "I know this is easy for me to say, but I'll bet even in a couple of hours, when the sun comes up, this won't look so bad."

She watched his eyes go over the ugly, demoralizing mess with obvious skepticism.

She had to keep talking. She wasn't sure why, but she felt as though he was slipping away from her. "I know you're insured. A janitorial service, a couple of days with a construction crew and some good carpenters, and this'll all be—"

He drew a deep breath and took her hand, turning to lead her away. "I'm taking you home," he said. "It's late and cold and..."

She stopped him at the batwing doors that hung crookedly, charred and burned, like the edges of a pirate's map. "Come home with me, let me make you a cup of coffee and we'll plan a strategy for—"

"No." He tugged her after him, through the doors, through the charred part of the dining room and into the mall, where the hose was being reeled up. He left her for a moment to speak to the firemen who remained, then he walked Jocelyn to the car. Way out on the dark river, sea lions barked stridently.

Rob drove home in silence. When he let her off at her grandfather's, she asked simply, "Are you coming back?"

He avoided her eyes. "I've got to make a lot of long-distance calls—attorney, insurance agent, suppliers...."

"You know what I mean," she said quietly.

His expression was carefully neutral. "My clothes are there," he said.

Clever, she thought. *Well done. When you're no longer in shock, I'll make you pay for that.* She forced a smile. "All right. See you later."

JOCELYN PUT THE KETTLE on and paced her grandfather's kitchen. This was not happening. She was not going to let it happen. She was not going to let Rob back away from what they shared because of some confused notion that every time he lost a restaurant, it was because he loved someone.

She'd been afraid of romance, but his persistent attention had given her courage to take a chance on love again. If his love was genuine, then she could do the same for him. If it wasn't—if it was just the shell of romance and not the real heart of it—then she'd accept the end of their relationship.

Chapter Fifteen

Nathan's ancient washer squeaked as it agitated, and the dryer roared rather than hummed, as though it fluffed a grizzly.

With two days to the bazaar, the Senior Center Committee in full control of all the details and her grandfather that morning declared safely ambulatory with the aid of a cane, Jocelyn took the day off to tidy Nathan's house and catch up on laundry before moving back to her apartment.

She folded Rob's white shirts, T-shirts and cotton briefs into a separate pile, fighting another dream that tried to turn her grandfather's basement into the little room off the kitchen in Rob's cottage on the bay. She saw tiny socks, diapers, shirts and rompers that had once been Lindsay's and then Robin's and had now been handed down to her.

She let herself enjoy the scene for one moment, then closed her eyes on it. Dreams were a comfort, but there were times when a woman simply had to face reality. If Rob had awakened this morning feeling the way he had when he'd left her last night, her dreams were history.

The sudden appearance of a French bouquet of flowers in front of her face made her blink and look again. Was this a remnant of the dream, or was it real? Then her nose caught the spicy scent of carnations and the sweetness of honeysuckle. Rob! She turned, a joyful laugh erupting from her. Then she looked into his eyes.

His mouth was smiling, but everything else about him was not. His eyes were sad and tired, and despite the smile, his expression had no sparkle. When he'd been teasing her, scolding her, wooing her, that sparkle had always been so definite a part of him.

She reached back to turn off the dryer. "Hi," she said warily.

He wore jeans and a thick, clay-colored sweater over a chambray shirt. He handed her the flowers, his smile still in place.

"Thank you," she said. "What's the occasion?"

"Do I need one?" he asked.

She was suspicious; he could see it in her eyes. He wasn't as good at this as he'd thought. He knew it was because he'd gotten in deeper than he'd intended this time. He felt a desperate need to get away. Life had taught him that he didn't get to keep things—not fathers, not wives, not dreams.

"Nathan looks well," he said, leaning back against the folding table. "He came to the door with his cane, boasting about you and I having to find someone else to smother with attention."

Jocelyn nodded. She even smiled as she folded a bath towel. If Rob could behave as though nothing were wrong, so could she.

"The doctor was very pleased. I'm moving out tomorrow." She pulled a double-bed sheet out of the dryer, arms wide as she struggled to fold it on the length.

Rob took one end from her and held as she shook it out. The distance between them made it easier to say what he'd come to say.

"I won't be able to make the dance after all," he said lightly, as though it didn't really matter to either of them. "I've got a million details to attend to and—"

They were eye to eye for an instant when Jocelyn brought her end of the sheet to his. The clear, level look in her eyes told him she saw right through him. He took the corners from her, and she reached down for the fold and stepped back to straighten it.

"You don't have to explain," she said. "I think I knew last night when you wouldn't come back with me that you've chosen the restaurant over me."

"Joss..." he said, genuinely horrified that she thought so.

She came forward with the third fold and took the sheet from him. "Oh, I know it isn't because you love it more than you love me, it's because it's safer. It's a place to hide." She put the sheet on the pile of clothes, then turned and crossed her arms, leaning against the table. "I know all about hiding. I did it in weird clothes because they kept people at a distance. You do it in a restaurant because it's a good excuse for working instead of loving."

"Had I been there—" he began heatedly.

"The fire would have still broken out," she said, interrupting, "because the wiring was faulty. Laurel told me."

He was getting angry now. She was so damned calm, and so clinical about it, when his insides felt like a Jacuzzi.

"I won't be easy to replace, you know," she said softly, her large eyes pinning his. "Oh, you'll find another woman who'll fall for your romantic line, just like I did, but sooner or later, it'll come down to right where we are now. Do you love her and take the chance that you'll be left again, or do you find a convenient excuse to chicken out?"

Rob turned to the stairs. "I don't have to listen to this," he said.

"Yes, you do," she insisted in an amiable tone.

Near the furnace, he turned back and asked, "Why?"

She picked up his pile of clothes and held it to her chest. "Because I have your underwear."

He folded his arms and considered her, the charged atmosphere between them sparking. The anger in his eyes became something allied but very different.

He came toward her. ''I could report it stolen,'' he said softly.

She tossed the clothes at him, abandoning all semblance of casual control.

''Take it!'' she shouted. ''And get out! But I'm going to the dance without you, and I'm going to find somebody else!''

He reached for her, but she backed away, hitting at him. He blocked her defense until she was backed against the dryer with nowhere to go.

Overpowering her physically was easy. Resisting being emotionally overpowered by her himself was not. She fell against him, sobbing.

He held her to him, leaning down to rest his cheek against hers. ''Why don't you just come home with me,'' he whispered, ''and we won't worry about tomorrow.''

God, that was inviting. It would give her what she needed at the moment, and dismiss her concerns about the future. But, then, the day after would come and there she'd be again—in the same predicament she'd warned him about only a moment ago.

She let herself hold him, relishing being held one more moment, then she pulled away. ''Thanks, but I want more than romance from you.''

He shook his head grimly. ''Joss, I warned you in the beginning...''

She nodded, picking up her bouquet. ''I know. All you promised was hearts and flowers.'' She gave him a wry, sad look. ''You did come through on the flowers.''

''Jossie!'' Nathan bellowed from the top of the basement stairs. ''Come up here!''

He sounded so desperate that Jocelyn dropped the flowers onto the folding table and ran, Rob right behind her.

"What is it, Gramps?" she demanded as she topped the stairs into the kitchen. He pointed to the living room doorway where Charlie stood.

"I've come to say goodbye," Charlie said, her face red and blotchy from crying. She clutched a handkerchief in her hand.

"What...?" Jocelyn held her sister at arm's length and tried to draw her toward the sofa, but with the help of the ballast of her pregnancy, Charlie held her ground.

"I'm leaving Chris," she said, mopping at the endless stream of tears on her face. "I can't take it anymore. I love him and I wanted to work it out, but I don't think he cares anymore. He was all sweetness and light at Phyl's yesterday, then he left before breakfast again this morning. I'm flying out to Mom and Dad's. I'll call you from there."

"Charlie, wait!" Jocelyn tried to stop her as she turned for the door. "A pregnant woman as far along as you won't be allowed on a plane. Have you talked to Phyl?"

"Before I left," she said. "Then I'll drive to San Diego."

"What if you go into labor on the highway?" Jocelyn demanded, playing for time.

"I've still got a couple of days. I'm—I'm okay."

"But you're upset. Gramps!" Jocelyn turned to her grandfather, imploring him to do something.

"Charlene Alexis," he said, pulling himself up sternly, his stature undiminished by the cane, "you will sit down and we will talk this out."

She gave him a quick hug. "No. I'm going."

"You have to talk to Chris before you leave," Jocelyn said. "This is the coward's way..."

But Charlie wasn't listening; she was steaming toward the door at full waddle. From outside came a screech of brakes, the slam of a door and footsteps advancing at a run. The door burst open again and Chris stood there, coatless, his tie yanked away from his throat, his dark hair mussed. His eyes were anguished and distraught.

At the sight of Charlie standing there, his entire being seemed to fall several inches. He leaned a hand against the doorjamb and put the other to his heart while he gasped for breath.

"Charlie," he said. "Thank God."

She tried to push past him. "I'm leaving, and you're not going to stop me," she said between gulps and sobs. "It's too late, Chris."

"Honey, let me explain," he said gently, blocking her way.

"No!" she shouted. "When I wanted to talk, you wouldn't listen. Well, I don't feel like talking anymore."

"Well, you'd better change your mind," Phyllis said, suddenly appearing behind Chris, "because I'm parked behind you in the driveway and I'm not moving until you've heard him out."

"I will not be bullied into—" Charlie said intrepidly, only to stop when Phyllis and Jocelyn pushed and pulled her toward the sofa. Each took an arm and leaned her unbending body backward until she could sit. "God!" she said, folding her arms in a temper over the mound of her stomach. "Will I ever stop being the little sister?"

Phyllis and Jocelyn looked at each other. "No," they replied simultaneously.

ROB DIDN'T LIKE BEING closed in the kitchen with Jocelyn, Nathan and Phyllis while Charlie and Chris ironed out their problems in the living room. Nathan knew there was a problem with Joss and him, and Rob could have sworn that Phyllis already suspected it. He did his best to sit quietly and listen to Phyl's story and try to act invisible.

"She did the same thing to me," Phyllis explained, helping herself to coffee from the warming pot on the counter. "Came to say goodbye. When she told me she was going to stop to see you, too, I left the kids with my neighbor and ran by Chris's office. When I told him what we suspected about him and what she was doing, I thought he was going to have a stroke. So I drove him over here myself."

"I was not playing around!" Chris's voice shouted from beyond the door. "I was working toward my C.P.A. so I could get a raise so we could get the down payment for the house you want so badly. I took a test-prep class at the college." His voice quieted, and Phyllis continued the story for those gathered in the kitchen.

"He wanted to surprise Charlie," she said, "so he told her he was working late instead of telling her the truth. He didn't want her to get her hopes up in case he didn't pass."

"What about the brunette?" Jocelyn asked.

"Would you believe a lawyer friend trying to help him study? Her husband teaches the class Chris took. That's why I saw them together in the college parking lot. The afternoon you saw them in the restaurant lounge, she'd been coaching him for a couple of hours and he was going to Portland the next day to take the test. It was sort of a good-luck drink."

"Charlie said he left before breakfast this morning."

"An early meeting. I checked." Phyllis sighed. "So we were mistaken. Love conquers all, after all."

Jocelyn turned to Rob, her expression bland. "Hear that, Donnelly?"

Rob pushed his chair back and caught Jocelyn's arm. "Excuse us." He nodded politely at Nathan and Phyllis as he drew Jocelyn out the back door. They stood together on the walk in the chilly sunshine.

"I'll come back for my clothes another time," he said, his face devoid of all expression. "I just don't want to sit around...I mean, I can't..."

She nodded and folded her arms. "What about Phyllis's dinner?" she asked stubbornly. She knew he'd presumed she'd just forget it.

Surprise registered in his eyes for a moment, then he looked up at a starling on the telephone wire. "I've got to meet with the insurance people, talk to carpenters, call—"

"Right." She cut him off. "Well, while you're burying yourself in work, I'm going to the dance. I might even find a man who's willing to love me. Who'll marry me and give me babies and make every day Valentine's Day. Will you be sorry if that happens?"

He leaned down to kiss her lightly on the cheek, his eyes filled with misery. "Eternally," he said. "Bye, Joss."

Jocelyn watched him walk away, feeling everything she'd become try to crumble. But she squared her shoulders and swallowed a sob. She didn't want to live without him, but she could. She could.

"I CAN'T DO THIS." Jocelyn slapped the snooze alarm on her clock radio and pulled the blankets over her head. She heard rain hitting the roof and beating at the windows of her apartment.

It was February 14, Valentine's Day. The day of the bazaar, Phyllis's dinner and the Valentine dance. The day she would be spending with hundreds of people, but alone.

The ache that had begun in her stomach in the middle of the Old Cannery's blackened kitchen two nights ago had now swelled to fill her entire being. Everything hurt—head, heart, hopes, dreams. Physically and emotionally, she'd fallen victim to a beastly little cupid and his arrow.

She gave her blankets a listless toss and sat up. Rob had warned her to keep her backside covered, she reminded herself wryly. She should have listened.

She groaned and put both hands over her face. The last thing she wanted to do today was smile and sparkle and have to remember the million details that would make the bazaar a success. And she didn't want to see Rob. She missed him as though a part of her had been amputated, but she didn't think she could bear to look upon his face.

The sound of her doorbell made her groan again, but galvanized her into action. She pulled on a robe and padded to the door. She was greeted by the sunny faces of her sisters and their husbands. Then she was pushed aside as they marched in and took over her apartment.

All the decorations, folding chairs she'd borrowed from the Senior Center for the vendors to sit on, signs she'd made to post near the pier and a strongbox of change she'd picked up the night before at the bank, sat in the middle of the living room carpet.

Phyllis put her hand on her hips and frowned. "You're not dressed," she said. Then, after a quick look into Jocelyn's eyes, she gave her sister a hug and smiled. "No matter. We'll take care of this while you shower. Everything's going to the mall?"

"Yes, but . . ." Jeff and Chris were already hefting boxes and bags.

Charlie waddled toward the kitchen, blowing Jocelyn a kiss. "I'll make you some breakfast." Then she stopped Chris, who was loaded down with things to carry out, and reached up for his kiss. He gave her an adoring smile before obliging.

Jeff rolled his eyes. "They've been kissing since we picked them up."

Phyllis pushed him toward the door with his burden of chairs. "Don't be jealous, dear. If you hadn't forgotten how, I'd—"

Jeff leaned both chairs against the pile of boxes, grabbed Phyllis by the hair, bent her backward and kissed her into silence. She arose pink-cheeked and uncharacteristically ruffled.

Despite her personal misery, Jocelyn had to smile. It was wonderful to see Charlie happy, and a ruffled Phyllis was a rare treat.

Jeff winked at his wife. "Later, baby," he said, and followed Chris out the door.

Phyllis smoothed her hair and caught Jocelyn's indulgent expression. She put an arm around her sister and led her toward the bathroom. "We're here to help, not to do everything. Get a move on."

"Phyl?" Jocelyn stopped her in the hallway, her eyes filling. She knew why her family had come to help, and she appreciated the gesture. She needed them today. She put her arms around her bossy, snoopy older sister and hugged her fiercely. "I love you," she said.

"I know." Phyllis's voice sounded strained. "I love you, too. Have faith, okay? This is going to work out."

Jocelyn pulled back and shook her head. She knew Phyllis wasn't talking about the bazaar. "It isn't," she said gravely. She had to accept it.

"I think it will," Phyllis insisted, turning Jocelyn toward the bathroom. "The man isn't stupid. Now, hurry up."

MARY, FREDDIE AND JOHN were already setting up their table when Jocelyn and her family arrived. Nathan supervised from a chair on the sidelines. With a sympathetic glance, he pulled Jocelyn down for a hug. "How's my girl?"

"Fine, Grandpa." She handed him a thermos Charlie had prepared. She was careful not to look in the direction of the charred wall of the restaurant. "Need some coffee?"

He indicated the steaming cup at the foot of his chair. "Got fresh. Griff and Laurel have coffee going at one of the waitress's stations in the restaurant. They brought rolls, too."

As though on cue, Griff appeared at the dining room doorway. He waved Jocelyn over with an arm still swaddled in bandages. With Phyllis directing the transferral of everything they'd brought in the truck, Jocelyn hurried to him.

"How're you feeling?" she asked, smiling. "You look great."

Laurel waved from a long table they'd set up with cups and cream and sugar. Her smile was as wide as Griff's.

"I'll bet you've had excellent nursing," Jocelyn teased.

"I have." He put an arm around her and asked gently. "How are you doing?"

"Fine," she lied bravely. She judged by the sympathy in his eyes that that hadn't been a frivolous question and that he knew it was over between Rob and her. She tried to divert the conversation. "The smell of smoke isn't as bad as I remember," she observed.

"Rob had a janitorial service come in yesterday. They stripped the kitchen and blew out the smoke. He didn't want your bazaar to be affected by it. He sent Laurel and me down to make coffee for the shoppers. He even rented a small refrigerator to replace the one he'd promised you."

She swallowed painfully. "That was thoughtful."

"He is generally," Griff said with a frown. "Except when he's being stupid."

Laurel joined them, handing Jocelyn a cup of coffee and a maple bar. Her obvious happiness lifted Jocelyn's spirits.

"My loan was approved," she announced.

Jocelyn hugged her with the arm that held the bar. "That's wonderful. I guess I'd better get myself down to the bank to cosign."

"No need. Griff did it." She beamed up at him. "Our names are going to be together on a lot of things."

Jocelyn laughed with them. That was wonderful news. Why did it hurt so much?

"Joss!" Jeff called from the restaurant doorway. "Where do you want the signs?"

"I'll be right there!" she called. She smiled from Griff to Laurel. "So, I'll see you two at dinner tonight?"

Laurel nodded. "You bet."

Griff sighed, holding up his hands. "If these things don't fit in my suit jacket, I may be a little casual, but I'll be there."

"See you then." Jocelyn hurried to Jeff, waving at the happy twosome over her shoulder.

DESPITE THE RAIN, the shoppers arrived early, bought big and stayed late. The fishermen's wives were out of chowder after lunch, and Freddie sold her last dozen cookies in the middle of the afternoon.

Crocheted goods and embroidery went like items on the sale table at Saks. Chris and Charlie, shopping arm in arm, bought booties, bibs, rompers and bonnets. Phyllis bought crocheted dolls for Lindsay and Robin, and Jeff ate all day long.

Jocelyn operated on automatic pilot. She knew what she had to do and how she had to behave. Though she was busy every moment, the clock dragged from hour to hour. She wasn't sure how to feel about that. On one hand, she was anxious for the interminable day of noisy good cheer to be over. On the other, the end of the bazaar only meant dinner at Phyl's, followed by the dance, both events she would attend unescorted.

She tried to concentrate on how much money the bazaar was bringing in and planned to cross her lonely bridge when she got to it. Or jump from it.

"WHAT IN THE HELL are you doing?" Griff, in a dark suit and tie, the arms of the coat slightly misshapen by his bandages, stood in the middle of Rob's kitchen and stared around him in concern. Every kitchen cabinet was in the middle of the floor, except the corner one Rob was prying off the wall with a crowbar.

Rob wore faded jeans and a sweatshirt that looked as though whoever had worn it last had been shot at close range.

"I've been wanting to refinish these since I moved in," he said, grunting when the cabinet refused to give. He glanced at Griff and smiled thinly. "Whoa. Studly. How do you feel?"

"Good. How do you feel?"

"Like hell."

"There's a cure for that."

Rob ignored him and worked on the cabinet. Griff walked up to him. "All she did was love you, man," he said quietly. "Why are you doing this to her?"

"She's gorgeous and wonderful," Rob replied without looking at him. "She'll find somebody else."

"She wants you."

"She'll get over it."

"Damn you!" Griff swung at him with a bandaged arm and winced when his injury connected with solid muscle.

"Griff!" Rob said in concern, backing out of his reach. "Are you . . . ?"

"You're the one who made her vulnerable," Griff shouted. "I warned you, you were going to hurt her. What's the matter with you? Did you think she was just another chick you could romance and leave?"

"No." Rob tossed the crowbar down and took a rag from his back pocket. "I knew from the beginning she would be different."

Griff studied him while he wiped his hands. "Then if she's different, why are you doing this to both of you?"

Rob tossed the rag down, put his hands on his hips and said quietly. "Because I'm still the same. I don't get to keep things."

"What?" Griff's voice cracked with disbelief. "You half raised me and I'm still here!"

Rob gave him a fractional smile. "Hardly a recommendation." Then he sobered and shook his head. "It doesn't matter now...."

Griff walked around him to look into his eyes. "Oh, yes, it does. You were too gutless to go down there today, but you should look into her face. It matters. It matters a lot." Griff put his muffed arms on either side of Rob to hold him still. "Remember when you dragged me away from the gang?"

"Griff..."

"Do you remember?"

"Yes." Rob shifted his weight. "I remember."

"Do you remember what you said that night while your mother patched you up?"

"It doesn't really—"

"You told me that life was full of easy ways out. That I could spend my life looking for a fast way to gain status and make a buck, like your father did, or I could live a real life and work for those things. Well, love comes the same way, pal. It costs you. So your childhood wasn't perfect. So you've logged a few losses. Who hasn't?"

Griff walked around Rob again when he tried to turn away. "That leaves you with a good sixty years left, Rob," he said relentlessly. "You had a father who screwed up and left. You had a wife who was a witch and cheerfully took you for everything she could get. Don't punish yourself for that by rejecting Jocelyn," Griff went on earnestly, "because that wasn't your fault. It just happened the way it did because that's life. Give yourself a break, Rob. Love her. Let yourself see what real love can be like. I have a feeling you two could make it last forever."

Rob picked up the crowbar, avoiding Griff's eyes. He felt numb, almost dead. "You're going to be late picking up Laurel," he said.

Griff raised his bandaged hands and growled impatiently. "If I had fingers, I'd drag you out of here like you dragged me fifteen years ago." He turned angrily and stalked to the open door. "You need something to fall on your thick head!" he shouted, and disappeared.

Rob concentrated on the recalcitrant cabinet, turning off the yearning. He couldn't love anyone forever. No one could love him forever. He'd get hurt again, and worse, he'd hurt her. She deserved better.

She wants you, Griff had said. *You should look into her face....*

Trying to tune out his torturous thoughts, Rob wedged the crowbar between the cabinet and the wall and applied all his strength. He swore with a startled shout when the cupboard gave. He braced his arms to hold it, the door fell open and something hit his head, bounced off his shoulder and fell to the floor.

THE SCANDINAVIAN CLUB WAS decorated in pink-and-white bunting over the lace-draped windows. Pink ribbons dangling paper hearts hung from the old-fashioned wall sconces, and bunches of dried flowers were mounted in doily cones on the walls between the windows. Dreamy music came from a small band on the stage.

Jocelyn stood near her family's table and absorbed the wonderfully romantic hearts-and-flowers effect, thinking it ironic that she'd finally come to a point where she could appreciate it when it was out of her life forever.

"I think they've out-schmaltzed your bazaar," Phyllis observed, holding Jeff's arm. "Isn't it therapeutic to pull out all the stops once in a while and let yourself be sappy?"

"Don't get carried away," Jeff advised. "Tomorrow, we still have to clean out the garage."

Phyllis smiled up at him. "My Don Juan."

Laughing, Jeff swept her onto the dance floor. In the black-sequined dress she'd lent Jocelyn two short weeks ago, she looked like an ad for some exotic designer. Across the floor, Charlie and Chris swayed dreamily in each other's arms, and on the sidelines, Mary and Nathan chatted with their friends. Judging by their expressions, they discussed the unheard of success of the all-community Valentine project.

"I'm glad you decided to wear the dress," Laurel said, appearing suddenly beside Jocelyn and stepping back with a critical eye. "Redheads who refuse to wear red are missing the chance to make a very dramatic statement."

Alone, Jocelyn thought while outwardly thanking Laurel for the compliment. *The only statement I'm making is— I am alone.*

Somehow, being dumped a second time was far worse than the first. Not only were her feelings hurt, her pride decimated and her belief in herself as a desirable woman severely shaken—but this time, she knew real loss. Deep, dark, uncompromising loss. She had the courage to face it and endure it without retreating into her armor, but it hurt abominably to look into a future without Rob.

"Want to dance?" Griff appeared on her other side, a bandaged arm gallantly extended.

"No, thank you," she said, smiling affectionately at him. "You should be dancing with Laurel."

"I intend to," he said. "But right now, I'd like to dance with you."

"You don't have to...."

He grinned. "You can rest assured I won't get fresh. I can't. No fingers."

"And I'll be watching," Laurel threatened. "Be careful, Jossie. I've found those hands to be pretty dangerous."

Jocelyn was passed from Griff to Chris to Jeff to John to the mayor. She detected a not-very-subtle conspiracy to keep her dancing until she was too tired to think.

As the mood of the evening mellowed into its romantic surroundings and the band ignored fast numbers in deference to all the close embraces on the dance floor, all the dreamy-eyed whispers and the promising looks, Jocelyn balked as Jeff tried to pass her to Griff. The band had begun a velvety, tantalizingly slow rendition of "My Funny Valentine."

"No." She pushed Griff's arms gently away and beckoned Laurel, who was sipping punch with Nathan and Mary. "I absolutely insist that you dance with Laurel."

"Joss..." Griff began.

"No," she said again. She took a step back and cried out in surprise when she collided with something solid.

She turned to apologize—and stared up into Rob's dark eyes. They were as honeyed, as velvety as the music swelling around her. Her heart stalled, and her breath caught.

He smiled, something sweet and fresh in the gesture. "You're not supposed to step on my toes," he said, "until we start dancing."

Though everything else inside her seemed to have shut down, she felt a sharp flare of joy. She squelched it as quickly because it just couldn't be.

Rob turned to Griff. "Beat it, oven mitts," he said. "I'm cutting in."

"'Bout time." Griff turned to Jocelyn with a broad smile and a bow. "I leave you to less-intriguing but more capable hands." He danced away with Laurel.

Jocelyn was vaguely aware of her family gathered in a corner, watching. She still couldn't speak.

"May I have this dance?" Rob asked, his expression sobering, his eyes darkening further. She noticed that a red rose protruded from the breast pocket of his dark suit.

I'm going to die, Rob thought. *If she turns on her heel and walks away as I deserve, I'm going to die. My life will go on, but the important part of me, the loving, trusting part that hasn't seen the light of day in twenty years will cease to exist.* Love ached in him while he waited.

Jocelyn opened her mouth to speak, tried to nod, but succeeded in neither.

Rob saw the confusion in her eyes and had to touch her. He put a hand to her cheek. At the silky touch of her, he forgot all the things he'd planned to tell her. Moody music played and couples danced by, glancing interestedly at him and Jocelyn. He didn't see them. He was aware of nothing but her.

"Jocelyn . . ." he whispered.

Jocelyn struggled to pull her scattered wits together. His touch suggested things, promised things she'd been sure only a moment ago could never be hers.

"Rob?" she asked. Then she saw for the first time a bright red mark several inches long near his hairline. She put her fingertips to it, wondering if she were dreaming. But his flesh was warm to her touch. "What happened?" she asked.

He stared at her another moment, then pulled the rose out of his pocket. He raised an eyebrow and laughed softly. "Something fell on my head."

She frowned in concern. "What?"

He handed her the rose. "Swinburne," he said. He smiled, his eyes desperate with love. "If I may paraphrase?

Our lives will grow together, in sad or singing weather. If you'll be what the rose is, I'll be like the leaf." •

Jocelyn looked from the love brimming in his eyes to the rose she held. It was tied halfway down the stem with a pink bow—from which dangled a marquis-cut diamond in a gold setting.

A cry escaped her. She quickly covered her mouth, the eyes showing above her hand wide with shock.

Rob held his breath and tried to read her expression. Shock. Indecision?

"Jocelyn, will you marry me?" he asked urgently. "I can't live without you another minute. I *won't* live without you. I love you. I *believe* in love. I—"

He stopped midsentence when she flung her arms around his neck, sobbing.

The music and the dancing had now stopped and everyone stood around them in a wide circle. Phyllis and Charlie came halfway toward them.

"What?" Phyllis asked, half worried, half hopeful. "What?"

Jocelyn hung from Rob's neck, still crying, but he was strongly aware of being unembarrassed. He glanced around at their silent, waiting audience, and said candidly, "Well, I'm not sure. Jossie, was that a yes?"

"Yes!" She raised her head to repeat loudly, tearfully, "Yes!"

The crowd remained silent.

"What," Phyllis demanded, "was the question?"

In answer, Rob put Jocelyn on her feet, took the rose from her and yanked the loop of the bow that dropped the ring into his palm. He took her left hand and slipped the ring onto her third finger.

Phyllis screamed, Nathan shouted, Charlie and Laurel burst into tears, and cheers and applause erupted from the rest of the room.

Rob wrapped Jocelyn in his arms and pressed her to him. "There you have it," he whispered. "Flowers and my heart."

"Rob, I love you," she whispered back, holding him so tightly, she couldn't tell her heartbeat from his. It occurred to her that perhaps they were no longer separate.

They were smothered in a hug that involved Phyllis and Jeff, Charlie and Chris, Nathan and Mary, and Griff and Laurel.

"Oh, God!" Charlie said excitedly. "Oh, God!"

Phyllis put an arm around her. "Relax, sis," she said. "I warned you this would happen."

"It isn't that." Charlie shook a hand at her and concentrated on something in the air above their heads. Then she closed her eyes and winced, reaching blindly for Chris. "It's time! Bethany Lynn is on her way."

For the second time that evening, everyone on the dance floor stopped. Phyllis took charge of Charlie, while Jeff and Rob supported Chris, who had turned green and seemed about to collapse.

"What can we do?" Laurel asked as she and Griff followed the parade to the door.

"Can you relieve our baby-sitter?" Phyl asked, helping Charlie into her coat. Charlie was already doing her breathing exercises. "I hate to ask, but this might take a while."

"Of course." Griff took the house keys from Jeff.

"What about us?" Nathan asked, his cane in one hand, Mary under the other arm.

"Call Mom and Dad," Phyllis said. "Tell them their third grandchild is on the way."

"And tell them they should come home for a wedding," Jocelyn said, taking Charlie's other arm as they stepped out into the rainy night.

In Phyllis and Jeff's station wagon, Chris recovered sufficiently to sit with Charlie in the middle seat and time her contractions.

Rob and Jocelyn huddled together in the back as they raced across town to the hospital. "The hospital's going to get tired of seeing us," Jocelyn said.

"They'd better get used to us," Rob said, holding her against him and bracing himself as Jeff took a turn with skill but considerable speed. "A passel of kids will keep bringing us back."

She looked up into his eyes, her own still filled with wonder. "Is that really what you want?"

He leaned down to kiss her. "You are what I want—and whatever comes with you."

She shook her head at him, smiling. "That includes this family. You're crazy."

He nodded agreement. "Certifiable. Carstairs told me so. I got him out of the shower to open the jewelry store for me. I stole the rose from the bouquet he always has in the window."

She kissed his chin and rubbed her cheek against it, marveling that they finally belonged to each other. "Swinburne would understand, though," she said.

Epilogue

In the doctors' parking lot of Salty Harbor Memorial Hospital, perched on the roof of a blue Mercedes bearing a vanity plate that read BABIES, Percival and Rupert watched Charlie and Chris and their entourage crowd into emergency.

At the door, Rob held Jocelyn back, pushed her into a shadowy corner between a pay phone and the door and kissed her deeply, lingeringly.

Rupert raised a fist in the air and shouted, "Yes! What did I tell ya?"

Percival nodded, hooked his bow on the Mercedes's antenna and leaned back on an elbow. "You did good, Rupe. I'm putting you up for a raise."

"Naw."

"Why not?"

Rupert pointed his bow at Rob and Jocelyn as they walked arm in arm into the hospital, gazing into each other's eyes. He heaved a satisfied sigh. "That's why. Don't need it."

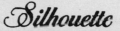

Silhouette Sensation

COMING NEXT MONTH

IN DEFENCE OF LOVE
Kathleen Creighton

Brady Flynn was fascinated by Michael Snow, but she hadn't meant to get mixed up in his personal life, or in the danger which surrounded him. But when a speeding car nearly ran them both down, she was suddenly *very* involved.

Taking Brady home worked out really well from Michael's point of view. Trapped by the weather with a gorgeous woman whose warmth and enthusiasm for living were infectious, nobody else knew where he was. He was safe. He just wasn't so sure about his heart . . .

A RISK WORTH TAKING
Judith Duncan

Photographer Walker Manley's cranky disposition kept the world at bay—until he fell hard for Riley McCormick. He knew he didn't deserve her and was determined to resist his tormenting need for her.

Riley, however, was not a woman who backed down from a challenge. She didn't know his secrets or understand his reasoning, but she was certain that if he'd let her in, her love could free him. But was she strong enough to break down his barriers?

Silhouette Sensation

COMING NEXT MONTH

FLANNERY'S RAINBOW
Julie Kistler

Jack McKeegan's whole life changed when he went to a St. Patrick's Day party at an isolated pub and had a few drinks with a little old man in a green suit!

Flannery O'Shea came home the next day and discovered Jack asleep in her bed. Somebody had apparently wandered off with his clothes, his car and a very important contract! When Jack started talking about leprechauns, Flannery began to wonder if her eccentric grandfather had been up to mischief. . . But Jack seemed to hold *her* responsible!

ONE SWEET SIN
Linda Shaw

When her ex-husband sent out a plea for help, Allyson Wyatt took a deep breath and contacted R.T. Smith, Daniel's best and oldest friend and *her* nemesis.

R.T. was the perennial bad boy made good. To be a Major in the Marines by the age of thirty-four was no mean achievement. He would help Daniel despite the history, the one sweet sin, he and Allyson shared. But he wished Allyson was not involved. One look at her and his blood ran as hot as ever. . .

NOW YOU CAN ENJOY
4 SILHOUETTE SENSATIONS, A CUDDLY
TEDDY AND A MYSTERY GIFT FREE

♥ ♥ ♥ ♥ ♥ ♥ ♥ ♥ ♥ ♥ ♥ ♥ ♥ ♥ ♥ ♥ ♥ ♥

Now you can enjoy 4 Silhouette Sensations, a
cuddly teddy and a mystery gift absolutely FREE
and without obligation. Then if you choose,
you can look forward to receiving your new
Sensations delivered to your door each month
at just £1.85 each (post & packing free) plus a
FREE newsletter packed with author news,
competitions offering great prizes, special offers
and lots more. Send no money now. Simply fill
in the coupon below at once and post it to:-
Silhouette Reader Service, FREEPOST,
PO Box 236, Croydon, Surrey CR9 9EL.

— — — — — — NO STAMP REQUIRED — — — — ➤

Please send me, free and without obligation, four specially selected Silhouette
Sensations, together with my FREE cuddly teddy and mystery gift - and reserve
a Reader Service Subscription for me. If I decide to subscribe I shall receive 4
new Silhouette Sensation titles every month for £7.40 post and packing free. If
I decide not to subscribe, I shall write to you within 10 days. The free books
and gifts are mine to keep in any case. I understand that I may cancel or
suspend my subscription at any time simply by writing to you. I am over 18
years of age.

Mrs/Miss/Ms/Mr _____ EP47SS

Address _____

_____

_____ Postcode _____
                                   (Please don't forget to include your postcode)

Signature _____

mps
MAILING
PREFERENCE
SERVICE